The Writings and Opinions of
Dean Wesley Smith

Introduction
On Site Research

This last winter I took a road trip from my home on the Oregon Coast to Las Vegas, Nevada. Now that is not a short drive and even longer in the winter, so I hoped to do some writing along the way and maybe while in Las Vegas.

I managed to keep up my blog along the drive and talk about the idea of writing a novel while in Las Vegas while visiting with friends and playing some tournament poker.

It seemed like a fun idea at the time.

Turned out I was right.

So I checked myself into a very nice suite in the Golden Nugget Casino and Hotel in downtown Las Vegas, set up my writing computer on a nice desk in the suite, and then took a walk.

It was a crisp but clear night in Las Vegas, and the parties were going on as always. I left the Fremont Street Experience and headed up Ogden Street toward the Ogden Condos, a huge, block-wide building that towers over downtown Las Vegas. Two of my characters in my novel series Cold Poker Gang have penthouse apartments there.

I figured since I was in Las Vegas, I might as well write a Cold Poker Gang novel. I explored around the Ogden Condos, then walked toward the Strip through a pretty seedy part of town, especially at night.

About ten blocks toward the strip I stopped and looked up at the Stratosphere Casino. I was in such a position that it made me remember the old Landmark Hotel and Casino owned by Howard Hughes and if I had been standing on that corner back in the 1980s I would have been able to see it.

The Landmark used to tower in the air as the highest building in Las Vegas, a replica of the Space Needle in Seattle.

Now I am showing my age. I have been going to Las Vegas since 1972 to play cards, often professionally. And I love the city and I remember clearly exactly where the Landmark had stood.

Thanks for the Support

Dean Wesley Smith

Standing there on that street corner, I knew instantly I had to write something about the Landmark. So I turned around and headed back to my suite. I had no idea what the plot might be, but I knew it had to do with my two retired detectives who lived in the Ogden and the book would also have something to do with the old Landmark Hotel and Casino.

Now, here, in this issue, you can read *Ace High: A Cold Poker Gang Mystery,* the results of that walk that night, all written while in a wonderful suite in Las Vegas.

And you can read the entire book made up of all my blog posts about the writing of *Ace High: A Cold Poker Gang Mystery.*

I sure hope you enjoy the read as much as I did the writing.

—*Dean Wesley Smith*
May 28, 2017

Smith's
MONTHLY

*Every Month Original
Novels, Stories, and Articles*

USA Today Bestselling Writer
Dean Wesley Smith

TABLE OF CONTENTS

Coming Next Issue in *Smith's Monthly*

THE ADVENTURES OF HAWK

Smith's MONTHLY

NUMBER FORTY
JANUARY, 2017

*Original Stories,
Novels, and Articles*

DEAN WESLEY SMITH

THE ADVENTURES OF HAWK

USA *Today* Bestselling Writer

DEAN WESLEY SMITH

THAT OLD TINGLING

A Marble Grant Story

Marble Grant, superhero, discovers a lot of training goes along with being dead.

But with the training, she felt like a kid again, only thankfully she didn't have to start all the way back in diapers.

Just about the point she gets the hang of the basics of being a Ghost Agent, she meets her new partner, Sally Glass, Sim to her friends,

Two hot women ghosts with attitude. What could possibly be better?

That Old Tingling
A Marble Grant Story

One

WHO KNEW THAT so much training went along with being dead. I felt like a kid again, only I didn't have to start all the way back in diapers.

But I did have to learn how to use restrooms, since it seemed ghosts had to pee and eat and everything else and for a woman having the lid up on a toilet was a critical factor. I couldn't lift a lid yet.

One of the very first lessons I learned was to check to see if some woman was in a stall before sticking my head through the stall door to see if the lid was up.

Learned that lesson the hard way. Ugly hard way. I'll never get that sight or that smell out of my memory. Four hundred pounds, almost nude, and clearly the poor woman had eaten something very, very wrong.

Rotten fish and dead animal under a bridge kind of wrong.

Luckily the poor woman didn't hear me gasp, cough disgustingly, and stumble back and through the wall and right into the men's room. Let me tell you, that morning I heard noises from the stalls in that men's room I didn't know were possible for a human to make.

A girl could get real traumatized being dead, of that there was no doubt. Jewel said when I returned to the breakfast table that I was almost ghost white. Ghost-white skin didn't match my purple hair or my bright yellow blouse no matter how dead I was.

I also had to figure out how to eat and start learning how to actually touch something physical and move it. You know, things like toilet lids. My trainers of the dead, Jewel and Tommy, said that would take me time.

As with everything else they taught me, they had been right.

After three months of training, I knew how to control live people, knew how to eat and dress with ghost food and clothing, and could get around pretty well by teleporting, just as I had as a superhero.

I was feeling pretty darned good about it all, actually.

I also had learned more about sex by being inside of people's heads than I had learned dating men and women both for over a hundred years. Wow, some folks out there really were kinky. I mean I liked to experiment and I sure enjoyed sex, but some of the stuff I saw in people's minds just made me look away.

Damn tough when you are in a person's mind, let me tell you.

My best friend of the last hundred years, Patty, who was still alive and a superhero like I used to be before a bullet implanted itself into my forehead, helped me get a nifty and large two-bedroom condo in Las Vegas on the fifth floor of the Ogden Building downtown.

Her boyfriend, Poker Boy, seemed to have more money than Fort Knox and he bought the place and all the furniture and fixtures I wanted, as well as all my clothes.

I kissed him on the cheek and told him I doubted I would ever be able to pay him back. He had just laughed.

Patty told me later that was his embarrassed laugh. Then she told me he would never miss the money in the slightest. Seems Fort Knox couldn't match his money. Playing poker and investing the money smartly over time had clearly been good for him. Besides, he figured the condo was an investment since I sure couldn't own it or sell it.

Patty had helped me shop for clothes. Ghosts could take and wear the ghost part of any clothing. But if I actually had the physical clothes hanging in my closet, I could always wear the ghost part of the outfit any time I wanted.

Now Available
from all your favorite booksellers
in trade paper and electronic editions.

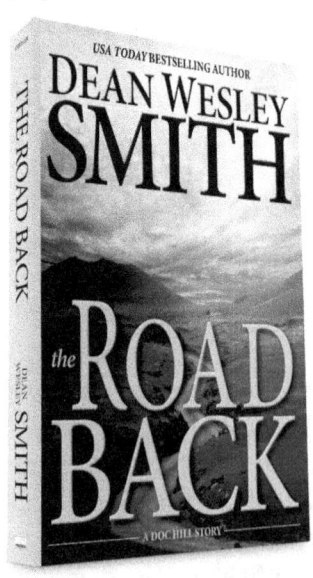

And no damn laundry. I just tossed the dirty clothes in a basket and a day or so later the ghost clothes vanished. They went back and joined their real part in the closet, all neat and fresh just as I bought it for me to use again.

Didn't get better than that.

So Poker Boy had given me and Patty an unlimited credit card and I now had my bedroom and a hall closet full of brand new clothes and shoes and sexy underwear, even though I doubted the sexy part of the underwear were going to get used any time soon.

The vibrator that Patty helped me buy got used regularly to cure that old tingling, especially when I happened to stumble into an attractive man or woman and read their thoughts and their likes and dislikes in the bedroom.

Those images from those people's minds made for some good before-sleep fantasy workouts with that vibrator.

Yeah, kind of being a voyeur, I know, but a ghost does what a ghost can do.

I decided to not fill my extra bedroom closet with clothes just yet. Never knew when someone alive or dead would need a guest room. So Patty and I furnished it with a large bed, wooden dresser, and a reading chair with lamp.

One thing for certain, it was great to have rich live friends when a person was a ghost. Made living a ton more comfortable. I had had a nice place in Boise before I died, but nothing like this condo.

Everything in it was ultra modern and clean and the couch and chairs in the living room were actually comfortable. I had dozed off numbers of time already watching movies on that couch.

The kitchen was enough to make me want to learn how to cook, even though I lived in a city with some of the best restaurants in the world I could get food from at any moment.

I had gotten into a habit at night for dinner of going to a new restaurant and bringing back to my place one of their specialties. Something different every night sure kept things interesting in the food department.

The view of the condo was toward the Strip and the balcony had a glass table and five surprisingly comfortable chairs. On warm evenings I usually ate dinner out there, just enjoying the feel of being lucky.

Yeah, I know, I had been killed and I was now a ghost.

Still I felt damn lucky.

Two

I WAS ENJOYING one of the sweetest-tasting peach daiquiris on my balcony just before sunset four months after I had died when Jewel and Tommy appeared.

I had yet to jump to get dinner, but I had plans on trying a barbeque plate from a place in the MGM Grand where Patty worked. She said it was wonderful.

Jewel and Tommy both had on their normal jeans, expensive shirt and blouse, and tennis shoes. Together they were the most attractive couple I had ever met. Stunning model-like looks. Tommy had those wide shoulders of a cop and Jewel was thin and trim and always looked perfectly together.

Did I mention they were also two of the smartest people I had ever met as well. Both had higher degrees and Jewel had been a medical doctor. And on top of all that, they were just flat nice people. Go figure.

"Sorry to bother you without checking ahead," Jewel said. "But we figured you would want to join us."

I took a long drink of the daiquiri as I stood. "You know me. Always up for an adventure. Where are we headed?"

"Your partner is about to join us," Jewel said.

"Damn right I want to be there," I said, laughing.

I had been hearing since almost the moment I discovered I was a ghost that I would have a ghost partner at some point joining me. I knew nothing at all about this person. No one would say a word since the person was still alive. So it had sort of been one of those nagging events coming that I had mostly just put out of my mind.

Jewel smiled. "Then let's go."

And the next thing I knew I was standing in a hot, dry desert on the shoulder of a two-lane paved road. The sun looked exactly like it had from my condo balcony, so I figured I was somewhere in the desert southwest.

"We're fifty miles to the north of Las Vegas," Tommy said.

The two-lane highway stretched off into the distance in both directions. There was not a building or a soul in sight. A slight breeze was doing some wonderful things with my nipples through my thin blouse and my long purple hair was blowing slightly around my shoulders.

I had on my evening kick-around-the-condo sweat pants and tennis shoes. I certainly hadn't dressed for this occasion.

We stood there on the edge of the road in the fading light for a good minute with nothing happening.

"We in the wrong place?" I finally asked.

Never was one for just standing and waiting. Another nice thing about being dead, I seldom had to stand and wait for anything.

Tommy pointed to the north. In the distance I could see a single light coming toward us. That would be the first car to pass us since we got here.

Only it became clear fairly quickly that it wasn't a car, but a motorcycle. And it was moving at an insane speed.

As the motorcycle was about to flash past us, a coyote jumped up from the ditch beside the road and the motorcycle hit the creature square in the side. Neither the poor coyote, or the motorcyclist, had even an instant to react.

I watched as the motorcyclist in black leathers and black wrap-around helmet went sailing past us about thirty feet in the air over our heads.

The impact of the cyclist hitting the road was an awful sound.

The cyclist started doing uncontrolled cartwheels along the pavement.

To one side of us the remains of the coyote landed in two parts.

On the other side of the road the big black motorcycle was doing cartwheels out into the desert brush, flipping parts in all directions like a stripper shedding clothes.

I wanted to be sick.

That accident had to be one of the most horrid things I had ever witnessed.

Hands down the most violent.

Being a superhero in the real estate and hospitality areas didn't much call for extreme violence.

Three

THE THREE OF us stood there on the side of the road without talking. I don't think any of us had expected the intense violence of that accident. That cyclist must have been going well over a hundred miles per hour.

The body finally slid to a stop about a football field's distance away from us and a moment later the cyclist in all black, still wearing a helmet, was sitting on a rock to the right of the road closer to us than the body.

"That's our signal," Jewel said and led the way as the three of us walked up the road toward the cyclist.

I was working on taking deep breaths, pushing the image of that accident out of my mind so that I could focus forward. This person was supposed to be my future partner. Certainly he or she was someone who liked to take risks.

If nothing else, that might get interesting at times.

The three of us stopped near the cyclist who looked up, face hidden by the black faceplate on the helmet. Then two gloved hands came up and took off the helmet, shaking loose long blonde hair.

Sitting there on the rock, newly dead, was one of the most attractive women I had ever seen. She had deep blue eyes, high cheekbones, and a short nose.

She looked completely stunned and even with that look she was beautiful.

"What happened?" she asked, looking at us.

"You had an accident," Jewel said.

The woman shook her head and took off her gloves, tucking them into her helmet in a practiced move.

"Not likely. At that speed I would be dead. And I don't even have a scratch on me."

None of us said a word. We just let her slowly figure it out for herself.

Finally Jewel introduced the three of us.

"I'm Sally Glass," the woman said.

"Where are you from?" Jewel asked.

I was impressed at how calm and level Jewel sounded. I was still having trouble getting my heart under control from the violence of that crash and also the beauty of the woman sitting on the rock in front of me.

I was attracted to women as much as I was to men. And clearly Sally was my type.

Also, her name sounded very, very familiar.

The more I looked at Sally under those motorcycle leathers, the more I realized she was about my size and shape at five-eight. That would be helpful in getting her some clothing.

The nagging feeling I knew her kept getting stronger like a bad itch in a place I couldn't scratch.

"Boise," Sally said, pointing back north. "Wanted to spend a few days in Vegas and clear my head a little.

"I was from Boise," I said, working to keep my voice as calm as I could. "I worked real estate there among other things."

Sally nodded. "Banks and construction, among other things. And you look very familiar."

"I was thinking the same for you," I said.

Jewel glanced at me and nodded. She was about to say something when Patty appeared.

I suddenly felt very relieved that a real live person was here.

"Patty," Sally said, standing and sounding happy.

"Hi, Sim," Patty said.

The two women stepped toward each other hugged on the edge of the road.

"I was hoping to get to see you on this trip," Sim said.

The moment Patty said "Sim" I knew who this woman was. She was also a superhero in the banking side. Patty had always talked about getting the three of us together at some point, but it had never happened. Seems Sim and Patty had met about fifty years ago when Sim became a superhero.

But now we had finally met, in the middle of the desert, with Sim's broken body crumpled in a pile beside the road about fifty steps away.

"So what is this all about?" Sim asked.

"You had an accident," Patty said.

"That's what they—Oh, crap, I'm a Ghost Agent."

Sim suddenly looked like she needed to sit down again and Patty moved to Sim's right and I went to her left side and we braced her.

"You are a Ghost Agent now," Jewel said. "Tommy, Marble, and I are all three Ghost Agents. Marble is also a superhero like you."

"I'm dead?" Sim asked. "Really dead?"

Jewel nodded and pointed to the body.

Sim looked around until she spotted her own body and then nodded. "I knew there was no way I could survive an accident at that speed. Did you see it? Must have been spectacular."

"Violent," I said, enjoying holding her up a little more than I probably should have at that moment. "And I'm afraid to say the coyote you hit didn't make it either."

Sim laughed and shook her head.

"So you hungry?" Jewel asked.

Sim frowned. "I was really hungry before all this. One of the reasons I was going so fast. And I still am. Do ghosts eat?"

"Take it from a newly-made Ghost Agent as well," I said. "We do eat and everything tastes better than you can imagine."

Jewel and Tommy both nodded to that.

Sim looked at me, then nodded. "You were killed in a double murder in an alley in Boise about four months ago. Right?"

I nodded.

"I remember when that happened and was surprised Patty wasn't more upset than she was when I heard it was you."

I laughed. "She's been helping me. Wait until you see the condo she and Poker Boy got me to live in."

"Can't wait," Sim said and smiled at me.

I damn near melted right there in the desert. Working with this woman was going to be heaven. And if she didn't like women as a sexual partner, my poor vibrator would get a regular workout.

Patty looked at me. "All right if Sim borrows something to wear?"

I laughed. "Never a problem. I think we bought me more than enough."

Patty turned to Jewel and Tommy. "How about the three of us meet you at the Golden Nugget buffet in fifteen minutes."

"We'll be there," Jewel and Tommy said and vanished.

A moment later we were out of the slight wind of the desert and in my condo.

The idea of getting to help train Sim to be a Ghost Agent over the next months had me excited to say the least. But watching her strip naked in my bedroom topped any thought of that being the most exciting.

Her body was amazingly like mine. Thin hips and small breasts. Only she was a natural blonde where I was a complete brunette when I didn't color my hair one color or another.

And we were almost exactly the same height.

I showed her how to turn on the water in the bathroom so she could take a quick shower. When she came out with wet hair and a towel around her, she looked even more stunning.

"Kind of strange how the towel still just stays on the rack in there while I dry off with this same towel."

"Everything has a ghost component," I said. "Jewel and Tommy will explain everything."

"Wait until you taste the ghost component of food," I said. "Better than anything you have ever tasted."

"I am so starved right now cardboard might taste good," she said and dropped the towel to start to get dressed.

I had to turn away or simply melt into a puddle, she was that beautiful.

And I was that horny.

The only slight imperfection she had was a scar on one hip that someday I would ask her about, but not tonight.

Later that night, as Sim changed clothes once again to get ready for bed in my guestroom, I decided seeing her naked was by far the most exciting thing of the day.

By a long ways.

Two hours later, when she knocked on my bedroom door and came in and asked me to hold her, I knew from here the days would just get better.

I had considered myself lucky as it was.

But I remembered that first night after I had died being scared and uncertain about everything. I wish Sim had been there to hold me.

But now I could hold her.

And that was all that mattered.

I had just gotten factors luckier to have her as a partner.

We fell asleep in each other's arms.

And she never used the guest bedroom again.

Dead or alive, that would have been just fine with me.

But honestly, being dead made it even better.

~

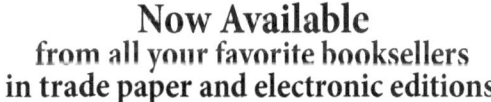

USA *Today* Bestselling Writer

DEAN WESLEY SMITH

A Bryant Street
Story

THE MAN WHO LAUGHED
ON A RAINY NIGHT

Bradford Borne loved rainy, April nights.

He loved to move the body of his dead wife on rainy April nights every year.

He loved how the rain hid his work, covered his tracks, protected him.

But on Bryant Street, even a simple task like moving a body becomes twisted.

The Man Who Laughed
on a Rainy Night
A Bryant Street Story

BRADFORD BORNE STOOD in the Oregon rain in front of his three-bedroom ranch-style home in the suburbs of Portland. On his right was the flowering plum tree his wife Radella had planted fifteen years before, the year before she died.

Actually, he had planted it on her insistence. She had sat in a lawn chair eating chips while he had done the work.

But now, to protect against the rain, he wore his dark raincoat and a wide-brimmed rain hat, rain pants over his normal tan slacks, and shoe protectors over his brown leather dress shoes. The rain didn't even touch his glasses. He was completely protected from the storm and the chill evening air of late April.

The homes along Bryant Street were silent in the late hours, the blinds pulled on every home, the televisions flickering light to dark and then light again, shadows projected against the windows indicating all his neighbors were in their normal evening zombie state.

The rain also made seeing very far difficult, so he was convinced no one would see him at all. And this time of night on a weeknight, most every one of his neighbors was home in routine. No chance a stray car would pass by tonight.

And the sound of the rain would cover and dampen any sounds he happened to make.

A perfect night to move his dead wife Radella.

Soft ground from the spring rains, no one to see him.

Perfect. Just perfect.

This would be the tenth or maybe eleventh time he had moved Radella in fifteen years. He sometimes couldn't remember.

The first time was because of a sewer issue with the city. Two years after he had buried her the first time, the city needed to run a sewer line to get everyone in the subdivision off their septic tanks. To connect to his home, the new sewer line would run right through where he had buried Radella.

So he dug her up one rainy, muddy night, dealt with the mess, and moved her to the other side of the garage. It had been a long and horrid night.

But as the months went by after that night, he realized he had actually enjoyed the task. He had enjoyed the fear of getting caught, the physical stress and the labor. It had made him feel alive again, something he hadn't felt since the first year of marriage to Radella.

And since the night he had buried her in the first place.

So the following year, again in April, he moved her again, this time to the back corner of his fenced-in backyard, making sure he left no signs at all of anything being disturbed.

He felt so alive after that second time that he ended up meeting a new love of his life.

The official story was that Radella had left, gone back east. He had filed for divorce and faked her signature and was free of her legally. No one really asked about her.

So he married Marilyn that fall and by April Marilyn was going the same way as Radella had gone. Eating, not interested in much of anything but television, yelling at him for every little slight or misstep.

In six months after their marriage, he had become her house slave, the short little man who went to work, earned the money, and then waited on her when he got home.

In late April of that first year of his marriage to Marilyn, she took a five-day trip back to Florida to visit family and he took the opportunity to move Radella again, giving himself that new feeling of life.

By the following April he was almost dead again, his emotions shut down, his caring for life gone.

So on a dark, rainy April night, as Marilyn slept, he smothered her with a plastic bag and buried her in the yard.

He didn't bury her close to Radella. It was a very large backyard with a high wooden fence around it all. Lots and lots of room back there.

Then, when Marilyn's family in Florida asked about her a month later, Bradford had said she had left him with a man named Roger and he knew she was planning on driving to Florida. They didn't seem surprised and said they had never understood what he had seen in her.

He had filed divorce papers and forged her name and they never found her.

And again, no one really ever asked about her. He clearly made poor choices when it came to love.

Or maybe the choice was to marry someone just like that. He could never figure that out.

In late April of that same year, he moved Radella again, trying his best to get some feeling and zest back.

It worked.

So every April, like celebrating an anniversary, he moved Radella one rainy night and Marilyn another.

Neither Marilyn nor Radella had been a light woman on the days of their deaths. Radella had topped over three hundred pounds without clothes and Marilyn had been close to that. Now after all the years wrapped in plastic and tarps, neither woman had gotten lighter.

And Bradford hadn't gotten any younger or stronger.

Bradford was a tiny man by anyone's standards. He owned and ran his own small grocery store just one mile from his home and he had met both Radella and Marilyn when they were still thin.

Radella's death had been different from Marilyn's. He hadn't actually killed her. Not exactly, anyway. One day, as he was serving Radella dinner, she choked on a large bite of steak, medium rare as she liked it, and he sat and watched her die. He didn't feel guilty or sad or anything. In four years she had killed any part of him that showed that kind of emotion.

So he had wrapped her in a large plastic sheet, securing both ends completely. Then wrapped her in another plastic sheet and secured it solidly as well. That evening, actually, was the most he had touched her since their honeymoon.

He left her the next day in the pantry and bought a very heavy tarp and brought it home with him that night. He wrapped her in that and tied it securely with rope.

That night it rained and the digging was easy, and it made him feel alive but he didn't notice until he had had to move her because of the sewer problem.

Now it was April again. It was a dark, rainy night. It was time.

He laughed and took one more look up and down the deserted street. Tonight he would move them both on the same night. How much fun would that be?

He got his shovel and went to where he had buried Radella last year and started to dig, carefully cutting away the sod so he could replace it later. His plan was to move Radella to the back side of the house near the back deck, then move Marilyn into the hole Radella had spent a year in.

He had a tarp beside the hole for the dirt and the rain splattering on the tarp was almost hypnotic.

He was paying no attention at all, just enjoying the feeling of the work and the rain when he suddenly realized he was too deep.

Radella wasn't here.

He was sure he had buried her right there last April. But she wasn't there and a very dead, very heavy woman wrapped in plastic and a tarp didn't just vanish.

He stopped and walked around the large backyard. In fifteen years she had been in eleven places. Or was that just ten. He was getting confused clearly on where in the large backyard she was.

Ahh, well, he would at least move Marilyn tonight.

He finished preparing the hole he had dug, then went over to the end of the wooden fence to the left of his home, near his bedroom window, and started digging, again putting the sod carefully aside and the dirt on another tarp.

And again he got too deep.

Marilyn wasn't there.

For a moment he felt panic, something he hadn't felt in decades. How could he forget where he buried both of his wives?

He once again walked around the backyard trying to jog his memory from last April.

Or was that the April before?

All the Aprils seemed to run together. Had he not been able to find them last April either?

Finally he went and sat in the rain on his back step, letting the water running off his hat calm him.

Then, after a few minutes, he just started to laugh.

Both ex-wives lost. They were here somewhere, he was sure of that, but where was the question.

He sat and just laughed as the rain poured over him, clearing the air, softening the ground, making it a perfect night.

He honestly didn't need to know this year where they were. Next April he would try again to see if he could find them.

Laughing to himself, he went back to work filling in both holes, patting down the sod, cleaning up what dirt had gotten off the tarp by hosing down the lawn in the rain.

When he was all done, you almost couldn't tell any work had been done in those two areas and the rain was starting to ease just slightly.

He cleaned and put away his shovel, cleaned off the tarps and hung them to dry in his tool shed. Then he went in his back door and took off his rain gear.

He felt tired, but alive.

Very much alive.

Alive enough to get through another year.

He started a pot of coffee and stood in the window and watched the rain while it brewed, smiling to himself.

Next April he would find them.

And move them both.

They were out there somewhere.

He was sure of that.

And that was all that mattered.

Now Available
from all your favorite booksellers in trade paper and electronic editions.

DEAN WESLEY SMITH

USA TODAY BESTSELLING AUTHOR

GHOST AGENT

THE POKER CHIP

A GHOST OF A CHANCE NOVEL

DEAN WESLEY SMITH

WRITING A NOVEL IN FIVE DAYS WHILE TRAVELING

The Tricks and Techniques of Writing Fiction
While Away from Home

A WMG WRITER'S GUIDE

One of the most prolific writers in modern fiction writing shows you how he does it.

Author of over one-hundred-and-fifty novels, USA Today *bestselling writer Dean Wesley Smith gives an intimate day-to-day, minute-by-minute account of how he wrote a full novel in five days while traveling.*

From tips on how to prepare for the writing to what to do when the trip gets in the way, Dean deals with it all. A moment-by-moment account of what it feels like to write a novel in five days while traveling.

And yes, he wrote this book while writing the novel. A don't-miss read into the mind of a prolific and bestselling fiction writer.

Writing a Novel in Five Days While Traveling

Author Note

These chapters, including the introduction were written as blog posts on my blog starting on January 9th and ending on January 16th, 2017, with an epilogue blog two days later.

Not only do I talk about the writing, but about the trip itself and the writing experience and my worries.

I hope that if you are thinking of trying to write while traveling that this book of blog posts will help you.

I sure had fun.

INTRODUCTION

YUP. A CRAZY idea. Especially considering I have not once been successful at writing while traveling.

How's that for a negative start?

So I figured it was about time to teach myself how to do this and as I figure it out I might as well write this nonfiction book as well as the novel.

Win—win. If I pull it off.

Otherwise, it will be an entertaining failure for you all to watch right out here in public.

And what's really silly is that I will be doing all my normal e-mail, normal workshop stuff, and still doing the CFO job for WMG while I am gone. I will be cutting nothing out.

Yup, nothing will seem different from your end except the content of these blogs.

So if you have questions or want to sign up for a workshop, feel free. I will be doing all my normal computer work every day, three times per day.

Some Considerations to Start

Today is Sunday and I will not start the novel until Wednesday. But I am doing these nonfiction introduction chapters each night ahead of that while traveling.

My first consideration in getting ready for something this crazy is that I do not have a laptop computer. I have an old iPad, but don't use it much at all anymore.

I use massive Mac computers with second screens. I have three set-ups like that. One for my internet at home, one for my writing computer, and one in my WMG office.

So as this trip got near, I thought about buying myself a laptop and then carrying a second screen and keyboard with it. Good idea until I realized how silly that was. I would be carrying a second screen, so I could just carry my large Mac just as easily.

So this morning around 10 a.m. I put a pillow in the back seat of my car (a very smooth-riding Cadillac CTS), carried my big internet computer out and put it on the pillow, screen toward the seat. Put another pillow between the screen and the seat and then covered the entire thing

with a blanket and strapped it in with a seat belt.

Easy and it rode like a charm.

The real advantage of driving: I can pack as much as I want. And I don't much care for flying these days, so driving is more fun anyway.

So now I am sitting in front of my big internet computer in a really nice hotel suite somewhere south of Eureka, CA. I have just finished doing all the work for the coast anthology workshop and got out the next story for the writers to write.

And I have answered all my e-mail earlier and am now writing this introduction.

This desk and chair is actually as comfortable as my chair at home after I put two pillows under me to get me to the right height.

Why Do It This Way?

I think trick number one in trying to write while traveling is to be comfortable. If you normally write on a laptop, do that. I normally write on a big screen, so I am doing that.

Again, many writers have learned how to do this. I have never done any writing while traveling. So some of this stuff I am discovering might seem logical if you write and travel. I am always up for tips in the comments. (grin)

If I had to fly, I never would have considered doing this.

What to Prepare?

Since I am doing this blog every night on how to do this (or how to fail at it in spectacular fashion) I had Allyson at WMG mock-up a cover for this nonfiction book. That is for decoration here and also to keep me motivated.

Second, since I never write with any outline or anything, I figured I would at least pick a title and a series to write in to give myself a jump. And since all five days of writing this will be while I am hanging around with friends and playing poker in Las Vegas, I might as well pick a series set in Vegas.

I have two series that are set in Vegas: Poker Boy and the Cold Poker Gang mysteries. Poker Boy is in the book I stopped writing to do this, so that left the Cold Poker Gang mystery novels. (Couldn't make it easy on myself, could I?)

The two characters in the last novel live about three blocks from where I will be staying, so that will be fun. I came up with a title for the novel and Allyson did a mock-up cover for me which I really, really love.

I have no plot or even idea for the book and won't until I sit down to write. Not even going to give it a thought. But if you are trying something like this, it might be an idea to plan ahead a little or work on a project you have already started.

So now, after nine hours of driving today, I have another nine hours tomorrow and then a bunch of assignments for workshops to do.

The Traveling Three Days Before Starting a Novel

Since this is a book about travel, I figure I had better detail out each day a little.

I left Lincoln City on the Oregon Coast about 10:30 a.m.

Storms were burying Portland and the I-5 corridor in ice and I-84 was shut down. So my only safe choice was to hug the coast going south to stay out of most of the mountains.

I learned today that my memory of making that drive twenty years ago wasn't accurate. Going down the Redwood Highway (101) in torrential rains was not fun in the slightest. The weather people called it an "atmospheric river of moisture" and it was. Wow.

I stopped four times along the way, once in Newport, once in Florence, once in Coos Bay, and once in Eureka. Took about nine hours.

In the summer that would be a two-day drive because of traffic, but thankfully I had none today. No one was stupid enough to be on the roads today but me, I guess.

The drive down the Oregon Coast was stunningly beautiful, even in the winter and pouring rain. I forgot how really beautifully alien and remote this part of this country is. If you have time, worth seeing, folks. But caution, this is a long, long ways from anywhere.

Checked in, got my computer set up, got some snacks to eat, did my e-mail, and then watched television for a while until it was time to do workshop stuff and then write this.

So tomorrow another nine hours of driving.

I will have chapter one of this nonfiction book tomorrow night from farther south on this crazy trip.

Onward.

CHAPTER ONE

SECOND DAY OF traveling and I will be starting the novel in two days. So doing introduction and preparation chapters first for the nonfiction book as I go along.

A sort of writing travel book.

Sort of.

SMITH'S Monthly

Besides the cover and the series the novel will be in, do I have anything plotted out for the novel? Nope.

Not a thing and I'm not going to, actually. I didn't even think about it once today.

But I have done a few basic preparations besides making sure I had a computer with me that I could write on.

But before I get to those helpful hints, let me tell you about my second day of travel. After all, that's part of this book, how travel influences the writing of two books.

Yes, that's right, I am writing two books. These chapters will become the nonfiction book and then I will also write a novel in five days if all things work out.

And yes, we will also bundle both the nonfiction book and the novel together at some point and have them both in Smith's Monthly, of course. I suppose that will make it a third book. (grin)

The Second Day

Today started off with a panic, actually.

I got up early, ahead of my alarm and glanced out the window to see if it was still raining. I had spent the night on the third floor in a nice suite hotel to the south of Eureka, CA. I intended to go back to bed for another hour or so.

To my surprise and then shock, right outside the hotel was a massive river. (Didn't see it the night before because of the darkness and heavy rain.)

To say this river was angry would be an understatement. Colored in dark brown and moving so fast that floating debris seem to just flash past the hotel.

And the only thing between the river and the hotel and my car in the parking lot was a tall, artificial levee with a sidewalk on top of it.

And the water was flowing within a foot of that sidewalk and people were standing up there staring, including a few official-looking folks.

So much for going back to bed.

Last thing I wanted was to see my Cadillac floating down the river. Less than an hour later I was packed and pulling away from the hotel. Official people were still standing on the banks. No idea what happened, but it didn't look positive.

9:30 in the morning and I had a nine hour scheduled drive ahead of me.

Well, that didn't work out so well. After the monsoons that hit (and are still hitting) California, it took me eleven hours of driving before I was in this hotel room in a suite hotel in Fresno, CA.

At one point during the day, Kris was on the phone with me from our home in Lincoln City, Oregon, trying to help me find a way around some flooded and closed roads in north-central California. She was on her computer and I was trying to figure out where I was.

At that point I had already been dealing with flooded-out roads and closed roads for five hours.

You see, I had to somehow get from Highway 101 to Interstate 5 and I didn't want to go through San Francisco. With Kris's help through the road closures and stopping for directions once, I made it to I-5 and then went south, finally cutting across from I-5 to Fresno on what I thought would be a fairly short distance.

Nope.

And even though the map says straight, not straight… Road just vanishes in places.

Two very friendly guys in one service station in a tiny town in the middle

24

of nowhere got me back on track and two friendly policemen in Fresno helped me find the hotel.

And then I was so tired, I went into the lobby of the wrong hotel and the poor clerk couldn't find my reservation until I finally noticed I was in the wrong hotel. My hotel entrance was across the parking lot.

Fifty feet away.

I had parked in front of the correct hotel, walked into the wrong hotel.

The nice clerk said that happened a lot. Duh, putting hotels with similar names within fifty feet of each other in the same parking lot with California-level sucky signs... I suppose it would happen.

After getting all set up here in the room, I didn't want to go out for dinner because I was exhausted and didn't want to get lost again, so a television dinner (advantages of a suite hotel) and the last part of the National Championship College football game and I went to work on the workshop assignments.

Then a fifteen minute nap, then back at the assignments after a walk around the hotel to wake up.

It was a day.

A second day.

Some Suggestions on Getting Ready

When I was planning this trip, I knew that the first three days were going to be too much driving time to do much. And I had workshop assignments to do.

I did not expect a seven hour drive to be ten the first day and a seven-nine hour drive to be eleven the second, but I had planned no fiction writing, so it worked out.

So *Suggestion #1:* Look clearly at the trip ahead to see where fiction writing hours are available and realistic.

Realistic is the key.

Suggestion #2: Figure out what else you have planned.

For me, this trip I knew I would be doing workshop assignments and I knew

---

how long that took. And I knew that I would be doing work on the Anthology coast workshop, and I knew how long that took. So I planned out both.

Realistic is the key here as well. If a trip to see a tourist place is on the schedule, give that extra time. And give driving extra time.

Suggestion #3: Do a daily plan for the entire trip to see if fiction writing is even possible. If not, take the trip and leave the novel for when you get home.

For me, on this trip, the first three days are just marked travel. I knew I wanted to do these first nonfiction chapters, but I didn't mark them down for fear I wouldn't get to them.

Almost didn't tonight.

As the days go by, I will detail out my day each day and how it fit in my original plan, or if it did at all. I expect to have to adjust as I go along.

So that is *Suggestion #4:* Be prepared to be flexible. Never know when roads are going to be washed out on you in a state suffering from a drought.

An Observation from Day Two

I am from Idaho. I have driven back roads that I thought rivaled anything in the country as for pure beauty and scary and narrow and twisted. And I've been on a few back roads in Oregon as well. Not as tough as Idaho roads, but a few were close.

Today I learned that Idaho and Oregon back roads are freeways compared to some places in California. Who knew? California is known for its jammed freeways, not the twisting, narrow monsters I ended up on today. Beautiful scenery, sure, but wow...

Northern California above the wine country is another country. Or it might as well be. It's so isolated in places,

I saw three VW mini-vans from the 1960s and one even had a big peace sign on the back.

Not kidding.

CHAPTER TWO

THIRD DAY OF traveling and I will be starting the novel tomorrow. So doing these introduction and preparation chapters first for the nonfiction book as I go along.

Travel Today

I have my computer set up just fine where it will sit for the next five days.

And today was a much easier drive than the previous two days by a long ways. I left Fresno, CA, around 11 a.m. and was in this suite in Las Vegas before 6 p.m.

I went out for dinner by 7 p.m., then a long walk to do some research for a

friend (not for the coming book), then did the workshop assignments I needed to do for the rest of the night.

So now I am ready to start writing fiction tomorrow.

Again, I do not have a clue what the book will be about. But let me give a few more hints about getting ready to do something like this. And a couple of warnings if you are thinking of a challenge like this.

Hint #1: Attitude is everything. Once I decided to try this, I started working on my attitude.

Positive attitude.

Every time a negative thought or worry crept in over the last four or five days, I would go back to the basics. The basics are the hours this will take.

I have the hours in the next five days. So if I use the hours correctly, I can enjoy poker tournaments, spending time with friends over lunches and dinners, do my e-mail and business stuff, and still write this novel.

What do I mean by the hours? I know that to do 8,000 words of fiction in a day, I need to spend about 6 hours or so at it. Maybe a little longer. So I picked 7 hours per day of writing time to be safe. That's what I mean by hours.

Hint #2: Plan the days ahead to convince yourself you have the time. I have no intention of following some silly plan while here, and no way I can control my friends or if I go deep into a big poker tournament.

But I had to lay it out ahead of time to make sure the hours really were possible. There are seven hours per day for five days easily on this trip.

Hint #3: Plan on not thinking about the book. In other words, I plan on just getting out of my own way, slamming my critical voice into a corner to whimper for five days, and write a clean novel.

I will not rewrite this. (I never rewrite anything anyway.)

So I will be writing clean and if all things fall into place I will have a finished 40,000 plus novel by the end of five days.

This is back on the attitude point. Attitude and belief are everything.

And planning to have a good attitude and a belief that something is possible.

Some Basic Warnings

Warning #1: If you are deathly afraid of failure, never try anything like this. About a thousand things could go wrong to derail this or any challenge like it. I am prepared for failure if it happens. Not afraid of it.

Warning #2: If you don't have all the myths of writing cleared out of your system, don't even think of trying this. If you have to write perfect, this challenge will kill you dead. If you write sloppy, this challenge will be a waste of time. If you think everything you write is important, run from this idea.

And so on and so on.

Warning #3: If you don't know exactly how many words you can write in an hour, tested over time, don't try this. Chances are you will be wrong about your writing speed and you will just set up for an automatic failure.

This gets deadly when you think you can write at a certain speed and suddenly a story becomes important to you for some critical voice reason, so you slow down, and the challenge pressures you into madness.

Warning #4: If the fear of doing something like this kills the flexibility I talked about in the first chapter, run away from this idea. Fear often makes people very rigid and if you are naturally one of those people, find other ways to challenge yourself.

Also, if you are normally a ridged schedule person in real life, the needed flexibility to do this kind of challenge will kill you. Avoid completely.

Warning #5: If you can't handle an emotional up-and-down ride, don't try a challenge like this one. No chance on the planet this kind of thing will not be a bumpy ride emotionally.

For me that will be part of the fun. Writing into the dark completely will mean at times I will be stuck. And when stuck here, there are lots of other things for me to go do.

Uh-oh...

What Will Happen Next?

Each day I will do a chapter here about the day, the details of the day, and how it shaped up and how I did with the writing.

You will be able to follow the progress of the word count and when this book and the novel are eventually bundled together, you will be able to see exactly what I wrote on any given day.

I will also detail out how I am feeling. Tired, excited, and so on.

In other words, the ups and downs of the ride through the writing of the book.

So here we go.

I have driven three days to get here to Las Vegas. And tomorrow my friends start arriving.

And poker tournaments start.

And tomorrow I start a brand new novel called *Ace High: A Cold Poker Gang Mystery.*

Not a clue what it will be about, but it will be set here in Las Vegas, I know that much.

Stay tuned. The ride should be interesting, if nothing else. Just hope I can keep this ride on the tracks.

Observations from the Day and Pictures of my Suite in Vegas

Some pictures of where I will be writing. This suite in Vegas is huge and comfortable. I will not be suffering. (grin)

First picture is looking from the front foyer past the living room area toward one window. This is a corner suite on the 17th floor. Fantastic views.

Second picture is of where I have the computer set up.

For some reason, every time I come to Las Vegas, I realize how much I feel at home here. Not sure why I have to learn that over and over.

I suppose it feels like a second home because since 1972 I have been coming here to play poker (and in the early days play in gin tournaments). And then for a time I played blackjack.

And I paid my way through architecture and law school mostly in this town playing cards.

And no matter how much the town grows, to me it still feels the same.

It's good to be back.

CHAPTER THREE

FIRST DAY OF writing on the novel. Here we go.

And as planned, it didn't happen exactly as planned by a long ways.

But it still happened and I got just over 8,000 words done.

So day one success. Not as planned, but remember I said flexible was the key on this and today I was flexible.

Detailing Out the Day

I made it out of bed by noon and by 1 p.m. I had showered, gotten dressed, had a bunch of water and a power bar and was sitting down at the computer to first get my e-mail, then write.

It took me about five minutes to just look at my e-mail, then I got to writing.

In the first hour (remember, I have this broken down into seven hours of writing per day), I managed to get 1,400 words and a really nifty start for one of these mystery novels. I'm using an old Las Vegas hotel, now torn down, as setting in the prolog.

I took a five-minute break and then in fifty minutes did another 1,450 words. Two hours down and right on schedule. Hot damn.

It was 3 p.m.

I took a break and went and played some blackjack, then took a walk down the block to a famous toy store. I had talked to the owner at one point and at some time in the future our two WMG collectable stores will work with his on buying large collections. That should be fun when we get to it.

I got back a little after 4 p.m. and set back to write. And that was when plans started to go sideways. They were having big planning meetings at WMG and I needed to be part of it at times. So every ten minutes or so the phone would ring.

I still managed to get some writing done over the next two hours, about 1,000 words, actually.

Then my friend Jim, who was flying in today, texted me that his plane was having some problems and he was still sitting at the gate in Idaho.

So for the next hour between texts and phone calls, I managed another 500 words, which I considered a miracle to be honest.

So finally around 7:30, with 4,300 words or so done, I took a nap.

After the nap I watched a little news and then did another hour session of 1,300 words.

A short break with texts coming in from my friend about his airport adventure, I wrote another 1,200 words. (My plan was to have dinner with him at 7 when he arrived, then later on come back to the room to write. That plan had long since been tossed out.)

So by the time ten-thirty in the evening rolled around, I hadn't had dinner and my friend was headed to the hotel in a shuttle.

I went looking for him and we went to dinner around 11 p.m.

Great time, great seeing him again. Jim and I have been friends now for 51 years. So really, really great seeing him again.

This will be a fun week.

Finally around 2 a.m., I left the bar and headed back to the room. I talked with Kris for a time and then went to writing again. In one hour I got another 1,100 words and got the novel to 7,900 words.

I walked around for a little bit, then came back and got just over a hundred words before deciding 8,000 words was enough for the day.

So lots of business, a ton of e-mail, about fifty texts and two-dozen phone calls, all while on vacation and writing.

Plus a two-hour dinner with a great friend, some exploring, an hour in a bar, and some blackjack.

And 8,014 words.
Day one down.
On target.

Some Points

Someone asked why 40,000 words?

Well, to start with, I grew up in the 1950s and 1960s, where the standard length of most novels was between 30,000 and 50,000 words. Very few went over that, especially in commercial fiction.

So I grew up with that length, it feels right to me, and my mind works in that length. I have said often I always hated that New York changed the form of literature by forcing writers to bloat out books so that the publishers could make more money and sell their books for more money.

So when I was allowed by the indie world to write what I wanted to write, all my novels now end up between 35,000 words and 50,000 words, with most coming in around 40,000. And these Cold Poker Gang mystery novels are all coming in around 40,000, at least the first six or seven of them.

Flexible is Everything

Today I wanted to be in contact with my friend while he was trying to make it down here. I enjoyed the texts. And I really enjoyed being part of the planning of the coming year at WMG. Some great stuff happening in this new year that has me excited, actually.

So with the writing, I had set my mind that I needed to be flexible and right off the bat that mind-set kept me going.

When traveling, flexible thinking is everything.

And since I wasn't stressed about getting back to the writing and staying on schedule, I had a really fun experience. Jim and I were sitting at the bar near the poker room and this chatty, half drunk young girl and her completely drunk

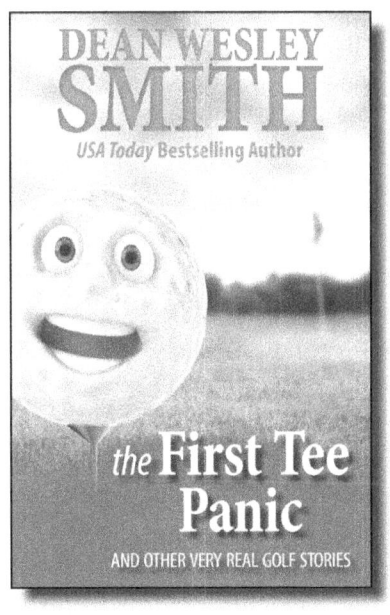

sister sat down at the bar next to us. The really drunk sister tried to show me how to play blackjack on a bar machine.

Considering I paid my way through architecture and law school playing blackjack, that was funny and I played along with her, taking her slurred advice because she could "feel" the cards on the machine.

I doubt in her state she was feeling much of anything, to be honest.

The really chatty girl had just turned 21 today which was the reason they were out drinking. They had sent mom back to the room an hour before. The chatty girl asked me about my NASA jacket I was wearing, asked me if I worked there. I said nope, so she asked me what I did for a living. Since they were both feeling no pain, I decided to mess with them a little.

I said, "I sit alone in a room and make shit up."

The poor girl said what? Clearly confused.

Her sister wasn't yet passed out. I figured the bartender was going to have to call the mom to come get the drunk older daughter at any moment.

"You asked me what I did for a living," I said to the younger birthday girl. She nodded. So I said, "I make my living by sitting alone in a room and making shit up and people pay me a vast amount of money to do that."

Jim was laughing at this point and the older sister's head was going for the bar, so I suggested the younger sister get her older sister to a bathroom fairly quickly. She had that look that drunks get right before they throw up.

The older sister slurred, "Good idea."

And the two staggered off with Jim and I both laughing. I really shouldn't

pick on young, drunk kids, but an old guy has to have some fun at some point. (grin)

And that brings me to my third point of the night.

Don't Forget to Have Fun

If you can't have fun writing and traveling, what in the world are you doing either for?

Just saying.

The Writing of
Ace High: A Cold Poker Gang Mystery

Day 1: Words written: 8,000.
Total so far: 8,000.

CHAPTER FOUR

SECOND DAY OF writing on the novel and it was difficult, as I expected. For a couple of reasons I'll talk about below.

But it still happened and I got just over 7,600 words done.

So day two was a success. Not as planned, but as expected.

Detailing Out the Day

I made it out of bed by noon and by 1 p.m. I had showered, gotten dressed, and was headed for lunch in the buffet with the guys.

I was exhausted and my shoulders felt like rocks. Writing this many words (over 9,000 yesterday not counting e-mails) is a physical sport to not take lightly. I did my best to set up this hotel room in a comfortable fashion, but even at home, writing 9,000 plus words in a day would have frozen up my shoulders the following day.

Back to the room around 3:30 p.m. after some fun discussions and too much food.

So I took a nap. (The afternoon poker tournament was cancelled for some reason, so didn't even have to face that decision.)

Woke up feeling even worse, but managed to sit down and get 1,200 words done by 5:30.

A short break and another 1,300 words by 6:30 p.m.

Another nap, barely waking up in time to meet the guys at 8 p.m. for dinner. Feeling a little better by then, but not much.

We made it back to the Nugget after dinner by 10 to play in the 10 p.m. poker tournament, but I only had 2,500 words and was still feeling like crap at that point. So I skipped it and came back to the room.

A third short nap and I got to writing around 11 p.m.

Between 11 p.m. and 4:30 a.m., with short breaks, I wrote 5,100 more words. I was going to push more, but still had to write this chapter of this book.

More WMG Writers' Guides
from all your favorite booksellers
in trade paper and electronic editions.

So 7,600 words of fiction for the day. Another day on target.

Two down, three to go.

Some Expected Problems

I have been writing long enough to know that the second day after a sudden jump to a large day of writing is always painful.

The third day, tomorrow, I expect will be easier, and from there I expect this to be a cruise to the end. At least physically.

But a couple of real issues face you when traveling.

Exhaustion

No one I know doesn't get tired while traveling. Lots and lots of obvious reasons for this. When trying to also write, I discovered my brain (from the new stuff around me) feels overloaded and scattered. And the exhaustion doesn't help.

It takes a real focus to just not say, "To hell with it."

So when traveling, expect exhaustion to hit on the second day after you arrive. If you are trying to hit a deadline or a quota as I am this trip, expect exhaustion ahead of time and be gentle with yourself. Notice I took three naps today.

And didn't play poker.

Physical Issues

Yes, typing is a physical thing. And it takes practice and work to build up to a level like I am doing this trip. But if you have been following my blog, you know that lately I haven't been working at this level on my writing. I've been doing many other things.

So suddenly I jumped to over 9,000 words. I expected the rock shoulders this morning. Didn't like them, but I had Advil with me to help and took the Advil right before a nap.

I expect tomorrow the shoulders will be stiff and sore still, but not as bad.

In other words, practice at levels of production helps the stress. And helps the muscles get used to that level of production. Just be prepared for that even if you are ramping up production at home.

Focus Issues

This is a problem that hits on the second and third days of something like this. The only way I know to deal with this issue is to set your goals firmly ahead of time and then through the various distractions and exhaustions, keep the goals firmly in mind.

Today I found that tough. And to be honest, if I had had a laptop sitting here, I might not have opened it. But having this big screen sitting here glowing at me sort of kept me reminded every time I woke up that I needed to be focused.

More WMG Writers' Guides
from all your favorite booksellers in trade paper and electronic editions.

I didn't expect that, but it turned out to be a nice bonus. Go figure.

Tomorrow will be another focus issue day because I have numbers of things planned. So I will talk more on this topic in a coming chapter.

So now I am going to go get six hours of sleep so I can again meet the guys in the buffet tomorrow morning for breakfast at one.

The Writing of
Ace High: A Cold Poker Gang Mystery

Day 1: Words written: 8,000.
  Total so far: 8,000.
Day 2: Words written: 7,600.
  Total so far: 15,600.

CHAPTER FIVE

THIRD DAY OF writing on the novel and it turned out to be one of the types of days I was worried about having when doing the planning.

The vacation part of the day and a bunch of business completely overwhelmed the writing hours.

And there was a lot of business stuff.

So I ended up with 3,800 words, but still it was a really fun day, which is the main reason I am traveling here. So maybe there will need to be an adjustment on this nonfiction book. I'll talk about that below.

Detailing Out the Day

I made it out of bed by noon and by 1 p.m. I had showered, gotten dressed, and was headed for lunch in the buffet with the guys.

I felt much better today than I did yesterday, as I expected I would. Shoulders were free and nothing really hurt, even though I had only gotten about six hours of sleep.

We sat around for two hours in the buffet eating great food and talking, then headed for the poker room for the 3 p.m. tournament.

I lasted until the fifth round. Just ran into a couple better hands and by 4:30 I was headed for the door to come up here and write.

I spent about two hours on business stuff and e-mail because, to be honest, today had some really fantastic business news. So I was in a wonderful mood even though it was 6 p.m. and I hadn't written a word.

I managed 800 words before taking a very short nap.

Then at 6:45 I met the guys to go flying, meaning the zip line. That took two hours before we got done with that at around 9 p.m. Fantastic fun. I will put the video from the head gear I had up on my YouTube channel.

Back to the buffet we went and we ate there until around 10:30 when they went to play in the nightly poker tournament and I came back up here to write.

I got started by midnight after more e-mail and a walk to the store for water and snacks and such.

I managed 1,400 words before the guys texted me that one of them had won the tournament and they were headed to the restaurant for pie.

Off I went with them, getting back to the room around 3:30 a.m.

I got started again writing and did 1,600 more words, bringing the total on the novel to 3,800 words for the day. Way off the pace I hoped to set, but what the hell, it was a fantastic business day and a really fun day with old friends.

Adjusting—A Backup Plan

Since I wanted to finish the novel by Sunday night, which is looking more problematic at the moment, I do have a backup plan. You see, I have two more days of travel (at least, assuming I can get over the mountains between here and my home) after I leave Las Vegas.

So WMG would basically do the cover so that the FIVE was crossed out like an editorial mark and the word "six" would be added. I'm not saying that's going to happen, but it has always been the backup plan.

And if you try a challenge like this, with unknown real-world events possible, set up a backup plan right from the start. That will keep you sane.

I'm not pushing that plan into motion until the end of the 5th night. I've been known to rally and I honestly don't know what will happen in the next few days. So anything is possible.

But the backup plan is in place.

And the book itself is going along great. Very twisted mystery, as normal for this Cold Poker Gang series, and I have no clue where it is going. I'm just letting my detectives figure it out and I'm typing as fast as I can to keep up with them.

Great fun all the way around.

A fun day, great business news, wonderful food, fun writing, and fantastic friends.

I honestly don't give a crap that I didn't get a few more words done. 3,800 words in one day is more than most writers do and I really need, at times, to keep that in perspective.

And today I did.

The Writing of
Ace High: A Cold Poker Gang Mystery

Day 1: Words written: 8,000.
 Total so far: 8,000.
Day 2: Words written: 7,600.
 Total so far: 15,600.
Day 3: Words written: 3,800.
 Total so far: 19,400.

CHAPTER SIX

FOURTH DAY OF writing on the novel and it turned out fine, but I didn't make up any ground. But I had a great day both writing and on the vacation part.

I ended up with 8,200 words, but had been hoping for a few thousand more. I might still get some more in, but I'll add them on to tomorrow if I do since it's 4 a.m.

Detailing Out the Day

Once again I made it out of bed by noon and by 1 p.m. I had showered, gotten dressed, and was headed for lunch in the buffet with the guys.

Yes, we are eating most meals in the buffet because, to be honest, it's fantastic and they keep changing the food from day to day, so it's been different every time we have eaten there.

And besides, I have two novel series, including the one I'm writing, that use that buffet as a setting.

Can't figure out I like the place, can you? (grin)

We sat around for two hours in the buffet eating great food and talking, then we all headed back to our rooms. I went

to write and nap and they went to watch the football games and nap.

I managed 3,800 words and did my e-mail and such between 3:30 and 7:30, plus got a nap. Not bad.

Back to the buffet for dinner.

We ate there until around 10 when they went to play in the nightly poker tournament and I came back up here to write.

I managed another 3,300 words by 1 a.m. when I got a text that they were both out of the tournament and were heading for a restaurant to get a snack. I joined them and managed to get back here to the room around 3 a.m.

I finished up another 1,100 word session by 4 a.m. to stop and do this chapter.

So even though I have a backup plan if I can't finish the book, I am still feeling that finishing the novel is possible by tomorrow evening.

So not going to change the cover or the title of these chapters just yet. I've been known to have some big days and I honestly have no idea where this book is going or how long it will be. If it goes too much past forty thousand words, it will take a sixth day. But if it comes in at forty thousand or a few thousand under, five is still possible I think.

So right now, since I have some ice tea in me and don't feel that tired, I think I'll do another session or two.

Just might finish this in five days while traveling after all. We shall see.

A Couple of Things About This Challenge I Realized Today

Focus. Doing something like this requires a focus I wasn't sure I would be able to do. I didn't change any of my vacation plans today, but instead of coming back to the room and turning on the television and watching one of the football games, I sat down to write.

Also, when left with a choice to sit in a poker tournament I didn't feel like playing in or go write, I picked writing. My focus was on what I was having fun with and this novel and this writing is great fun.

Alone. Not a chance in the world would I try this kind of thing if I hadn't been traveling and staying in this suite alone. Nope. I wouldn't even think of trying it if Kris was traveling with me.

Back to focus for a reason for that.

The Writing of
Ace High: A Cold Poker Gang Mystery

Day 1: Words written: 8,000. Total so far: 8,000.

Day 2: Words written: 7,600. Total so far: 15,600.

Day 3: Words written: 3,800. Total so far: 19,400.

Day 4: Words written: 8,200. Total so far: 27,600.

CHAPTER SEVEN

FIFTH AND FINAL day of writing on the novel and it turned out fine. Yup, got the book finished. Go figure. I'll explain more below.

I ended up with 9,500 words today including the 1,600 I did after I finished yesterday's chapter here.

Book came in at 37,100 words. But I might need to flesh out the ending because I figured out the end, was tired and did a lot of "and then this happened…"

And actually, all the novels in this series have run from 36,000 words to 43,000 words, so this is spot on for length for the series.

However, more than likely (as I run back for the spelling check that I do for every book) I'll cycle through the last part and add another thousand or so words on that ending.

Why that happens on things like this I'll talk about below.

Detailing Out the Day

Once again I made it out of bed by noon and by 1 p.m. I had showered, gotten dressed, and was headed for lunch in the buffet with the guys.

The last morning of this ritual.

I ended up eating ten meals in the Golden Nugget Buffet during my six days here. And never really had the same food. I have never seen a buffet that had consistently great food and changed it up every meal and every day.

And not just changed up one or two things, but across the board.

Except the bread pudding was there every meal. Damn it.

So after two hours of talking and such, I came back to the room, watched a little of the Packer's game, then went to work.

I managed 3,100 words and did my e-mail and such before turning the television back on and watching that fantastic finish on that game. Wow, just wow.

Then I wanted to do some research, so I went out for a walk. Just to put the neighborhood of where my detectives live back in my mind clearly.

Then I came back into the casino. I was going to cash in $30 in chips I had in my pocket, but decided to play some blackjack for a few hands instead. (Remember I paid my way through college playing blackjack down here and in Reno.) I seldom play anymore. But I thought it would be fun for a very short time.

Found a single-deck $10 table and sat down. I was the only one there. Thirty minutes later I walked away from the table after tipping the dealer $10 with $300. But compared to poker, playing basic strategy blackjack is deadly dull.

Only question I had was should I split 7s against a 12. Of course I should, odds slightly in my favor, but it took me a fraction of a second to remember that. (grin)

After that I went back to writing and managed another 2,800 words before heading back to the buffet for dinner right at the end of the second football game.

Back to the buffet. Sounds like an SF movie.

Only Jim was left, my friend for over 52 years now. We basically sat and talked until they kicked us out. (They put away all the food and started cleaning the carpet.)

Always great seeing him.

After that I managed another 2,000 words to get to the end and also did a bunch of workshop stuff. I also packed one of my bags and took it out to the car so I would have to make one less trip tomorrow.

So it turns out that I don't have to change the title of this nonfiction book.

I actually wrote a complex and very twisted mystery novel in five days while on vacation with my friends. And I wrote it into the dark and without a starting idea.

And as I said earlier in this book, this is the first time I have ever been able to write on the road, let alone an entire novel. So it has sure been a learning experience for me.

I wrote an entire novel in five days and also wrote this nonfiction book which I will finish up tomorrow. And yes, later on we will package the novel with these chapters so you can see everything I did.

A Couple Major Realizations

Deadline. I really wanted to get the novel done today. I didn't want to be working on it after a long drive tomorrow. So that desire of doing the five-day book while in one spot put on a pretty amazing feeling of deadline.

Not sure I liked the deadline part, but it worked this time. I have tended to shy away from deadlines as I have gotten older. I wouldn't do this again just for that reason alone.

Rush to the End. That is what ended up happening for this book some. I always feel that way on every book I write, but most books I have the time to make myself slow down, but this one had to come in under deadline.

The moment I figured out how the book was going to end, right before I went to dinner, I didn't want to spend another moment writing it. The book was done in my mind.

So those last 2,000 words were tough since I kept moving to do other things. Now I really understand why you should never, ever have the Internet on your computer. Yikes.

I know, for a fact, I did some scenes cut short or in summary instead of actually having the characters walk through the scene. But I'll do that on a last cycle of those 2,000 words later. If they need to be cycled. I won't know until I get home.

Tomorrow night (after I drive about twelve hours on my way back north) I'll do the final chapter in this nonfiction travel book on writing.

A summary, an epilogue, a bow on the silliness of it all.

But for now the novel is done and I'm actually amazed it came out as twisted and complex as it did. Sometimes my creative voice can really entertain me.

Great fun.

The Writing of
Ace High: A Cold Poker Gang Mystery

Day 1: 8,000 words written. Total so far: 8,000.

Day 2: 7,600 words written. Total so far: 15,600.

Day 3: 3,800 words written. Total so far: 19,400.

Day 4: 8,200 words written. Total so far: 27,600.

Day 5: 9,500 words written. Final: 37,100.

Epilogue

I AM WRITING this from the comfort of my office at home, the day after I got back, which was late last night.

I ended up having to fight a pretty nasty storm coming in, but made it fine. The drive from Las Vegas to the Oregon Coast took two days, with a stop in Redding.

As I said, the novel came in at 37,100 words. But I know for a fact that I will need to flesh out the ending slightly because I figured out the end, was tired and did a lot of "and then this happened…"

So more than likely the final word count will be closer to 40,000.

Won't be a rewrite. Just replacing a summary paragraph with a chapter. 9,500 words plus a chapter of this nonfiction book was a lot of words on the last day in Las Vegas.

Detailing Out the Trip

The trip took ten days, leaving on a Sunday morning and arriving home late on Tuesday night.

I drove just over 3,600 miles and stayed in four hotel rooms along the way, all suites.

I drove our Cadillac CTS which had no problems other than the last day the interior lights burnt out or shorted or something. No real issue, just annoying as I was trying to find that last hotel in Redding.

I took my big iMac, full keypad, mouse pad, wrist pad, and everything. I

wrapped the computer in a soft blanket, put a pillow against the screen, put the screen toward the back seat against the pillow, sat it on another pillow, and then used the seatbelt to strap it in. It rode like a charm and was easy to carry in and out.

In each room I adjusted the office chair at the desk in the suite, then put two pillows from the bed on the chair to get me up high enough that my hands and arms were in a good position.

On the trip I wrote the 37,000 plus words on the novel and about ten thousand words on this nonfiction book, plus all my standard e-mails, including three nights of doing assignments in hotel rooms.

So I figure my total word count on the trip was just over 60,000 words total.

Looking Back

Crazy Idea.

I honestly have no idea how this idea even came up, let alone why I was stupid enough to try it. I thought about it for about two weeks ahead of time before I mentioned it to anyone.

Of course, Kris just said, "Sure you can do that."

I mentioned to her I had hated to write on trips and never had before in almost thirty years and she just shrugged.

I think I wanted her to give me a good, logical argument against trying it. She refused and just left me out there to dangle in the stupidity of my own idea. (She has done that a great deal over the years, especially with the really stupid ideas like this one.)

Writing a novel in five days is a push even when at home, decks cleared, and food stocked. But doing it in a hotel room

in Las Vegas while enjoying time with my friends and playing some cards?

Seriously?

In hindsight, just flat crazy.

The One Secret

Sitting here safely at home, the one thing I realized I did correctly was not panic at all. I just kept the writing fun. And I didn't let the writing stop me doing anything I really wanted to do.

In other words, I kept it in perspective and flat didn't really care if it didn't work.

A couple nights the guys were headed to midnight food around 1 a.m. and I went and sat with them. I met them for breakfast and dinner every day. I played in a poker tournament and a bunch of blackjack. (Yes, I came out ahead.)

And one evening I spent a bunch of hours with one of my friends doing the Fremont Street Zipline. Great fun.

So the secret was that when there was an hour, I sat down at the computer and wrote.

Since I was also getting my e-mail and such on the same computer, I limited myself to e-mail in the morning and once in the evening, for the most part. That also helped.

I had also done the math, meaning I knew about how many hours I was going to need to write a novel. About 40 hours. Or about eight hours a day.

Which meant that with all the stuff I was doing on vacation, sleep was going to get a short shrift.

But I managed to sleep six hours every night. And get a nap every day.

Perspective Was Everything

This challenge wasn't as important as having fun with my friends in Vegas. I write novels all the time. This one wasn't any more important than anything else I do.

And that kept the critical voice under control. I only had a few times where I felt stuck on what to type next. Once I took a short nap, the other time I went out for a walk to the condo complex my characters were living in.

By the time I got back, I sat down and started typing.

I never once had any idea about where the novel was going and a couple times I left the room after a session to go have a meal with the guys and I was laughing because the book had twisted on me.

I had a blast writing the novel and I sure hope it shows in the book if you read it. One really twisted mystery that kept me entertained for five days.

My Conclusion

This was a writing exercise. It created a novel and this book, which is great.

The reason, deep down, as to why I do this, is twofold.

One: I get bored easily. Challenges are fun for me.

Two: I admire the old pulp writers, the men and women who thought nothing of writing a novel in five days. I read about the pulp writers all the time.

I had a big computer, they wrote with manual typewriters, for the most part.

I did it for one trip, many of the old pulp writers maintained that pace for a decade.

Writers of this modern era are for the most part lazy. Writers think that writing an hour a day is "hard work" and too much for their poor brains to deal with. Writing forty hours a week, as I did, is just too much for most modern writers to grasp. And the very idea would kill an English teacher dead.

Writers of this modern era are scared most of the time. So they must spend months outlining to make sure their novel is dull and won't have energy. And heaven help them if they waste a precious word along the way.

Writers of this modern era are in a hurry to be successful. So they write to market, to what others want them to write.

So this writing exercise was for me, to prove to myself that once again I was born too late as a writer. I wanted to prove to myself that I flat don't belong with all the lazy, whiny writers of this modern time.

I figured any pulp writer could write a novel in five days.

But could they do it while traveling?

Sure, but not as easily.

So for me it felt like a way that for a few days I could hang my hat with some of the pulp writers of old.

It was great fun.

And I hope you all enjoyed following along.

Missed the last Ghost of a Chance novel?
It's available from all your favorite booksellers
in trade paper and electronic editions.

Introduction to
Last Man Out

I would normally never write an introduction to a story like this, but I wanted to say a word about the very-much-missed editor of this story, Roger Zelazny. Now I knew Roger, he had been a friend for decades, but I seldom talked to him on the phone. Our friendship existed mostly at conferences and over dinners and at parties.

And as an editor and publisher, I had bought a number of stories from him over the years as well.

So the day he called, I was surprised. He started off by saying, "Dean, you used to be a golf professional, didn't you?"

I said I had.

"And you used to play cards for a living, both poker and blackjack, right?" Roger asked.

I again said I had, surprised he knew so much about me.

"Great," he said. "I need a story in either one of those areas for an anthology I'm working on."

He then told me the details and limits and payment amount and then pretty much hung up.

Instead of me buying stories from him, he wanted to buy a story from me. Strange how life works that way.

So I came up with an idea for a story around a special golf tournament. But by the very nature of the subject, golf tournaments are mostly dull unless it's the final day of a major tournament. So to get past the nature of the dullness, I had added sex to the golf tournament and gave the story a moral, something golf seldom gives you either.

I called Roger back and asked him about the sex with golf. His only response was, "I figured, Smith, that you would come up with something off the edge. Write it and let me decide."

So I wrote it. And he loved it. And he went to bat with the publisher for keeping it in the anthology.

Even though I was a golf professional for a lot of years, I seldom write about golf. In fact, this is one of the very few golf stories I have ever written. And it's all thanks to Roger Zelazny.

We all still miss you.

~

Dean Wesley **Smith**

USA Today Bestselling Writer

**In Golf and In Life
Beauty Rests
Just Below the Surface**

O LAST MAN
OUT

Golf Professional David Moore never expected a naked woman to be the prize for winning a golf tournament.

Yet there she sat beside him in the golf cart.

So perfect. Not even a drop of sweat.

An afternoon to remember that beauty really exists only skin deep.

Last Man Out

One

THE HEAT OF the sun already had the front nine of Troutdale Memorial Country Club sweltering and it was going to get hotter before the day was through. A slight breeze brought the faint odor of cooking bread across the first hole from Eddy's Bakery to the west.

My stomach rumbled at the smell, but I ignored it. I had been on a diet for weeks in a somewhat-successful effort to slim down. I didn't need hunger on top of a long afternoon baby-sitting ten men and their stupid golf tournament.

I wiped a finger around the inside of the neck of my new yellow Izod shirt and glanced at the blonde beside me in the golf cart. She seemed to be staying cool enough. It was lucky we had the cart to get a little breeze between shots. Otherwise we would have cooked out here.

About twenty yards in front of me on the first green a poorly struck putt caught the right edge of the cup and spun out, stopping two inches below the hole on the right.

I sighed. That was the end of the road for Dr. Fred Ashley. An eight on the first hole. He got the dubious honor of being the first man out.

A few moans, laughter and some good-natured kidding from the other nine contestants followed the missed putt.

I didn't say anything and neither did the blonde.

She and I had shared a cart for the twenty minutes it took the ten men to play the first short par four hole and I had yet to even ask her name. I glanced at the shiny blonde hair and the huge chest and then headed the cart through the pines for the second tee. She looked vaguely familiar, as if I had seen her in a magazine or something. Knowing these guys and their stupid tournament, anything was possible.

Dr. Ashley threw his putter into his bag and started back up the middle of the deserted first fairway toward the equally deserted clubhouse. We'd be lucky if there was one beer left in the bar by the time we finished this crazy tournament, as mad as the doctor looked.

The other nine contestants followed me toward the second tee.

Nine players left. Eight holes to go.

The rules were easy. The player with the worst score was eliminated on every hole until only one was left after the ninth hole. Under normal circumstances a Sole Survivor tournament was a fun and very challenging tournament.

But these ten members had rented the entire golf course, clubhouse and all, for their private annual tournament. It had cost them over five hundred dollars each and they had changed the rules to the Sole Survivor slightly. After every hole the survivors were going to be rewarded.

"All right, Debbie," Harry Braden said. "Give us our first prize."

Debbie got slowly out of the cart, gave the now silent nine men a big smile, unbuttoned her blouse, and tossed it into the back of the cart with the cooler of beer. She wore a bright-red lace bra that barely contained two of the biggest breasts I had ever seen.

She strutted in front of each man, not even breaking into a sweat, which, for some reason, made her seem even more unreal than the huge breasts did.

The men applauded and made rude comments as she bowed for them and then climbed back into the cart beside me. I tried not to look at her out of the corner of my eye as the men hit their tee shots.

Strange job I had.

As a golf professional, I had often found myself doing all sorts of bizarre tasks. But never had I run a tournament like this. Actually, for this tournament I had had no choice. The Executive Board of the golf course—my boss—wouldn't allow these men to hold their strange tournament unless I went with them and acted as rules committee and chaperone. Guess the Board was afraid they'd tear up the course or something like that.

When I took the head professional's position earlier this year the outgoing professional had slapped my back and mentioned this tournament. He said it was almost worth him staying. That had made no sense to me at all, since he was moving to the best country club in the state.

But now I was starting to understand.

I kept the cart to the back of the tee box as the men hit their shots and headed for the green. Then I turned to the woman and stuck out my hand. "David Moore," I said. "Head golf professional here."

The blonde smiled and shook my hand. "Pleased to meet you, Mr. David Moore. My name is Debbie. Debbie Kramer."

She let go of my hand and before I could add another word, she said, "And please don't ask me what a nice looking girl like me is doing in a place like this."

I laughed. "At least not until the seventh hole. That's the toughest hole on the course."

She laughed back, a high, clear laugh. "Deal."

I headed the cart over the bridge and down the path in the direction of the pack of men. I could feel the sweat dripping down my back and arms. It was going to be a hot afternoon in more ways than one.

Two

JIM FISHER, THE Plumbing King, had the worst score on the next hole and headed back for the clubhouse. Debbie took off her shorts and did the parade number around the tee again for the eight remaining men. Her lace panties matched her bra. I watched her move under the thin lace and tried not to think about going home that night to my wife.

Paula had let herself, as they say, "go" over the last few years and sex was not what it used to be before the kids. I still loved her. That much I was sure of. But it was not much fun going home most of the time. The last year she seemed to always be harping about something. So under the excuse of this new job I spent much of my time at the course. Better to hear golfers complain about the condition of the course than a wife bitch about how I didn't do enough for her or the kids.

Debbie had to put a towel down on the hot cart seat before she could join me back in the cart.

"Two things left to take off," I whispered as one of the men hit his tee shot. "What about the last five holes? Didn't you come a little under-dressed?"

Debbie patted my leg and laughed. "Just you wait and see."

I sighed and went back to watching the golf shots. Hot was not going to describe this afternoon at all.

Craig Stevens of Stevens' Hardware missed a short putt on the third hole and headed for the clubhouse.

On the forth tee Debbie took off her bra.

The men whistled and clapped and I couldn't help but stare. There was not one sign of a tan line. Amazing.

Bouncing down the next fairway with her sitting beside me was damn uncomfortable. About halfway to the green I turned to her. "Money good?"

She nodded. "Yes, the money is nice. How about for you?"

I shook my head, thinking about how Paula was always complaining about how little I made and what a failure I was. She said I paid more attention to how I dressed and my public image at the course than I did to our home.

"No, I'm afraid it's not that good. Golf professionals on local courses like this one don't make that much. You have to be out on the tours before you really make the big money. I tried that, but just couldn't stand the grind, what with the kids and all."

She touched my bare arm with the softest hand I had ever remembered feeling. "Maybe you should do what I do."

I turned and looked at her for a moment, then broke out laughing. "Actually, when you think about it, I sort of do."

She kept a straight face for a two count, then joined me. It was impossible to not stare at her chest as she laughed. I tried. I really did. But it was impossible.

"So how much," I said after we stopped laughing and I somehow managed to stop staring, "if you don't mind my asking, are you going to get for this afternoon?"

She shrugged, which was a motion I hoped she would repeat often. "I don't mind. They are giving me two thousand, plus tips."

I whistled. "That will buy a few drinks."

"That, plus tuition next semester." I must have frowned, because she laughed and added, "Vet school. I'm a second year. One afternoon's work for an entire semester of tuition. Not bad, huh?"

"Not bad at all," I said. "On second thought maybe I should think about doing your job. Think I would pass the physical?"

I puffed out my chest and again she laughed.

The afternoon just kept getting hotter.

Three

A STRING OF profanity came from the direction of the fourth green as the dentist, Dr. Freddie Cramer was eliminated. I hadn't been following how many shots he took. I was glad though that it was him. He was the crudest of the men left.

He stalked off in the direction of the clubhouse and Debbie did the parade around the next tee box again, only this time completely nude. She had light brown pubic hair that was neatly trimmed and everything about her seemed perfect.

Too perfect.

She rejoined me in the cart, adjusting the towel on the seat, but not covering herself. I took a deep breath and headed down the edge of the fairway of the short par three to get to the next tee.

I parked the cart so we could see the green and we sat there in silence, her nude and seemingly cool, me dressed and sweating. Down the fairway the remaining men took an agonizingly long time to hit their shots at the green.

"You're kind of down to the nitty-gritty," I finally said as the last finished and the herd started toward us. "Is it time for me to ask the 'what's a nice girl' question, yet?"

"Not yet," she said. "Seventh hole. You promised." Then she smiled. "Besides, you shouldn't always trust what you are seeing. My boyfriend taught me that."

"Boyfriend? He knows you do this?"

She smiled. "Actually he's helping me with the afternoon."

"Huh?"

She put her fingers to her lips and shushed me as the men came up to the green. "Seventh hole," she whispered.

I studied her nude perfect body for a moment and tried to remember if there was ever a time that Paula had looked like that. Then I reached back into the cooler and got us both a cold beer. She looked cool enough, but I knew I needed one.

Richard Grant took a double bogey five on the hole and headed for the clubhouse with a longing look at Debbie. After he was a distance away and the remaining five men were gathered on the tee box drinking beers, Debbie got up, moved over to the bench and laid down. Then, very slowly, she put one leg up on the back of the bench and ran her hands over her body.

All over her body.

Over *all* of her body.

All of us just stared.

I know my mouth was open.

Most amazing thing I had ever seen on a golf course in all my years as a golf professional.

After a very long fifteen seconds she stopped, rose and moved back over to the cart. She adjusted the towel on the seat and sat down beside me.

I thought my heart was going to stop.

I knew I hadn't been breathing.

"Jesus," Harry Braden said, moving up to the tee with an exaggerated limp. "How the hell are we supposed to hit a golf ball in this condition." He tugged at the leg of his pants.

"Hell, Harry," one of the other men said. "From what I hear you don't have enough to get in the way."

That broke the tension and everyone tried to get in their cheapest shot at the next guy.

Debbie sat beside me, legs crossed, smiling, cool and collected as could be.

Now Available
from all your favorite booksellers in trade paper and electronic editions.

I just kept sweating. This was pure torture.

Halfway down the next fairway Debbie broke the silence. "You like my show?" she asked.

"Are you kidding? It was incredible."

"Good," she said. "I was a little worried about this entire afternoon. Now I'm starting to get into it. This could be fun."

She was telling me? The most beautiful woman I had ever seen was sitting nude, beside me in a golf cart, with her legs slightly open. And she was saying it was going to be fun.

I was really starting to love this job.

Four

SHE WATCHED THE men hit their tee shots as I watched her.

Every detail of her body was nothing short of fantastic. Right off the pages of the top men's magazines. Way, way, way too good to be true. I had always thought the women in those magazines were a combination of good camera angles and airbrushing. But here sat Debbie, better than any picture.

"I know one thing for certain," I finally managed to say. "This is going to be a memorable day for me."

"That's a nice thing to say." She squeezed my leg. "I'll do my best to make it more so."

I just shook my head and dug us both out another beer.

Pete Beeker was eliminated next and headed through the trees to the clubhouse. I could just imagine the party back there in the bar as each man arrived and told his story of what happened on each

49

tee. I could see right now why this was an annual event. Maybe I should suggest this idea at the next Professional Golfers Association meeting.

Four men stood beside their bags as Debbie climbed out of the cart. She moved over to Harry, took his driver out of his hand and then moved over to the bench. She laid on the bench with one foot on the ground and the other foot up on the back. Then she took Harry's driver and licked the grip like it was a candy cane.

Then she did something with Harry's driver that I had never seen done with a golf club before.

After a minute she jumped up off the bench, walked back over to Harry, handed him his club and said, "I think you're up."

I wish I had a camera for the look on Harry's face as he stood there looking down at the grip of his driver. The rest laughed until finally Harry joined in.

Debbie winked at me as she climbed into the cart.

I was falling in love. It was way beyond lust.

Three holes left to play.

The competition got serious. All four men wanted to stay and watch Debbie's performance on the next hole. But they knew that the worst score couldn't. Somehow, some way, Harry regained enough composure to beat Alex Golden in a tie breaker. Even Debbie applauded the good golf and blew a kiss at Alex as he headed for the clubhouse.

Three men left: Harry Braden, Stephen Baker, and Stanley Haycraft. All three looked sweaty from the heat and excitement.

Debbie got out of the cart and slowly walked over to Stanley, smiling. I watched him as he licked his lips. He looked like he wanted to turn and run as fast as he could.

But before he could decide, Debbie reached him, took her hand and placed it between his legs. A few quick seconds and then she moved to Stephen and did the same thing. Then finally Harry. All three men just stood there, mouths open. I don't think a one even moved a finger.

She climbed into the cart beside me. She had this cat-like smile on her face, like she was enjoying the hell out of giving all of us blue balls.

At that point, I was glad my job was only driving the golf cart. No way could I have concentrated on hitting any stupid golf ball. This had to be the hardest tournament ever imagined.

Harry was still first up again and it took him two large gulps of beer just to get the ball to stay on the tee. I had never seen a man's hands shake so much.

After the three men managed to hit their tee shots and headed down the eighth fairway, I turned to Debbie. "Well, we finished the seventh hole. Can I do the standard line now?"

She laughed. "You really are curious, aren't you?"

I nodded. "Yeah, I think that describes it."

She turned to the air in front of the cart, put her hand against her ear and said, "John, what do you think?"

I stared at where she was talking and then back at her.

She listened for a moment and then nodded. Then she turned to me. "John asks if you can keep your mouth shut?"

"John?" I looked at the empty tee and the empty air in front of the cart and then back at her. "Who is John?"

Debbie laughed, her breasts bouncing as she did so. "Oh, I forgot I didn't tell you his name. John's my boyfriend. I told you earlier that he was helping me. He's a doctorial student in physics at the University."

Again I glanced at the front of the cart where she had been talking and the empty tee box beyond. Nothing.

This woman had flipped.

I was sitting in a golf cart with a naked insane woman.

"Can you keep your mouth shut?" She asked.

I nodded again. "Yeah. No problem."

Debbie looked at the three men who were now a good two hundred yards down the fairway, then again touched her ear. "John, can you break the illusion for a second?"

There was a slight shimmering in the air and suddenly Debbie was sitting beside me.

Only it was a very different Debbie.

This Debbie had much darker skin, and was covered with clear plastic straps around her much smaller chest, waist and boyish hips. Other strips extended down each arm and leg. Her dark brown hair was pulled up and taped to the top of her head with the same type of clear strip. She had a pimple on her left cheek and no makeup.

And she was sweating a lot. Maybe even more than I was.

"What the hell?" I rubbed my eyes and looked again. The naked, taped-up woman was still sitting beside me.

I shook my head. "Too much beer."

Debbie laughed. "Really something, isn't it? John's been working on this for years and he thinks he finally has it perfected. The Debbie you were seeing was nothing more than a very, very sophisticated illusion just above my own skin." She laughed. "Don't ask me how he does it. I don't have a clue."

I just sat there staring at her until she finally touched my leg. "You all right? You won't say anything, will you?"

I shook my head. "Not a word. As if I believe what I have just seen."

She pointed at the three men on the far green. "We better get going then. Don't want to let the winners down, now do I?" She again touched the side of her head. "John, bring it back."

The perfect, blonde Debbie shimmered back into place.

"Anything missing," she asked, looking down at herself.

"Not that I can see," I said, taking a moment to stare at the returned body before I started the cart down the path.

Stephen missed a five-foot putt that would have tied him with the other two. That left one hole to play between Harry and Stanley. Debbie met them as they came up on the last tee box. "There's a key in an envelope in the clubhouse for the room where one of you boys will meet me," she said. "But right now I'd like to give you a little preview of what the winner might expect.

She dropped down on the grass in front of them, opened up her legs real wide and for the next thirty seconds performed with the fastest fingers I had seen since Paula took me to a piano concert.

And all without breaking into a sweat or getting one blade of grass on her skin.

She was an illusion.

Yet I could not believe the woman under that illusion was really there. I wanted to believe in the blonde Debbie. I wanted to believe that she existed here, in front of me, being open and alive and fun and all sex.

Just like I had done as a teenager, I wanted to believe in the perfection of a woman.

But she was just an illusion.

Compared to who she is now, my wife Paula had been an illusion when I first met her.

Blonde Debbie squirmed on the grass and I thought of the other, taped-up Debbie, sweating and working to make vet school tuition under that illusion. It took a great deal of the effect away.

But it was still an amazing sight to watch.

Finally, she stopped, stood, climbed into the cart with me and looked back at the two men still standing on the tee box with their mouths hanging open and their golf bags in front of their flies. "I'll be waiting for the winner. Good luck."

She motioned for me to drive toward the clubhouse.

It took me a long moment to find the gas pedal.

The cart path up the ninth hole wound in and out of the trees. About halfway up the fairway, behind a small stand of trees, Debbie had me stop. "Better put some clothes back on the illusion," she said, laughing.

I watched her as she quickly put on her lace bra, then her skirt and blouse. She left her underwear in the tray between our seats. "A shower is sure going to feel good," she said. "And getting all this tape off of me."

She got back into the cart and laid her hand on my lap, right near my crotch. "And I want to thank you for being so nice."

"My pleasure," I said, telling her the truth. "You really going to be in that room with the winner?"

Debbie laughed again. "Yeah, but nothing will really happen. That is the one rule I set up beforehand with them: No touching. Only looking. John has the room completely wired. I'll be in the room putting on a great show, but the illusion will do all the work. Trust me, the winner won't know the difference."

"Oh, I believe you."

Debbie nodded and spread her legs so I could see the illusion of her crotch.

"You play better golf than these men do, don't you?"

I nodded. "I'm a professional. They're amateurs. I'd better."

"I'm a professional, too," she said. "At least until I get out of school."

She opened her legs even wider. "You interested in a quick show? No touching, though. Might mess up the tape."

"It wouldn't really be you, would it?"

She shook her head. "Nope."

I looked at her crotch and then at her beautiful face. "Thanks," I said, shaking my head. "But I think I will stay in the real world, such as it is."

"I sort of thought you might," she said. She grabbed her red panties and slipped them on in a motion that I was sure I would dream about for years.

Somehow I got her to her old Datsun in the parking lot and said good-bye. As she dropped down behind the wheel the illusion shimmered and was gone, leaving a taped-up, sweating woman. She waved to me from the car as she backed out. I liked the real Debbie more than the blonde magazine girl.

I went into the clubhouse and herded the losers out of the bar to the ninth green so that they could watch the end of their tournament.

Harry birdied the hole and ended up the Sole Survivor. I gave him the key to Debbie's hotel room and sat in the bar the rest of the day just thinking about Debbie, both the real and the illusion.

That night I took some flowers home to Paula.

After she went to bed I spent an hour in front of the mirror, just staring at myself, wondering.

How deep the real me was buried?

Missed the last Thunder Mountain novel?
It's available from all your favorite booksellers
in trade paper and electronic editions.

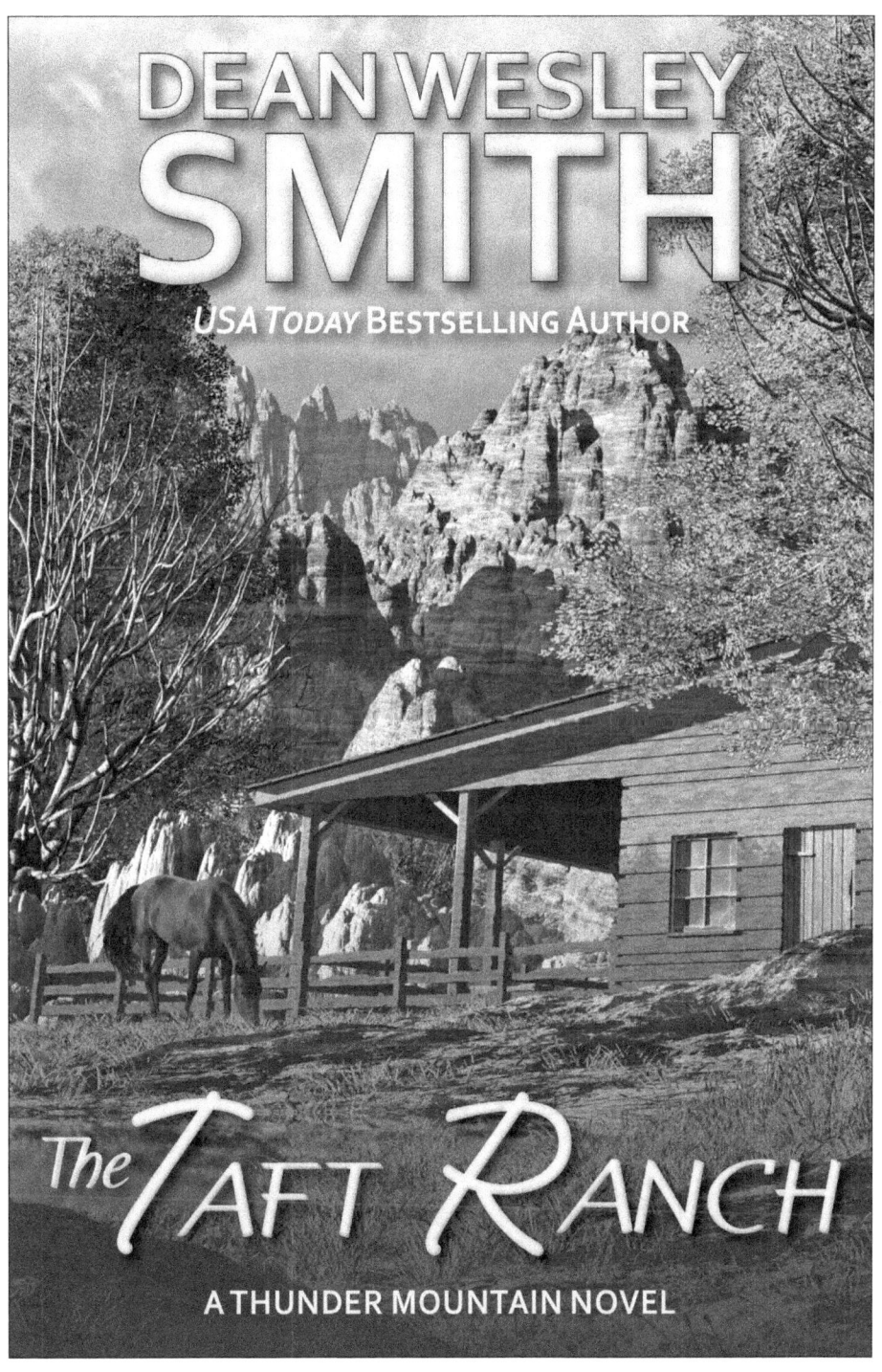

Dean Wesley Smith

USA Today Bestselling Writer

In the dead city
Carey found a life
and a future.

SHADOW
IN THE CITY

Carey went back into the dead city of Portland, Oregon, four years after something killed just about everyone. She mostly wanted to see if anyone still lived.

Instead, in the dead city Carey found a life and a future.

This story became part of my novel Dust and Kisses *in* Smith's Monthly *#1, a start to my Seeders Universe series of novels.*

"Shadow in the City" is based on the song lyrics of "Here in the City" by Janis Ian, written with permission for Stars Anthology *edited by Janis Ian and Mike Resnick.*

The lyrics this story is based on are reprinted here with permission from Janis Ian.

Shadow in the City

"You don't see many shadows here in the city
Only picturesque windows, all covered and dirty
Black and grey that once was new
Yesterday that once was you
No, I can't find my shadow in the city"

"Here in the City"
Janis Ian

Chapter One

SHE STOOD ON the abandoned freeway overpass and stared at the gray of the dead city of Portland, Oregon, and the deep blue of the gently flowing river below her. Four years ago the city below her had died along with the rest of the world. So why had she picked today, of all days, to finally go back?

Carey Noack was five foot two and didn't have an extra ounce of fat on her body. Over the last four years she had kept her light-brown hair cut short and out of the way. Today, for the final hike into the center of the big buildings, she wore a black sleeveless T-shirt, jeans, and her favorite tennis shoes.

"Man, Carey, how stupid is this?" she asked herself as she used a small towel from her pack to wipe the sweat from her face and arms. The weather had turned out to be one of those typical Oregon summer days, where the bright sun and clear skies made the air feel warmer than it actually was. It seldom got above seventy degrees where she lived, overlooking the sandy beach and the pounding waves of the Pacific Ocean, making today feel even worse.

She finished wiping off her arms, put the towel back in her pack, and grabbed the water bottle.

"Better keep drinking this," she said out loud before taking a long, deep drink of the warm water. She was going to have to be careful, make sure she didn't push too hard. She hated heat, and the last thing she would need would be to get heat stroke now.

Standing there on the overpass, it was hard to push away the memories of nightmarish last days she had spent in the city, and the last trip to the coast. It had been hot that week as well. The dead, staring bodies had been everywhere, filling the hot winds with the smell of rotting flesh.

She had simply run, trying to get away from the death and the smell. Of course there had been dead bodies in the small towns on the coast as well, and it had taken her some time to find sanctuary. The house she had taken, just north of Depoe Bay, sat on a rock ledge jutting out

into the ocean. The breezes were always off the water, and seldom did the smell of rotting flesh reach her.

Why, after four long years of living alone on the coast, was she back today, of all days?

Was she really that lonely? She knew that many, many nights, especially during the first year, she had simply sat and cried, trying to hold back the overwhelming feelings of sadness, shock, and loneliness. It was one thing to be a loner when the world was alive around her. It was another to be completely alone, talking to herself and her cats.

She missed her cats. She hoped she had left enough food for them to make it until she got back to the coast.

She had half expected that the buildings of the city would be crumbling and dead as well. But instead there was only evidence of lack of care. Windows were covered with dirt and film, weeds were growing thick in the cracks of the sidewalks, and nothing was lit.

The stoplights swinging lightly in the hot wind at the end of the overpass were now nothing more than dead eyes hanging over empty streets. It gave her the feeling that someone was watching her.

Carey shook off the feeling, took a second, long drink from the bottle of water, and stared down at the freeway. She had to be careful. There was no telling what waited for her there.

Damn she missed her cats.

The hot wind snapped at her short hair. At least now the winds didn't bring the smell of death as it had done the day she left. Four years of time had cleared that out, and she was grateful.

She picked up the backpack and shifted it slightly to make sure one strap didn't rub her shoulder too long. The pack contained enough water to get her by for a few days, plus food for two weeks, and extra ammunition for her rifle and the pistol in her belt.

She had spent a pretty good amount of time over the last two years learning how to fire that pistol and the rifle quickly and accurately. For some reason, she felt she actually might run into someone else alive on this hike. And since she was a woman alone, she didn't dare take any chances. But so far that hadn't been the case. Not even a sign that anyone had passed through the area at some point over the past four years.

Still, the small rifle felt good in her hands. A comfort. And for the rest of the walk into town she would carry it off her shoulder, loaded and ready.

Her hope, and her fear, was there *would* be other survivors in the city. She was convinced that a normal, sane person would have given up that hope by now; but still, here she was today, standing on the edge of the dead city, ready to check.

Carey sometimes lay awake at night listening to the waves pound the beach and rocks below her home and thought of people, and how nice it would be to talk to someone, or even listen to someone else talk. Just companionship. Four years of living alone had given her a lot of time to think, and she knew that simple, easy companionship wasn't going to happen. She was convinced she was going to die alone.

She glanced behind her, up the freeway the way she had come. Back that direction was home, with the comforts of generators for electricity, large screen television for running movies, and a converted neighbor's house full of more books than she would ever manage to read.

She couldn't believe that in all the death, she had managed to make the coast feel like home. The first year she had adopted two stray cats by slowly feeding them enough for them to trust her. Stingy was an old yellow cat who hogged the food, and Betty sat and purred while being petted, but never really left Stingy's side. Carey talked to them all the time.

She had also set up fishing nets and crab pots, and planned her days around finding enough food to keep going. During the spring, summer, and fall, she kept her gardens tended, with the biggest problem being keeping the deer out. She had built and stocked a root cellar, and filled another close-by house with canned goods she hoped would last.

Living like that, she had cut herself off from the sights, sounds, and reminders of what had happened to the rest of humanity. She knew how to be alone, how to live alone. That didn't worry her any more, since she had proven to herself she could do it. But for some reason the thought of *dying* alone scared her a great deal.

And she really wanted someone to talk to. Someone besides her cats. She had to find out if she really was alone, if the human race was going to die with her, or if there was still hope.

There had to be hope.

Considering the fluke circumstances that had allowed her to survive, she was certain that if there was anyone else, the numbers would be few. For a week before that last day, scientists around the world had been whispering among themselves about what seemed like a cloud approaching Earth, although actually Earth, and the rest of the solar system, were approaching the cloud.

No one was exactly certain what it was. Dust had been ruled out, with the leading theory being energy of some sort, visible only because of the light refraction it was causing to the stars on the other side.

Something out there was bending light, twisting it, ripping it apart, and Earth was going to pass right through that something. Even on the night side of the planet, no one would see the glow of the wave. It was just no big deal, just a scientific curiosity.

She had been a post-doc student in electromagnetics at the time, working at the University of Oregon with the renowned Dr. Addenson, the most famous man in her field. His main lab was down near the river in Portland, and she had taken an apartment in Portland, two hours north of the University of Oregon in Eugene, to work with him for the summer, and with luck, the fall semester. It had made being with her boyfriend, Sam, hard at times, since he was still in Eugene most of the time.

Dr. Addenson's belief was that Earth was about to flash through a low-level electromagnetic storm. It would take less than six seconds, by his calculations of the speed of the planet and the measurements they had managed to get of the cloud.

He had sent out a warning to others on his theory, to give them a chance to protect highly sensitive instruments. Strong electromagnetic pulses, like from an atomic blast, could shut down most modern equipment and destroy computers, but no one thought this wave was strong enough to do that.

Actually, no one knew what it was at all.

To prove his theory, Dr. Addenson designed an experiment with two dozen sets of sensitive electronic equipment, to monitor the effects of the pass-through. Part of the experiment was to have one set of control devices locked in a secure vault, designed to protect anything in it from any kind of electromagnetic pulse.

Carey had worked two long days and nights on the experiments, side-by-side with Addenson, getting them ready. Then, during the hour before the storm was to pass over, Dr. Addenson decided she should be closed in the vault along with the control-equipment to monitor them.

No one, not one scientist in the thousands who were aware of the cloud approaching, even thought it would be dangerous. So Carey didn't have any fear when she stepped into that vault and Dr. Addenson closed the door.

When she came out thirty minutes after the cloud had passed, Dr. Addenson lay dead on the floor.

It was a pure nightmare. It seemed that everyone had died in the midst of their normal activities.

The drivers of thousands of cars moving at all speeds had died instantly behind the wheels of their cars. The car wrecks were everywhere, clogging streets and smashed into buildings.

Out near the Portland airport dark clouds of smoke billowed into the air where some planes had crashed.

In an instant, the entire town had gone from a beautiful city to a nightmare filled with death.

Carey could barely remember stumbling out of the lab, checking for life in almost every body. She found Sam where she had left him that morning, still in her bed in her apartment.

Her mother was slumped over the sink of the family home in Beaverton, with the water still running. She had been preparing what looked like one of Carey's favorite meals, corned-beef and cabbage.

She had found her father in his office in the downtown area, slumped over his desk, his secretary slumped beside him.

Thousands and thousands of dead bodies, all seemingly caught in a moment in time. At first it seemed like a bad dream, then a nightmare she desperately wanted to wake up from.

Within hours it seemed the bodies started to smell, bloat up in the heat, look even more nightmarish as the maggots took over.

Finally, after two days of wandering around, Carey found herself back to the lab trying to discover what exactly had happened.

The instruments designed to record and test Dr. Addenson's theory told her the entire story of the storm passing over Earth. It had been electromagnetic, as Addenson had figured, but it had been resonating at the exact right band to shut down the human brain's electrical systems. All the signals that are constantly sent from the human brain to the heart and lungs were short-circuited.

In essence, people died before they even knew what had hit them. No one had been in pain, as far as Carey could tell, and no one had a chance to recover.

The storm's bandwidth had been very narrow. It had killed all dogs, but not small cats. She had discovered later that horses were gone, but not cattle. Rats, mice, most rodents were killed, but not most fish.

Deer had survived as well. And raccoons. And a lot of bees and insects of different types. She had no idea of the long-term effects the massive disruptions in the food chains would have, and she really had no way of actually measuring why some animals' brains were short-circuited by the storm and others were not. All she knew was that humans had drawn the short straw.

After sitting beside Sam's rotting body and crying for a few hours the next morning, she had headed for the coast to

 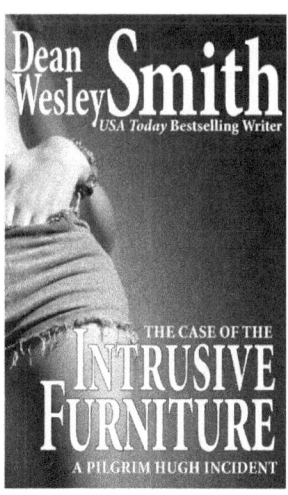 

get out of the growing smell and crammed city-of-death.

Now, four years later she was back.

Carey took another drink from the bottle of water, and studied the area in front of her. The freeway wound down the hill toward the main part of Portland that lay along the river. She could see most of the tall buildings, some of the riverfront, and all of the east side. Portland was still a beautiful town.

A few dozen cars were piled and scattered along the freeway where they had crashed when their occupants died. Wrecked cars was such a common sight for Carey, she often didn't even notice the bodies in them anymore. In these she could see the gleaming white of skeletons behind the steering wheels, their perpetual grins staring ahead.

She finished off the bottle of water, adjusted her backpack into place, and started off the overpass and down toward the empty, weed-littered freeway surface, her rifle in hand. Portland had been her home for a long time, a vibrant city she had loved.

Now she was back, and she had no idea what that would bring.

Chapter Two

HE WOKE WITH a start as the alarm on the computer beeped loudly, echoing through his penthouse apartment. At first Toby Landel couldn't figure out exactly what he was hearing. He had been dreaming about waking up in the morning in his old college dorm room, to his old alarm clock, and the dream had morphed into a nightmarish feeling of the alarm clock going off forever while he searched and searched under piles of clothes and stacks of books, unable to find it no matter how hard he tried.

He had done that, in reality, more times than he wanted to remember back in those days, and now, eight years later, the dream of it still haunted him.

But the computer beeping sounded different, more intense than his old dorm alarm clock, and the reality of its high-pitched, quick beat slowly replaced the ringing in the dream. He opened his eyes and stared at the white ceiling and wood beams over his head.

Something had triggered his security alarm again.

"Damn deer," he said, tossing aside the sheet and standing. He was nude, but since the morning seemed hot and bright, he didn't even bother to slip on his robe or slippers. He moved across the soft carpet toward the computer room, trying to push the sleep and the dream back completely. College was gone, his friends were gone, he was the only one left. And if he ever found that old alarm he'd smash it into a hundred pieces, just with the hopes that dream would stop.

Outside the expanse of open windows around him, the dead city of Portland looked exactly as it had every day for the past two years. But this morning the sun had already cleared off the haze, and he could tell without even going out that the air was hot and dry.

He had set up the penthouse apartment, on the fifteenth floor of what had been the Baxter Building, to cater to his every need. It had soft, rich carpet, big, expansive rooms, and an island kitchen in the center with bright lights and every appliance known to kitchens. He loved cooking, and used the kitchen almost more than any other area.

He had furnished the living room with a deep, comfortable recliner placed directly in front of a large screen television. He had also brought in a couch for the times he wanted to just lay down. To the right of the living room he had put together a weight and exercise room to keep his six-foot frame in top shape. He lifted every day, and ran on a treadmill facing the windows. He figured that he would never know when being in top shape would save his life.

Another recliner that matched the one in the living room, only because there had happened to be two of them in the furniture store the morning he had been looking, sat in front of a massive picture window that looked out over Portland and the Willamette River. Beyond the river and the east side of town he could see the snow-capped peak of Mt. Hood. He loved just sitting in that chair with a drink in his hand staring at the mountain.

Sometimes he sat there and read when it rained, watching the patterns of the water between chapters. When the world had been still alive, he never would have been able to afford a place like this. Now he figured he deserved it. Besides, who could tell him no?

The beeping continued, drawing him toward the computer room he had installed in the west corner of the big penthouse. He had been an electrician by craft before everyone had died, and had installed security cameras for a living for River Drive Security and Alarms. In fact, he had been installing a bank camera with his boss and two others the day everyone just died. He and Jenkins had been down in the vault when suddenly everything went silent on the comm link with the boss in the truck.

Jenkins had gone up to investigate, leaving Toby in the vault. Toby had never seen him again. By the time Toby had given up waiting, left the vault, and went to investigate, Jenkins was gone, and everyone else was dead. The only thing Toby could figure, in hindsight, was Jenkins had seen everyone dead, had freaked, and headed home to check on his wife and kids.

At first Toby thought that something airborne had killed everyone, and it would soon get him, so he had gone back inside. But after a short time of staring at dead bank customers and tellers, he knew that was stupid.

After that he had started to wander the streets, shocked at how people had died, staring at bodies, not really heading anywhere in particular for the first hour or so. Slowly it began to dawn on him that maybe he, and Jenkins, wherever he had gone, were the only ones left alive in a very large area.

Then, with one thought of his parents, it had become important to find out just how widespread this disaster had been.

His parents lived in Bend, a little resort city over the Cascade Mountains at the foot of Bachelor Ski Area. He had managed to make the six-hour drive to Bend in just under twelve, using six different cars when he came upon areas of the road that were jammed with wrecks. He had simply left the car and hiked until he found another car on the other side of the blockage.

All the way, he hoped they had been outside the influence of whatever it was that had happened, that he would find them alive and worried about him. As he got closer, the evidence told him that would not be the case.

He found his parents both dead, as well as everyone else in the small town.

For an hour he had sat in the middle of the main intersection, with the light changing from green to red over his head, honking a car's horn. The sound seemed impossibly loud, echoing off the buildings and the pine-covered mountains.

No one came and told him to stop.

He knew he was alone. Really alone, and the thought scared him more than he had ever been scared before.

The next few days were a blur. He had somehow managed to bury his parents next to his grandparents in the town's cemetery. Then he had gone down to his favorite bar and dragged all the bodies out onto the sidewalk and sat them at tables he had put there, posing each body as best he could in positions of drinking.

Then he had gone inside, alone, and filled the top of the bar with bottles of booze.. That day, and for days after, he had gotten so drunk he couldn't think.

It was finally the smell of rotting human bodies that had driven him away from the small town and out into a cabin way up in the Cascade Mountains, where he stayed for a long winter, waiting for nature to clean up the mess.

Then for a year he had wandered the Northwest, looking for anyone else alive, returning to Portland two years ago.

The computer alarm kept beeping, getting louder as he entered the room.

"All right, all right," he said, "I'm coming."

He expected to see nothing on the monitor, and to have to rewind a tape to see what had triggered the alarm. He had set up the system of motion detectors two years ago, using sensors that triggered cameras and ran off of batteries that he recharged every six months. He had installed the system when he realized the lights from the generator running his penthouse apartment could be seen for miles around the city. Most of the power had failed in the metro area, so his place stood out like a beacon at night.

And if anyone else was alive out there, he figured it would be better to know when they were getting close. The cameras, waiting with their motion detectors, guarded over twenty different ways into the city. About five times a week, deer triggered the alarms. But once, six months before, a ragged, insane-looking man with machine guns had come through, heading north.

The guy clearly did not bathe often, was dragging a pack in a wagon, and talked to himself constantly. No matter how much Toby had wanted another human back in his life, he couldn't bring himself to talk to the guy. The man was just too dangerous. Toby had watched him for two days with hidden cameras, but never let the guy know he was around.

The guy had done one good thing for Toby. He had proven that there were others out there, alive and surviving in some fashion. And ever since that day, Toby had been trying to figure out where they would be. He didn't know what had killed everyone, but something about being inside that bank vault had saved him. And if it had saved him, it had saved others, he was sure.

"All right," he said, dropping his nude body into the chair in front of his monitor command screens. The first thing he did was punch off the beeping alarm. Then he glanced at the control board. The motion had been on the old Interstate 5 headed south. Deer often went through there, since that area was between the hills and the river.

He flicked up an image from a camera he had hidden on a pole, expecting to see either deer, or nothing at all. The sight of a woman, standing on an overpass, shocked him to his very core.

His fingers fumbled over the controls for a moment before he brought up the zoom.

A woman, by herself.

He wasn't seeing things. She wore a black, sleeveless T-shirt, jeans, and tennis shoes. She had short, brown hair, light skin, and a clearly muscled body. He couldn't take his gaze off of her. In the last two years he would have never expected to see a woman, let alone a beautiful woman.

He stared at her image as she finished putting lotion on her arms and then took a drink of water. He would have been attracted to her even when everyone was still alive. He had kept the idea of ever meeting a woman again so tucked away in his mind, he wasn't sure yet if he was still dreaming.

As he watched, she headed off the overpass, a small rifle in her hand, walking with the assured gait of someone who had confidence to spare.

He wanted to shout at the screen that he was here, that she should wait.

It took only a moment before she was headed down the freeway toward town and out of his camera range.

The moment she disappeared he felt a jolt of panic go through him. "Oh, damn," he said.

His hands scrambled over the massive control board he had set up for the security cameras. Finally he managed to activate the next camera covering a section of the old Interstate 5 south of town. For a long moment he thought he had lost her, then she came around a large pile of wrecked cars and kept walking, right at him, as the motion-sensor alarm for that area started to ring.

She was too good to be true, an impossible dream.

He flipped off the alarm, sitting back in silence as he watched her stride toward him.

This could not be happening.

Almost the entire population of the planet seemed to be dead, yet here was a woman walking right into his life.

And just like back in his college days, he had no idea how to meet her.

The rifle carried with ease in her hands seemed to grow bigger.

At least back in college, trying to meet a girl didn't mean risking getting shot. But as he stared at this woman's face, he had no doubt that was a risk he was going to have to take.

Chapter Three

CAREY KEPT HER pace slow and easy in the hot sun as she headed down the freeway, moving in and around wrecked cars with their drivers still strapped behind the wheels, smiling sickly, skeleton-smiles at her.

She didn't let herself look inside the cars too much, because even after four years, those faces still seemed too human, too lifelike in their final poses. Especially the skeletons and mummified remains of the children, strapped in car seats, trusting their parents to take care of them. She didn't want to think about having children. At one point in her life she had thought she might like it. Now that thought wasn't allowed to the surface of her mind.

She stared ahead at the big overpass and the signs directing traffic to the downtown area, or along the bridge and beyond to Seattle.

Seattle. Wow, that seemed so far away. Maybe if there was no one alive here that she could talk to, she could take a look in Seattle some day?

Maybe.

Right now that seemed too far, too much to think about.

She made herself focus on the city in front of her. It seemed so familiar, yet so alien, especially walking along the freeway to get into town. She found herself staying to the road's edge, not that she needed to, just out of respect for old habits.

Ahead of her a half mile or so, the Marriott Hotel tower rose over the river. Her plan was to stay there, in one of the unoccupied rooms with a view. When working in town she had never had a reason, or enough money, to stay in such a nice place. It would be a treat.

She would find a good room, set it up as a base for exploring around the city, and maybe, if she had enough nerve to see Sam's body again, go back to her old apartment for some keepsakes. She planned on stocking the hotel room with food, maybe even get a portable generator in for electricity. But before anything, she would have to check the water, to make sure the water tanks of a place like that had enough good water to last her for a time. After a day this hot, she was going to need a shower.

Maybe with a little work, she could even make the place permanent. It hadn't occurred to her until just that moment that she could have a place in the city, a place on the coast, a place just about anywhere in the world she wanted.

Nothing was stopping her.

She moved along the off-ramp that led down to Front Street and then along the river front a dozen more blocks to the hotel. The grass along the river had turned to weeds, the sidewalks and streets were cracked and growing grass in places. But the city still had a beauty about it, with the blue river flowing through it, the mountains around it, and the green trees everywhere.

Can't Get Enough of Poker Boy?
These stories and more are available at your favorite booksellers.

The air smelled faintly of water and fish, and birds chirped and flitted from nests in the branches of the trees along the old park. She could see where birds had stained the edges of buildings, building nests in windows. Even though it was hot, she was lucky she had come into town on such a beautiful day.

Two blocks short of the hotel, something moved out of the corner of her eye. She snapped around, the rifle up and aimed, her blood racing.

A bird flittered away. She sighed and lowered the gun. "All right," she said out loud, "Calm down, and don't go shooting every little thing that moves."

"I'm very glad to hear you say that," a deep, rich voice said to her right.

She spun around, the rifle again up, her heart pounding so hard she thought it was going to jump right out of her chest.

She found herself face-to-face with a man about her age, with brown, unruly hair, twinkling brown eyes, and a large smile. He had his hands in the air like he had just been caught robbing a bank. He had stepped out of the shadows near an office building and was no more than ten steps from her.

He wore a plain white T-shirt, jeans and new-looking tennis shoes. He had the appearance of having dressed quickly, yet still seemed together and clean. He was also one of the best-looking men she had ever seen, even before everyone died.

It was as if time in the dead city around them froze.

Nothing on the street moved. The river sounds seemed to drop back to silence. She didn't even feel the heat.

She kept her gaze locked on his, the rifle pointed at his chest. She had hoped to find someone else alive, but she hadn't really expected to. And she had never expected to find someone so damn good-looking, and her age.

"I'm not going to bite," the guy said, smiling. His voice was deep and rich and matched his rugged face. His voice stayed level and didn't shake, even though she could tell he was worried about her shooting him.

Then he laughed. "Sorry for the cliché. I didn't know what else to say. I am unarmed and alone. In fact, until you showed up, I thought I *was* alone. Period."

Carey didn't lower her gun, and he didn't lower his arms. She had to get her wits about her, really find out who this person was, and what she had just walked into.

"How did you know I was here?"

"Security cameras," he said, pointing up at the top of a pole back down Front Street. "I have them on all the main entrances into town. A person living alone can never be too careful. But, to be honest, I was also hoping to find someone else alive, passing through."

"And you sit all day and watch your cameras?" she asked, now even more worried that she had run into a weirdo. Why hadn't she listened to her little voice when she felt she was being watched? Mistakes like that could get her killed.

He laughed. "Not hardly. In fact, you woke me when you stopped on the overpass. I have motion detector alarms."

She could feel herself starting to relax just a little, and her little voice wasn't screaming that this man was dangerous. She would have set up security cameras like that if she had thought of it, or known how.

She forced herself to think, slowly, giving herself time to calm down. One mistake, one slip, and she could find herself in a very bad situation. He was shorter than Sam had been, but still clearly very strong. She had to be careful, no matter how much she just wanted to lower her gun and hug this stranger and just talk to him.

"So where do you live?" she asked.

"Baxter Building," he said. "Been there for two years, in the Penthouse. How about you?"

"On the coast," she said.

He nodded, as if understanding that. "Yeah, I was up in the Cascades, in the forest, until the smell cleared."

"How did you survive?"

"Doing the security system in a bank in Beaverton. I was down in the vault, but I have no idea why that protected me."

"I do," she said.

At that his eyes lit up, and his arms lowered a little. "You do? Why? If you know that, it would help me figure out where there are more people alive."

Carey took a deep breath and ignored his question for a moment. Clearly, if he had been watching her, he had known she had a rifle, had known she would get the drop on him, and had risked being shot by introducing himself. The guy had courage, and really wanted her to trust him.

She motioned that he should lower his arms, and she lowered the rifle, keeping her hand on the trigger and the rifle ready to bring up quickly.

"Thanks," he said. He moved his shoulders around a few times. "I clearly need more reps on those hand-raising isometrics."

She smiled, and he smiled back.

How could the first man she had seen alive in four years have such a wonderful smile?

"So, do you have a name?" she asked.

"Toby," he said. "Toby Landel. An actual, native Oregonian, born and raised."

She actually laughed at that, since something like that mattered only to Oregonians.

"I'm Carissa Noack. People used to call me Carey. Also a native through and through."

It felt strange using her full name after four years. Strange, and yet somehow, normal, as if having and using a full name returned a little civilization to the world.

"How about I cook us both breakfast?" Toby said. "My stomach is starting to sound like an earthquake, and I bet you haven't had a good omelet since you left the coast."

"Omelet?" she asked, the word out of her mouth before she had a chance to stop it. She hadn't had anything like a real egg since she moved to the coast. On the hike in she had seen chickens, but hadn't been able to get close to any.

"Yeah, real eggs and everything," he said. "Honest."

"How? Here in the city?"

He nodded, smiling as if he was very proud of having eggs. "It seems chickens survived whatever killed everyone. So I went out into the country and trapped a few, including a couple of roosters, and set them loose in the Rose Garden."

"You're kidding?" she asked. The Rose Garden was the big basketball arena where the Portland Trailblazers basketball team had played.

"I'm not," he said, laughing again. "It does seem strange, now that I think of it. I just figured the seats would make great nests for them, plus it's big enough to hold a lot of birds."

She laughed at the idea. The Rose Garden as a chicken coop. How perfect. "What do you feed them? How many do you have?"

He shrugged. "Every few weeks I scatter a truckload of grain from some sacks I found in a warehouse down by the river. Every month or so I trap some more birds and turn them loose in there. The population seems to be growing. I try to go get the eggs I can find every few days, but there are always more than I can use. I take a bird every few weeks for a special dinner. I bet I have five hundred birds in there now, if not more."

"Amazing," she said.

"Thanks," he said, smiling. "I'd be glad to show it to you, right after breakfast. I would love to have someone to talk to while I'm cooking after all these years."

She stared at him for a moment. She had come back into town with the hope of finding someone else still alive. Now she had, and she didn't know what to do. She hadn't expected this, she hadn't expected anyone, let alone a great-looking guy who raised chickens and could cook.

"All right, Mr. Toby Landel," she said, swinging her rifle up on her shoulder, but making sure her pistol was within easy and quick reach in her belt, "let's just go see how good a cook you really are."

The smile that lit up his face almost melted her right there in the street. She had so wanted company, been so lonely for simply talking to another human, and clearly he had been the same way.

He indicated that they should head off down Front Street in the direction she had been heading. She knew the Baxter Building was beyond the Marriott Hotel a few blocks, so he was indicating the right direction.

She moved into a position beside him, matching him stride-for-stride, feeling just like a junior-high girl faced with talking to a boy on a first date.

She had no idea what to talk about, and in this case, she hoped he didn't turn out to be crazy. Actually, she had worried about that with boys in junior-high as well, so nothing seemed that different,

except that they were the only two people left alive in the city, and if he threatened her, she would have to kill him.

Chapter Four

IT HAD GONE better than Toby had hoped. She hadn't shot him. On top of that, she had actually accepted his invitation to breakfast, after a little bit of conversation.

It was also a fact that his cameras had not done her justice. Up close, her deep brown eyes and intense gaze melted him like no other woman had ever done before. Now granted, he hadn't seen a live woman in four years, but she would have had that effect on him before everyone died.

Now all he wanted to do was talk with her. He had not realized until he started speaking just how much he had missed interacting with humans.

"This is the place," he said, his arm sweeping around the penthouse that no one had seen but him in four years. "And that's Buddy."

Buddy was the big, gray-and-white cat that had adopted him when he moved into this building. Buddy hated going out, loved sitting with him while he read, and was a great companion.

Buddy walked up to Carey as she knelt down to pet him. "I've got two. Stingy and Betty."

"I bet you miss them," Toby said. "How long have you been gone?"

"Eight days," she said, petting Buddy as Toby went into the kitchen area and opened the refrigerator. He got out the eggs and some fixings to go in the eggs.

She stood and dropped her pack, putting her rifle on top of it. Then she moved over and looked at his kitchen. "Wow, you have everything in here."

"The advantage of not having to pay for anything," he said. "Feel free to look around as I get this started. The computer monitor room is up front in the corner, bathroom is back there on the left."

He watched as she hesitated, then decided to go ahead and look at his place. She poked her head into the computer room, then nodded. "You are good at electronics, aren't you?"

"Not as good as I used to be when I worked with it every day," he said, breaking six eggs into a pan. "I'm afraid my omelets are basically eggs mixed with green peppers and onions from my rooftop garden, and some canned ham. I haven't had the courage to try any mushrooms."

"That sounds wonderful," she said, smiling at him as she ran her hand across the back of the chair he had facing the window. "This is some view."

Now Available
from all your favorite booksellers
in trade paper and electronic editions.

"No one seemed to be using the place, so I figured why not," he said.

"Know that feeling," she said, smiling. "I'm using three different houses on the coast."

Silence filled the room, broken only by the sound of his fork stirring the eggs, and his knife cutting the pepper.

Finally she moved back over to the edge of the kitchen island and leaned on the counter. "You know, for four years I've been hoping to find someone alive, have someone to talk to; and now that we have met, I don't know what to say."

Toby stopped cutting and looked at her, letting himself be drawn into her deep, brown eyes. "I'm feeling the same way, to be honest. Like a high-school kid afraid to talk to the girl in the chair beside him."

She laughed. "I'm feeling more junior-high."

"I didn't notice girls back then," he said. "I didn't start paying attention to them until sophomore year."

For some reason that admission seemed to break the ice. He could feel it, and the sound of her light laugh filled the room.

As he cooked, they went through their backgrounds, his in Bend, hers in Beaverton. He had been a year behind her in school, and for some reason, even though they were both at the University of Oregon at the same time, they had no memory of seeing each other.

Over breakfast, which she ate without hesitation, they talked about their families.

When they were done eating, and he had refused to let her help clean up, she asked if she could use his bathroom. When he agreed, and warned her about the hot water being a little too hot, she had smiled like he had given her a perfect Christmas present.

As she was taking her shower, Toby took a cup of coffee and moved over to his chair in front of the window. How had he managed to actually meet another person, let alone a woman he was attracted to, and that he enjoyed talking with?

Had he dreamed the entire thing? Was the water running in the bathroom just his mind playing tricks on him?

And what was he going to do next?

Actually—more importantly—what was *she* going to do next?

Chapter Five

BY THE TIME Carey finished with the most heavenly-feeling shower she could remember in years, her mind had cleared some. She was still having a hard time believing that anyone else was left alive, let alone someone nice. But unless she was dreaming this shower and that fantastic omelet, Toby was actually out there.

She put on clean clothes, stuffed the dirty ones in her pack, put her pistol back in her belt and went out, dropping her pack beside the door before petting Buddy.

"Everything all right?" he asked from a big lounge chair half facing one of the floor-to-ceiling windows.

"Perfect," she said. "I haven't had a hot shower since I left home. Thank you."

"No problem," he said. "There is coffee on the counter in the big pot. Help yourself."

He suddenly jumped up, moved into the living room, and dragged the other matching chair back so that it sat at an angle, facing the window. Carey poured herself a cup of wonderful-smelling coffee and joined him.

"Sorry," he said, smiling at her as he finished getting the second chair in place beside the first. "Just not used to having guests."

She sat and put her feet up. "I know the feeling."

She enjoyed the silence and the fantastic view for a few moments. Then he asked, "You said you knew what caused all this?"

"I do."

"Would you tell me?" he asked, a look of hope in his intelligent eyes.

She sipped the cup of coffee and then smiled at him. "For a wonderful breakfast, a hot shower, and this cup of coffee, it seems I can do that."

He laughed and she started into a description about her old job, what she had been doing when everyone died, and what had caused it.

"Electromagnetic pulse?" he asked when she finished.

"Basically, yes," she said. "Just very weak, and at such an exact wavelength as to short out some animal brains, including humans. I was protected by the experiment vault; you must have been protected in the bank."

Toby jumped up and started pacing.

Carey sat and watched him move. Just doing something as simple as watching another human move was a joy.

"Do you know what this means?" he said, the excitement clear.

"No, what?"

"That there has to be others alive out there besides us. Maybe even an entire community of people. Maybe more than one community, in touch with others around the world."

"You're not making sense," she said. "Where? And how?"

"Cheyenne Mountain in Colorado, for one," he said. "There are lots and lots of people who work down in that mountain twenty-four hours a day. It's protected from electromagnetic pulses like we were, and they all would have survived."

She remembered reading stories of how Cheyenne Mountain was built to withstand a direct atomic hit. There would be people alive in there.

"And there were places like that under the White House, and on other military bases," he said. "And atomic subs were protected. If it's electromagnetic pulses that did this, then there will be lots of people alive out there. And they will gather in groups. All we need to do is find them."

He dropped into his chair and sat staring over the hot city.

Carey looked at him, then sat back as well, letting the idea that he had just given her sink in. She knew he was right. Suddenly the world on the other side of those windows didn't seem so dead.

Or so hopeless.

He was right, there were other people out there, somewhere, maybe trying to rebuild civilization. She had skills that she could offer them.

So did Toby, if that computer surveillance room was any indication.

"I am very, very glad you decided to come back to the city," he said, looking at her. "And that you didn't shoot me on sight."

"So am I," she said, smiling at him.

He turned to look over the city.

They both sat, silently, staring at the river and the mountains to the east. She had never felt so comfortable in a silence.

And now the silence wasn't because of death, but because of the chance of life. It was a silence of two people thinking. And what kept going over and over

in her mind was that now, maybe there was a chance she wouldn't die alone.

After what seemed like a very long time, Toby asked, "Want to go with me? See who we can find? Between the two of us, we can figure out where to look."

She stared into his eyes. She could see hope. And she could see trust. Without a doubt she wanted to go look for others with him. "I'd have to go get my cats," she said.

He smiled. "I think Buddy and I can help with that."

"Then the answer is yes," she said. "Let's go see who we can find."

"It's a long way to Colorado," he said.

"It's been a long four years for both of us," she said, reaching over and taking his firm hand in hers, enjoying the feel of his skin against hers. "I think we can make it."

He gently squeezed her hand and smiled. "So do I."

Missed the last Cold Poker Gang novel?
It's available from all your favorite booksellers
in trade paper and electronic editions.

ACE HIGH

A COLD POKER GANG MYSTERY

DEAN WESLEY SMITH

USA TODAY BESTSELLING AUTHOR

1991. The famous Las Vegas hotel The Landmark scheduled for destruction. A girl's body found in one of the old rooms. Impossible to even tell her identity or what happened to her.

Seventeen years later Cold Poker Gang members Pickett and Sarge take up the girl's long-cold case. And layer by layer they uncover one of the most twisted crimes in the history of the famous sin city.

A crime that still needs to be covered up with even more death.

Ace High *wins the award for the most twisted crime novel yet in the series of Cold Poker Gang novels. If you love great mystery books, grab this one.*

Ace High

A Cold Poker Gang Novel

Ace high means the best card you have at the end of a hand is an ace. No pairs, no straights, nothing else. Just an ace is your best card.
A very weak hand in most instances.
But not always.

AUTHOR'S NOTE

The characters in this book are fictional and any similarity to any person, alive or dead, is purely accidental. The Landmark Hotel did exist, but as far as I know, the events in this novel did not happen. This is a work of fiction.

Part One
COLD AND COLDER

Prologue

April 3rd, 1991
Las Vegas, Nevada

THE LANDMARK HOTEL, or as it was called before it was closed, the New Landmark Hotel, felt more like an ancient ruin to Steven Bell. And as a long-time resident of Las Vegas, that made him sad. In its glory, the hotel and casino had really been something to see, towering proud and gleaming over the valley. Now it desperately needed paint, the windows hadn't been washed in years, and weathered plywood covered all the entrances. It just looked worn out and tired as only a well-used and not-maintained building could look in the desert winds and heat.

Sad, just flat sad, that a building of such importance to an entire city had been left to rot.

He just hoped someone with a lot of money would come in and bring the Landmark back up to use. Maybe not as a hotel, but as offices and restaurants or a something.

Anything.

But after seeing the inside of the place, he was starting to doubt if that would ever be possible no matter the amount of money.

The Landmark had been designed to imitate the Space Needle in Seattle, thirty stories of tower with restaurants and a show ballroom with a huge dance floor at the top. For the longest time it had been the tallest building in the valley.

Most of the rooms and suites were in the buildings around the casino area on the ground floors, but some suites lined the sides of the tower all the way to the top.

Construction on the place had started in the early sixties, but it wasn't until Howard Hughes bought the Landmark that it opened in 1969. The hotel and casino went through numbers of owners after that, never really getting profitable until finally closing in August of 1990.

Clearly to Steven, no money had been spent at all to keep the place up in the last few years of its existence. Everything just looked worn or broken. The last guests before this place closed must have been disgusted at what they found. He would have been.

Now everything inside was to be liquidated and it was Steven and his crew's job to do an inventory. At first, when the court had hired him, he thought the job sad, but that thought vanished the moment he started through the place.

There just wasn't much worth selling left. Even worth selling or not, they had to inventory it.

Old blackjack and craps tables and such in the casino area might be worth something, but the casino had leased all its slots and those were long gone already. He and his crew of four found the beds in rooms were often rotted and the mattresses bug-infested. The wooden end tables and coffee tables in most rooms were worn and scarred. Lamps and their shades often were spotted with age or just broken.

All of the bar equipment was so dated as to be almost antique. And food had been left in the fridges and the pantries to rot when the place shuttered. If this place had sat like this in any other town but Vegas, the entire building would have been overrun by rats by now. As it was, he only saw some minor signs of mice. But who knew what was living in the walls.

He and the four people working for him had focused on the ground floor and casino area for the first few days. Now they were working their way up the tower slowly, leaving all the restaurant equipment and furniture in the top floors for last.

The afternoon of April 3rd was getting warm outside and the inside of the hotel was getting stuffy. He had already shed his outer shirt at lunch and was now in just a T-shirt and jeans. He had a work belt on his waist with most tools he would need including extra pens.

They had started at sunrise to avoid this kind of heat problem and in an hour they would call it a day. He couldn't even begin to imagine what this place would feel like without power and air conditioning in the summer. It would be like walking through an oven.

He was looking forward to getting home to his condo and showering off the smell of mold and rot.

He had climbed ahead of his crew to the twentieth floor, just doing a quick walk around the hall, making sure all doors were open as they should be.

Just as with every other floor, the carpet in the hallway was worn and everything smelled like it had been closed up far, far too long. The beam of his flashlight cut through the darkness of the hallway, with light coming in from the open suite doors to help some.

He stirred up a fine cloud of dust as he moved and the dust floated in the beam of his light. He desperately wanted to go throw open a few of the windows in the suites to get some fresh air in the place,

but then they would just have to close them. Wasn't worth the effort to even try to pry open rusted and old windows.

Ahead of him the hallway was even darker because the door to Suite 2017 was closed. He moved to open it, but it was locked. He tried the pass-key, but that didn't work either. More than likely the door was jammed shut.

"Munro, bring the crowbars," Steven said into his radio. "Got a stuck door on twenty."

"On my way," Munro said.

Steven moved on around the rest of the suite hallway, making sure all other doors were open. They were. So far, he and his crew had been forced to pry open or break open about thirty doors. He was just happy it wasn't a lot more. These old casino doors were solid.

Munro met Steven at the closed door and handed him a large crowbar. Munro was the largest man on the crew. Young, and with a wife and two kids, he never missed a day and was the hardest worker Steven had ever met.

Steven also knew Munro worked out at a local gym every day after work and had muscles on top of muscles. But when it came to heavy lifting and forcing a closed door, Munro was the best.

The two of them quickly had the trim off the door and with both bars jammed between the frame and the door, they managed to shove the door inward.

"Shit," Munro said, stepping back as a wave of dry, rotted-smelling air hit them. "What the hell is that?"

Both of them moved back along the hallway and away from the smell. Steven knew exactly what that smell was. Something had died in that room. He knew the smell of death from his days on search and rescue for the county.

And it wasn't the smell of fresh death, but old death.

Steven took out a mask from his tool belt and handed an extra to Munro. "Let me take a look first, decide what we need to do."

Munro nodded. Even in the pale light of the hallway, Steven could see that Munro's face was white. He clearly had never dealt with anything dead before.

With masks on, they went back to the now-open door.

Steven took two steps inside and stopped. Munro stopped right beside him, looking over his shoulder.

It was clear what had caused the smell.

On the bed was a naked woman.

Dead, very dead.

"Shit," Munro said and turned away, going back into the hall to throw up what he had had for lunch.

Steven just stared.

The mummified body still looked very human in the daylight pouring in through the window. She had long brown hair spread out around her head and she looked peaceful, with her hands crossed over her chest as if someone had placed her there, looking up at the ceiling, legs together. She had been young and thin.

And she had clearly been dead for some time.

A blue backpack lay on the bed beside her and her clothes, what looked like a white blouse, a white bra, and jeans were draped over an old chair. He could see nothing at all that looked like a cause of death.

In fact, she looked very peaceful.

He backed out of the room, making sure to not touch anything.

Munro was leaning against a wall, trying to catch his breath. The hallway now smelled of old death and Munro's former lunch.

Steven said into his radio to his crew. "Mark clearly where you left off and everyone meet at the truck at once. Don't depend on remembering where you were. We're done for the day."

More than likely they were done for the week. Crime scenes tended to do that to jobs.

Steven then patted Munro on the shoulder and the two of them headed for the staircase.

The hotel had gotten even sadder now. Its last resident was a young dead woman.

Chapter One

December 4th, 2016
Las Vegas, Nevada

RETIRED DETECTIVE DEBRA Pickett stood at the marble kitchen counter sipping on a cup of black coffee and watching as three kittens appeared at full speed from a hallway, chased each other through Sarge's living room, then through the new archway into her condo and out of sight.

It was amazing how much noise three kittens playing could make. You would have thought an entire heard of cattle had gone through the place as they scuttled along the wood floor.

Her black-and-white girl cat named Nose loved playing with Sarge's two orange tabbies, Pete and Ree. And now that Pickett and Sarge had finished the archway between their two condos, she guessed her cat was his as well and his cats were hers. They were still working out the details on this new living arrangement. It would take time.

She and Sarge now had two kitchens, enough bedrooms to hold a small convention, and two full living rooms and dining rooms. Maybe she should have just sold her condo and moved into his, but they had both liked the idea of combining the two condos. The building board hadn't objected once Sarge offered to pay for a remodeling of the building's fitness area and buy some new equipment. But they both had had to sign an agreement stating that if they wanted to sell either or both condos, the wall would have to be replaced completely.

She was actually surprised and very pleased that the board had agreed, even with Sarge's offer of a bribe. At some point, she and Sarge needed to have a conversation about how rich he really was. She was well-off from her divorce from the idiot who loved his secretary more than his money. But Sarge seemed to be at the next level of rich.

He said he never worried about money at all, which is why he had the most expensive and largest condo in the Ogden Building. He said it was his gift to himself.

She had felt the same way about her condo. And they both owned them outright.

Both of them were retired Las Vegas police detectives. Most retired detectives never ended up in paid-off penthouse condos, but they had both been lucky, if you consider lucky being her husband buying a new sports car and running away with his large-chested secretary and Sarge's father dying of cancer and leaving him a fortune.

Pickett sipped on her coffee again and watched the action as the three kittens returned at full speed and disappeared up the stairs. If the pattern lasted, they would soon end up lying in the sun taking baths in Sarge's big living room.

She had no idea what was going to happen if they decided to put a Christmas tree in here. It would be a kitten playground, she had no doubt about that.

This morning she had gotten up and showered before Sarge and had made the coffee. His cup was waiting for him on the counter along with the new file for the new cold case they had been given at the Cold Poker Gang poker game.

They were to meet Robin, another retired detective and her former partner, in thirty minutes for breakfast to talk about the case. Pickett loved those meetings. The three of them made an amazing team.

This morning Pickett wore her normal jeans, a cotton blouse, and a light sweater. She had her badge in a holder on her belt covered by a knit sweater and her service gun in a holster under her arm. She would hide that with a light brown jacket when they went out.

The weather today promised to be clear, but brisk in temperature, a perfect day as far as she was concerned. She didn't mind air conditioning in the summer, but her favorite time of the year was the winter. The weather actually changed at times.

And the coming holiday this year, with Sarge in her life, promised to be fun instead of depressing as it had been the last few years.

She had gotten out of the bathroom ahead of Sarge this morning. She kept her brown hair short because it was just easier to take care of and she never wore makeup. Not only was it silly at her age, but it felt awful in the summer.

Sarge said he liked the fact that she never spent much time in the bathroom getting ready. It seemed his ex-wife, who had left him for another man, spent far too much time in the bathroom by Sarge's measure.

Both of them had agreed that their marriages had been casualties of their job. It seemed that being a detective didn't leave much time and mental energy for making sure a marriage worked.

Sarge wasn't angry at his ex-wife in the slightest. He was still in contact with her and the guy she moved east with. He said he even liked the guy.

Sarge was far more forgiving than Pickett was with her ex-husband. Her ex deserved the young bimbo he got. Those large bimbo-breasts (as Pickett called them) had certainly cost him a lot of money.

She flipped open the file on the new cold case, a bizarre death from 1991. She loved the fact that she got to still work in an unofficial capacity as a detective because she was a member of the Cold Poker Gang.

The gang had been declared an official task force by the chief of police and the mayor. They were all unpaid and with no requirement to do paperwork. Their entire mission was to look into cold cases. So far the gang had an amazing closing rate on the cases. And had stopped a few active serial killers as well along the way.

None of them took credit, instead giving the credit to the active detectives who had to do the paperwork. That desire for no credit kept them on great terms with all the other younger detectives and made the chief look great to the mayor and the public.

The Cold Poker Gang met every week to play poker and talk cold cases. At this point, there were fourteen retired detectives in the gang, but only about ten showed up for the game on any given Tuesday. She and Sarge and Robin had decided they wouldn't miss a night.

And Sarge was the best player of the three of them. He seldom left a game without some extra money in his pocket.

But what was the most important to her was being able to carry her badge and

gun again and feel useful, even after she had retired. Being a detective had been her identity and now she had that back.

She actually had been too young to retire, but the divorce had made her lose focus a few years back and question everything, including herself. Now she was barely over sixty and everyone said she looked younger. She felt younger, especially now that she was back working and living with Sarge.

She felt she still had a lot of useful years ahead of her.

At that moment, Sarge came from down the hall, smiling at her. His hair still slightly wet from the shower.

He was the most handsome man she had ever met, she was sure of that. He had hazel eyes, thick gray hair, and a square jaw. This morning he was dressed in his normal jeans, dress shirt, and light jacket. He kept his badge where it always had been, on his belt on his right hip and his gun in a carry holster under his arm.

Just as she did, he always put on a light jacket to cover the gun and the badge.

He kissed her, then picked up his coffee as the three kittens came tearing back down the stairs. This time the two orange cats were being chased by the black-and-white. They stopped in the living room area, with one orange cat near the window in the sun, the other on the back of a chair, and Nose on the couch.

That was the end of the standard morning exercise for them. Now it was bath time.

Sarge just shook his head and laughed, then sipped his coffee. After a moment he pointed to the folder. "What in the world are we going to do with that?"

They had both read the thin cold case file last night and decided to just hold off talking about it until today with Robin.

Pickett just shook her head. "Might be our first stump. Not much to go on."

He nodded. "Having that same feeling. Maybe it will change after breakfast."

"Things always do look better after food," Pickett said, laughing.

With that, she closed the file and went to get her jacket from her condo, moving through the large new archway between the two living rooms.

Damn she loved this life and this job.

And she was falling in love more and more every day with Sarge.

How had she got so lucky?

Chapter Two

December 4th, 2016
Las Vegas, Nevada

RETIRED DETECTIVE BEN "Sarge" Carson stood beside Pickett as the long escalator took them up toward the Golden Nugget buffet. The sounds of the casino below were fading as the fantastic smell of eggs and bacon hit them halfway up.

"Just realized I'm hungry," Pickett said, turning and smiling at him.

"Suddenly got the same feeling," he said.

The six-block walk from their condos had been easy this morning. The air had a good bite to it, but wasn't cold enough to require more than their normal light jackets. The sky only had a few clouds in it and those were over the mountains to the west. It was going to be a beautiful December day that was for sure.

The buffet was separated from the escalator area by a wall of plants and fake windows. The buffet itself was huge with at least seventy or more tables in three large sections. Everything was decorated in brown and brass tones. Not gaudy like many restaurants in Vegas.

Comfortable, actually. And light, very light. That was one of the many reasons he loved it here. So many restaurants in Vegas thought dark meant mood lighting. He liked to see what he was eating.

Huge windows let in a lot of light on the far side. Those massive windows looked out over a large pool that seemed to always be jammed in the summer. Along the windows was the most popular area for tourists to sit in. He and Pickett always sat on the far side of the restaurant, away from the tourists.

All the regulars here did.

Sarge remembered his days of lying around a pool, mostly with his wife and daughter when Steph was young and he was still a patrol cop.

He had never been one for not moving and just being in the sun covered by too much smelly lotion. But those days watching Steph play and Andrea watching her closely were good memories.

It was Sarge's turn to buy breakfast, so Pickett went on in and to their normal table tucked back to the right from the entrance. All the staff knew them here since they were regulars, so before Sarge finished paying, two cups of coffee were on the table. He knew that would be followed by two glasses of water and two glasses of orange juice.

It was nice having the staff know them.

Sarge just headed from the cashier for the food, following Pickett.

He got started his normal morning three-egg ham and cheese omelet made fresh for him, then while that was being done, he got some fruit and a muffin from the pastry area.

He took the fruit back to the table, went back and got a freshly made waffle, covered it with syrup and then picked up his finished omelet.

He really was hungry today.

As he was sitting down, Robin arrived.

Robin had been Pickett's partner when they were both active detectives. They were known as the best detectives on the force. Sarge had heard of them far before he had gotten lucky enough to meet them after they retired. They had worked out of a different station than he did.

Robin was solid, with shoulders like a swimmer, and always dressed in a nice blouse and dress jacket that covered her badge and gun. Her husband Will had the city's largest private security firm. He protected some of the most famous people in the world when they came to Vegas.

He and his people were amazingly good on computers and Robin was one of the best. In the cases they had worked together so far, he and Pickett had done the leg work while Robin did the computer work. Sarge liked that agreement.

"Beautiful day out there, isn't it?" Robin asked as she approached the table.

"Better than most," Pickett said as she put her plate of eggs and ham on the table.

Robin dropped her coat and purse and the cold case file she had taken home in her spot, then turned and headed for the buffet sections while Sarge and Pickett both started in on their food.

When Robin came back, they all ate and talked about the cats for a time and how they were doing with the new archway.

Then, as Sarge was sipping on his coffee and his plates had been taken away, Robin got to the case.

"Any ideas at all?" she asked, touching the thin brown folder that they had been given by Andor, the retired detective who was the connection between the Cold Poker Gang and the actual working detectives.

"An unknown young woman found dead in a closed-up hotel," Pickett said. "No idea how she died, what she was doing there, or even exactly when she died, let alone how she got into the locked and boarded up hotel."

Pickett just shrugged.

Sarge shrugged as well. "I got nothing either."

Robin laughed. "We're going nowhere on this one."

"But we're getting there fast," Pickett said.

Sarge could only laugh and agree with that.

Chapter Three

December 4th, 2016
Las Vegas, Nevada

PICKETT FINALLY TOOK out her notebook and opened to a fresh page. Sarge got out his small pocket-sized flip notebook, and Robin pulled out her notebook she always used. It seemed that good detectives never trusted their own memories for anything and over the years she had come to appreciate the habit of writing everything down.

And bringing out the notebooks meant it was brainstorming time, even though none of them had any ideas at all.

"So we start at where we could dig out something," Sarge said. "Do we have DNA we could test run?"

Robin nodded. "We do, but it was run 25 years ago, which means it wasn't compared against much of anything at the time. I'll see if Will can push that through, looking for any kind of family hits as well."

Pickett nodded. Having Will and his people run it against databases might actually get a hit and have it happen within a day instead of months through normal channels.

"How about we take a run at the people who discovered her body?" Sarge said.

"Two guys working the hotel furniture inventory," Picket said.

"I checked last night." Robin said. "One is dead, the other is still alive. I got his address and phone number."

"That girl, from the photos, had been dead for some time, right?" Pickett asked.

"No way of really knowing how long since the mummification of the body made it almost impossible to tell," Robin said. "But clearly longer than a month or so."

"What happens if she was there when they shuttered and boarded up the place in August of the previous year?" Picket asked. That seemed to make sense considering what kind of heat it would take to mummify the girl.

"Possible," Robin said. "I'll check in on who did the shuttering and what that entailed. Someone should have some records on that."

"Manager of the place at the time?" Sarge asked.

"I'll find out," Robin said, picking up her phone.

Pickett knew exactly what Robin was going to do. She was going to have Will or one of his people do some quick research and get back to her fast, so they could plan.

"I need bread pudding," Sarge said, standing and smiling at Pickett.

"Me too," Pickett said, standing to join him.

"Make it three," Robin said before turning to talk with someone on the other end of her call.

The bread pudding in the Golden Nugget buffet was one of the highlights. Light, fluffy, sweet, and when the hot bourbon sauce was poured over it, an entire range of tastes came alive. One evening here, when eating alone and feeling sorry for herself, Pickett had managed four large servings of just the bread pudding. And had thought about going back for five.

That was before she had joined the Cold Poker Gang and met Sarge. She had never admitted that feat of bread pudding consumption to him.

When they got back to the table, Robin was done with her call.

"Will is finding out who was in charge of the shuttering of the Landmark and is running the DNA information."

They all sat there in silence, eating and thinking. Finally Picket came up with another idea.

"Missing persons," Pickett said.

"They ran it at the time," Robin said, nodding. "But again it was 1991. Our computers might get a hit now."

"Run it against missing girls from all over the country," Sarge said. "We can narrow the list down from there."

"That's going to be a lot of girls," Pickett said. "They weren't even sure exactly how old our victim was."

"I think getting the data would be worth the shot," Sarge said.

Pickett nodded. She agreed. It would be worth the search. And at this point all they were trying to do was catch any break at all.

"Anything with her clothes or pack that I saw in that picture?" Sarge asked.

Pickett opened up the folder at the same moment as Robin. There was nothing. The detectives at the time checked into that. Clothes and pack were all standard stuff that could be bought in any department store. And the poor girl had no purse or wallet or anything else that anyone could find.

Then Pickett had another idea she was almost afraid to voice considering some of their past cases. "Should we look for anything similar? Other young girls found naked and dead and in that position?"

Robin nodded. "We should."

"We should," Sarge said.

"We really should," Robin said. Then she sighed and wrote it down in her notebook.

The last thing any of them wanted was to find that pattern.

The very last thing.

Chapter Four

December 4th, 2016
Las Vegas, Nevada

SARGE FINISHED HIS bread pudding. The stuff was so good, so sweet, it was too dangerous to go for seconds. He had a hunch he could just keep going back for more and more if he let himself.

He pushed the empty plate away before he made a fool of himself by licking it clean.

"So one thing is bothering me," Sarge said after letting Pickett and Robin finish their desserts as well. "Why was she naked?"

"She wasn't sexually molested in any way that was obvious," Robin said. "But the mummification might have cleared anything not obvious out."

"Possible," Pickett said. "But that photo didn't have the feel of a sexual crime scene.

Sarge and Robin both nodded. They had all three seen their share of those over the years. And Sarge had no desire to ever see another.

But he had to tell them what he was thinking. "Am I being crazy, but the first thing I thought about when I saw that photo was that she was napping."

Pickett nodded and Robin opened the folder again to look at the photos of the scene.

"To me," Sarge said, "she looks like she took off her clothes to take a nap and just never woke up."

"If the Landmark had already been shuttered when she went into that room," Pickett said, "there would have been no power or air conditioning, so that room in late August would have been an oven."

"The water was turned off as well," Robin said, glancing up from the report.

"So they couldn't find anything that killed her because she died from excessive heat," Sarge said. "But why would she stay in a room that hot?"

That question bothered him more than he wanted to admit because he could only come up with a couple reasons, none of which he liked.

"Maybe the door just got stuck and she couldn't get out," Pickett said.

Sarge nodded. That was one thing he had thought about.

"She was locked in there," Robin said, softly. "I bet she was locked in there by someone. It says in the report that the workers had to pry open the door. No key worked."

Sarge nodded. That had been his biggest worry. If that was the case, this had gone from an unexplained death to a murder case.

"Photos of the door?" Sarge asked.

"In the master file," Robin said. "Andor only brought the cold case file

with the basics. I can access the master file online. I'll get the photos and send them to you when I get home."

"So we have a major hotel with hundreds and hundreds of rooms sitting empty," Pickett said.

"And the entire mess caught up in court proceedings, so who knew how long it was going to sit there," Robin said.

"And someone knew that and got in there and locked that girl in that room for some reason," Sarge said.

He didn't much like the idea, but it was a theory, which was more than they had on this case so far.

"Another pattern to look for in a computer search," Pickett said. "Evidence of use of shuttered hotels."

Sarge sat back, feeling a little shocked. There were always hotels and motels shuttered around this town. No one paid them any attention at all, it was so common. Sometimes the hotel or motel sat boarded up for years and years.

"So we go talk with the surviving guy who found the body first, then we find who was in charge of shuttering the place," Pickett said. "We have a plan."

"And I'll get all these searches going," Robin said. "Amazing how the three of us can scratch a hole into a completely rock-solid cold case."

"Assuming any of these ideas pan out," Sarge said, standing and putting a tip on the table.

"Buzz killer," Robin said, smiling.

"Well, that poor young thing had to get in there somehow," Pickett said, putting away her notebook and standing as well. "And someone, somewhere has to be wondering what happened to her."

"So let's see if we can give her and her family some closure," Robin said, nodding.

Sarge completely agreed with that.

The three of them headed for the exit and at the bottom of the escalator, Robin turned toward the parking garage and Sarge and Pickett headed through the casino toward Fremont Street to walk home and get a car.

Sarge had a gut sense this case was going to be a lot more than what it seemed.

He just didn't know what that would be.

Part Two
NOT JUST ANOTHER CLOSED HOTEL

Chapter Five

December 4th, 2016
Las Vegas, Nevada

PICKETT LAUGHED AS she and Sarge entered their condo complex. They had decided on the walk back from the Nugget to call their combined condos "The Complex." She kind of liked that, actually. With all the bedrooms and bathrooms and living rooms and kitchens, it felt like a complex.

And they had started to talk about what they were going to do for Christmas, but had gotten sidetracked.

Lying in the sun coming in through the massive windows of the main living room were three kittens. All of them were on the couch, all sound asleep. Two orange kittens were stretched out on their backs, feet in the air, one on each end of the couch and a black-and-white kitten was in the exact same position in the middle.

"Can they get any cuter?" Sarge asked, shaking his head and smiling.

"Probably yes," Pickett said, laughing. "They are kittens."

"Good point," Sarge said.

Sarge went to use the bathroom as she called a guy by the name of Munro Kristin. He had been one of the two men to break into that room and find the girl on the bed. Now Munro Kristin ran his own gym.

He told her he doubted he would have much to add after twenty-five years, but he did remember it like it was yesterday and would be glad to answer any questions they had.

And he was free in thirty minutes.
Perfect.

Ten minutes later, as they headed out the door, the kittens hadn't bothered to move. Sometimes cuteness almost got too much, but she and Sarge were both laughing as they left.

And that felt nice.

She drove her white Jeep Grand Cherokee. She tended to do most of the driving and Sarge seemed fine with that. She liked to drive and he clearly felt relaxed while she was driving, so as he said, it was a win-win situation.

It took her just fifteen minutes to get from the Ogden Condominium's parking garage to the Fitness and More Gym near the university. The place was modern and felt light and very clean. A dozen people were using different equipment around the large space and a man with far too many muscles was behind the counter.

He glanced up, saw them and smiled. Pickett was impressed. The guy clearly had a personality and liked people. And from the looks of the gray hair on his nearly-shaved head, he wasn't young either.

She introduced herself and Sarge and showed him her badge.

"Call me Munro. And what can I do to help you with such an old case?"

"Just trying to clean up some of the really old cold cases," Pickett said, taking the lead. "Glad you don't mind answering a few questions about it."

He shook his head. "Wish I could forget it. Seeing that dead girl on the bed has haunted me for all these years."

"Never saw a dead body before that?" Pickett asked.

No wonder he could remember so clearly. Trauma of seeing someone dead often did that to a witness. Or they went the other way and blocked it out completely.

"Still haven't beside her," Munro said. "Even in a funeral."

"So can you run back over what you did when you found the body?" Pickett asked.

"Steven, the owner of the company doing the inventory of the Landmark furniture and fixtures, called me up to the 20th floor to bring crowbars. He was scouting ahead of us and had found a door that the master key wouldn't work in and we needed to get it open."

"Was that unusual?" Sarge asked.

Munro shrugged, his massive muscles in his shoulders and arms moving like ripples under his loose T-shirt. "We had to break open a couple dozen doors in the entire place. But most of those were closets and back rooms and such. Steven always had me do it because of my strength. That was the only hotel room door the keys wouldn't work in, though."

Pickett nodded and glanced over as Sarge wrote that down.

"We had to pry off the molding around the door first," Munro said, "to get to the door. And then it took both of us on crowbars to force the door's lock enough to push the door open."

"Really stuck, huh?" Sarge asked.

"Bad," Munro said, nodding. "And when the door swung open we were hit with a nasty, rotting smell that drove us back down the hallway. Still makes me queasy to think about."

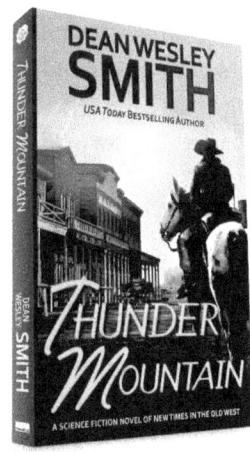

Thunder Mountain Novels Now Available
from all your favorite booksellers
in trade paper and electronic editions.

"So you didn't know she was in there at that point?" Pickett asked.

Munro shook his head. "Steven had a couple masks and we put them on and went back into the room. Steven stopped a few paces in and I looked over his shoulder and saw her naked and wrinkled there on the bed. No doubt she was dead. No doubt at all. And what really bothered me was that she seemed to be about my age at the time. I was twenty-five and had two kids and death wasn't something I thought was even possible at that point in my life."

"Yeah, that realization comes with time," Sarge said.

Munro nodded to that. "Came to me quickly that day, let me tell you."

"What happened next?" Pickett asked.

"I went back into the hall and lost my lunch," Munro said. "A moment later Steven backed out of the room, called the rest of the crew to go to the truck and then he walked me down the twenty flights to fresh air."

"Clearly Steven had seen dead bodies before," Sarge said.

"Steven worked search and rescue. He said he lost his lunch the first time as well."

Sarge laughed. "We all do. And trust me, it's better you never get hardened about seeing death like that."

Munro nodded to that.

"So you think that door was locked from the inside?" Pickett asked.

"Locked or jammed stuck," Munro said. "We opened all those other locked doors much easier now that I think about it."

Pickett watched as Sarge wrote that down as well.

This thing was strange to begin with, but now it had just gotten stranger. Did that girl lock herself in that room or was she locked in there by someone else?

Or had the door jammed by accident?

After only a few hours of studying this case, Pickett really wanted to know that answer and get answers to what happened in that room.

And more importantly, find out who that young girl really was.

Chapter Six

December 4th, 2016
Las Vegas, Nevada

IT WASN'T EVEN eleven in the morning and Sarge was already convinced that girl had been murdered. She had been locked in that room without food or water and simply died of dehydration and heat stroke.

What a horrid way to go.

Now he just had to figure out a way to prove that theory.

And if someone had actually murdered the girl, who and why had they done it? Figuring that out was going to be even harder.

He and Pickett thanked Munro and promised to tell him if they found out more about the girl, then headed for Pickett's car.

As they climbed in Pickett asked a simple, one word question. "Murder?"

"Convinced," Sarge said. "Hotel room doors don't jam like that and also not have the master key not work. Those old master keys in hotels worked for every door, which was one of the problems with them when someone lost one."

"That was back in the day before the security locks on the inside," Pickett said. "Robin and I worked a number of serial rapist cases right at the beginning of our detective careers where the rapist had gotten a copy of a master key in a couple of the older hotels."

"Yeah, as a patrol cop I responded on a few of those early on as well," Sarge said, pushing the memories back down. Hotels were so much safer today than they had been back thirty years before. Of that there was no doubt.

"So we need to get someone to talk to who worked on the shuttering of the Landmark," Pickett said. "I'm surprised we haven't heard from Robin on that yet."

Pickett grabbed her phone. A moment later she put the phone on speaker as Robin came on.

Pickett gave Robin a quick rundown on the information from Munro about the door, then asked, "Who do we talk with about the shuttering? Got a name for us yet?"

"Not yet," Robin said. "Turning out to be harder than I thought. But I think I found out who our girl is."

Sarge was stunned. He looked at Pickett whose eyes had grown round with surprise.

"You're not kidding us, are you?" Pickett asked.

"We put her DNA into the system," Robin said, "and it came back in less than an hour with a familial match. A brother. Her name was Heather Winston and she was 19 when she vanished. I'm sending you a picture of her from high school. She disappeared in August of 1990 between her freshman and sophomore year here at UNLV."

"So there is a missing person's case open for her?" Pickett asked.

"There is," Robin said. "The two cases should have gotten combined back in the day, but since the missing person's case was filed in August and she wasn't found until April the following year, it didn't happen."

"All those years of not knowing and the information was right in the files," Pickett said, shaking her head.

Sarge felt the same way, but it was a different world just back twenty-five years ago. Now the computers would have linked the two cases quickly. Back then it would have had to be detectives linking it and chances are she was reported missing in one area of town and found in another, so the detectives working the two cases didn't even know each other, let alone talked.

"Her parents still alive?" Sarge asked.

"No," Robin said. "They died in a car wreck up by Big Bear two years after she vanished. But her brother still lives here with his wife. He has three kids, all in college. He has his own accounting firm."

"You want us to tell him we found his sister?" Pickett asked.

Sarge hated that idea. But he knew that it had to be done and if Robin was sure about the identification, maybe the brother might help them figure out what happened.

There was never any way to know how someone would react after decades of not knowing what happened to a family member. Some were stoic and others fell apart. Either way, telling the family the bad news wasn't pleasant, but at least it gave them closure.

"I think you should," Pickett said. "It's a one-hundred-percent certainty from the DNA that the girl on the bed was Heather Winston."

"Give us his address and his work phone," Sarge said.

He wrote it down and then Robin said, "I'll get back to you as soon as I can with someone to talk to about the shuttering. But you should know that Heather Winston went missing a full week after the shuttering of the Landmark was completed."

"She didn't get in there ahead of time or during the process?" Sarge asked, again stunned.

"No," Robin said. "The shuttering was done a good week before, the doors locked, windows boarded up, and the entire place fenced in and locked up. Somehow she got it there after that process."

"Security service watching the place?" Pickett asked a moment before Sarge could."

"Already digging into that," Robin said.

"So we'll go talk with the brother and report back," Pickett said.

Robin hung up and Pickett glanced at Sarge. "At least we have solved one cold missing person's case this morning."

Sarge laughed. "We have, but just came up with a ton more questions on the case we are working on."

"True," she said as she started up the car. "Just trying to find a bright side of all this."

"I got a feeling with this one that there might not be many bright sides."

Pickett nodded. "I got the same feeling."

Chapter Seven

December 4th, 2016
Las Vegas, Nevada

THE BROTHER'S NAME was Bob Steven Winston. Pickett wasn't sure why the two first names, but she had sure seen stranger names in her years. He had had his own accounting firm since right out of college. He was two years older than Heather and looked like he was seventy, even though Pickett knew he was only fifty-six.

His office screamed money and just the massive decorative live plants in the huge waiting room had to cost a fortune to maintain.

Sarge told a receptionist who they were and that they needed to speak with Mr. Winston on a private matter.

Pickett introduced herself and Sarge when Winston came out and they both showed him their badges, then asked to talk with him privately.

He led them into a conference room off to one side of the lobby and closed the door behind them, indicating that they should all sit at the large oak table surrounded by ornate chairs.

Winston not only looked old, he moved like he hadn't had a day of exercise in thirty years. He was overweight and mostly bald, but his gray three-piece suit was expensive and tailored to fit.

"We're here about your sister, Heather," Pickett said.

Winston just shook his head. "Now what has she done?"

Pickett glanced at Sarge, then back at Winston.

Sarge sat forward. "Did your sister, Heather Winston, go missing in August of 1990? Two years before your parents' tragic accident?"

Winston nodded. "She did. Had us all scared to death. But she came home about a week later and wouldn't tell us what happened."

Pickett just sort of stared at Winston. Then she pulled out her phone and opened up the picture of Heather when she was in high school and turned it so Winston could see it. "Is this your sister?"

"Sure," Winston said, nodding. "She's gained a bunch of weight since then. So what's going on?"

"We seem to have made a mistake," Sarge said, standing before Pickett could say another word. "Our records show your sister's missing person's case was still open and we were just investigating. So it seems this one turned out all right."

Pickett and Winston both stood.

"Yeah, wish it had been that simple," Winston said. "After Heather came home she was never really the same. Mom and Dad were thinking of trying to get her professional help to deal with what happened during that time she was gone, but they died before they could force the issue."

Now Pickett was feeling even more stunned. And her stomach had clamped up into a knot.

"Sure sorry to bother you," Sarge said.

He nodded to Pickett and she followed his lead. Clearly he knew they needed to get out of there right now before one of them said something. They needed to find out first exactly what was going on.

And they sure weren't going to find it sitting here in this room; Pickett knew that without a doubt.

"Glad you could get it cleared up," Winston said as Pickett followed Sarge out the door.

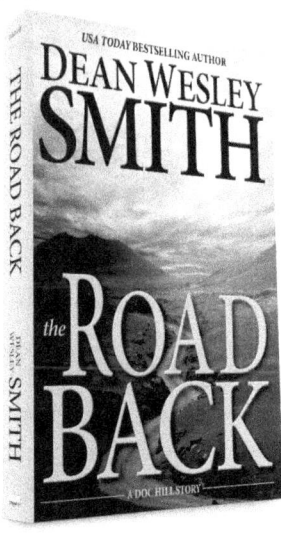
"So are we," Pickett said.

But this meeting had far from cleared up anything. It just had confused the issue even more.

And she had no idea at all what they needed to do next.

Not clue one.

Chapter Eight

December 4th, 2016
Las Vegas, Nevada

SARGE DIDN'T SAY a word until they were in the car with the doors closed. He didn't know what to say, actually. That was one thing he had never, ever expected to happen.

"What the hell was that all about?" Pickett asked, shaking her head and staring at the steering wheel.

"Let's see if we heard the same thing," Sarge said.

"Hang on," Pickett said. "Robin has got to hear this as well."

Sarge tried to calm his thoughts as Robin came on the phone and said, "That was quick. How'd he take it?"

"Well," Pickett said, "that's the problem."

"We were just about to go over what we heard in there so we are on the same page," Sarge said.

"First off," Pickett said, "when we asked him if he had a sister named Heather Winston, he said he did. And then asked us what she had done this time."

"What?" Robin asked.

"It gets stranger," Sarge said. "I asked him if his sister had gone missing in August of 1990 and he said she had, but came back a week later."

"A changed person," Pickett said.

"Serious?" Robin asked.

"Serious," Pickett said. "We showed him a picture of Heather from her graduation and he confirmed that was his sister."

"And then he told us," Sarge said, "that his sister was so different after the missing week that his parents wanted to take her for counseling and get her help."

"But they died before they could do it," Pickett said.

"Oh, shit," Robin said softly.

"We got out of there," Pickett said, "telling him that the mistake was that her missing person's case should have been closed but wasn't."

"I've got to sit down," Robin said.

All three sat in silence for a moment.

Then Robin broke the silence. "I'll dig into the Heather Winston still living."

"She has to be an imposter," Pickett said. "We're 100% on the DNA?"

"The body was the real Heather Winston," Robin said. "We have to assume that DNA off the body was collected correctly."

Sarge nodded. He had been wondering exactly the same thing. The alive Heather was most likely an imposter.

"Find out how much she inherited when the parents were killed," Sarge said. "And more details about the accident that killed them."

"You thinking the imposter killed them in some way?" Pickett asked.

Sarge just shrugged. That's exactly what he was thinking. But there was no proof or evidence. But the girl had a motive if she knew the real Heather Winston was found dead in a room.

"Something is really wacked out here," Robin said. "No doubt at all about that. And it would sure be nice to get some

of that modern Heather Wilson's DNA to test to see who she really is."

"We could stake her out," Pickett said, "see if we can get something from garbage or fast food or such?"

"Good idea," Robin said. "Give me five minutes to find her address and pictures, if there are any. I'll get one of Will's people to help me on this."

Robin hung up and Pickett started the car, moving it onto the road and away from the parking lot of the accounting firm.

Sarge pulled out his notebook and started writing notes about what had happened as Pickett pulled into a grocery store parking lot, parked and turned off the engine.

Just as she did, Robin called and gave them the address and that chances are the fake Heather was home because she worked nights at a casino on the Strip. And as best Robin could find, she lived alone.

"So we going to talk with her?" Pickett asked as she pulled the car out of the lot and headed toward the address Robin had given them.

"I think we have a logical chance to do just that," he said. "We talked to her brother, just needed to confirm a few details with her before we can officially close the missing person's case."

Pickett nodded. "And that would give us a better chance of getting something with her DNA on it."

Sarge agreed. He didn't like the idea much, but he agreed.

Ten minutes later they were walking up a gravel front sidewalk toward a small house in a very old neighborhood. The house had clearly seen better days and its white paint was peeling in a number of places. Dust seemed to coat the windows so bad they would be impossible to see out of.

A screen door hung loosely to one side of the main wooden door.

Sarge knocked loudly and he could hear movement from the inside.

A moment later a large woman dressed in a ratty brown bathrobe and worn blue slippers answered the door, a cigarette hanging out of her mouth.

A smell of burnt bacon came from the house mixed with the smoke smell. It was so dark behind the woman compared to the daylight that Sarge couldn't see much inside the house at all.

"Yeah," she said, standing in the door.

"Heather Winston?" Pickett said.

"Yeah?" the woman said.

Sarge just stared at that half-smoked cigarette as Pickett introduced the two of them and they both showed their badges. A number of cigarette butts littered the rock area beside the front door.

"We just talked with your brother a short time ago," Sarge said. "We are working a task force to close old missing person's cases and it so happened yours was still open. We just needed to check in with you to close the case."

"That was twenty-five years ago," she said, shaking her head.

"We were surprised when your brother said you were alive and that the case had never been closed," Pickett said. "So now we can get it off the books if you would help us with a couple details."

"Sure, what?" the woman asked.

"We just need to see a copy of your driver's license is all," Pickett said.

Sarge nodded. That might work to get them inside.

"Sure, hang on," the woman said.

She took the still burning cigarette and flicked it into the rocks beside the door, then turned to get the license.

Pickett smiled at Sarge and he smiled back. They had exactly what they needed.

The woman returned a moment later with her driver's license and Picket made a production of writing it all down, then they thanked the woman and apologized for interrupting her.

"No problem," she said.

They started to turn away, but as they did the woman closed the door solidly behind them.

"Got it," Pickett said.

Sarge watched as she took out a pair of tweezers from her small purse and picked up the still smoking cigarette. Then the two of them moved to the far side of the car where they couldn't be watched from any window, even if the fake Heather could see out of those dirt-covered windows.

Pickett put the cigarette out completely, then she climbed into the Jeep and opened the cigarette ashtray built into the Jeep's dash and put the cigarette in there carefully.

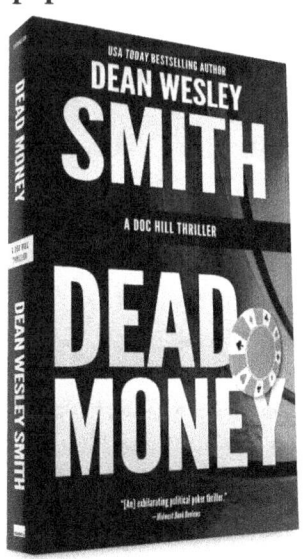

Fifteen minutes later they had dropped it off with Robin and were headed back to their complex to get some lunch and take naps. Both of them loved naps.

Both of them considered naps as one of the major benefits of retirement. And already they had gotten into a habit of napping in different places in the complex. They slept together at night, but napped apart during the day.

Both of them found that funny, but neither had suggested a change.

Sarge had no doubt that after this morning he was going to need a nap. Chances are his mind wouldn't let him sleep, but that didn't matter, he needed to try anyway.

Chapter Nine

December 4th, 2016
Las Vegas, Nevada

PICKETT ACTUALLY MAN-AGED to sleep for thirty minutes before coming awake thinking about the case and that poor girl in that hot room. What a horrid way to die, literally baked to death.

She headed into what they were calling their main kitchen, which was the kitchen in Sarge's condo. They had started to use her kitchen as a sort of large pantry and storage, which worked great.

She had just poured herself a glass of orange juice when Sarge came down the hall, yawning. His gray hair was sticking up in a few places as it sometimes did after he napped and he still looked handsome to her.

"Anything from Robin?" he asked as he too got a glass of orange juice from the fridge.

"About to call her," Pickett said.

At that moment the phone rang and Pickett laughed. "Great minds all on the same page."

Pickett clicked the phone on speaker. "We're both here. Any luck?"

"Well, not sure what we found would be considered lucky or not," Robin said. "First off, Will pulled about a hundred strings and we did an emergency push on the DNA off that cigarette. We should have enough preliminary results tomorrow to run it against some data bases."

"Light speed," Sarge said.

"Yeah," Robin said. "Not sure what kind of favors he now owes people."

Pickett laughed. Robin's husband Will was just amazing. He and Robin had been there for her through her messy divorce. Two better friends couldn't be found.

"Got you a name and address for one of the contractors who did the shuttering of the Landmark," Robin said, "and another name of the security firm who guarded the place."

"That will give us a start," Sarge said. Pickett agreed.

"Also did some research into the wreck that killed the Winstons up near Big Bear," Robin said. "Missed a corner and rolled their pick-up down a slight bank and into a tree. Both died of broken necks."

Pickett glanced at Sarge who was frowning.

"Let me guess, a straight road leading down into that corner," Sarge said. "And no autopsy done."

"Got it in one," Robin said.

Pickett just shook her head. The Winstons might have actually died in that wreck, and without anything else suspicious, no one would have thought to look beyond the tragic event. Now, after this long, proving otherwise was going to be damn near impossible.

"Any kind of inheritance?" Sarge asked.

"A big one. Both the kids got five million each."

Pickett was shocked at that. "The house we found the fake sister in sure wasn't a five-million-dollar home."

"Drugs," Robin said, "plus two abusive ex-husbands and then time in and out of jail for drugs and DUI. As far as we can tell, she blew through the money in five years."

"Wow," Pickett said and Sarge whistled softly.

But Pickett knew that wasn't unusual for people who came into money suddenly and didn't know how to handle it. Most lottery winners were broke within years as well.

"So where do we push at this afternoon?" Sarge asked. "I'm thinking the security end of things."

"I agree," Pickett said. "Somehow Heather Winston and maybe a number of other people got in there through the security firm."

Robin gave the name and number of the security firm and a man by the name of Crowly who had been with the firm since it did the security on the Landmark.

"Will says the firm is solid, keeps good records, and he has called the boss to ask them to help you," Robin said.

"Thanks," Pickett said. "We'll call him now."

"One more thing," Sarge said. "Would it be possible to do a search over the last few decades of people found dead in shuttered hotels and motels?"

"Sure, should be a simple task to run," Robin said.

"And would it be simple to add in other various reports around shuttered hotels and motels?"

Robin laughed. "That would be a ton of cases. But I should be able to put some order on it all. What are you thinking?"

Pickett was wondering the same thing.

"Something about this just feels off," Sarge said. "Like we are missing something. I feel like we are looking at a tree and not seeing a forest, but darned if I can figure out why I am feeling that way."

"Sounds logical to me," Robin said. "I'll see what I can pull together."

"Thanks," Sarge said.

"Yes, thanks. I'll call you after we talk to the security guy," Pickett said.

She hung up the phone and turned to the man she was deeply in love with. "You think we're stumbling into something larger again?"

"I hope not," Sarge said, laughing. "Just like you, though, I have learned to listen to that little voice nagging me."

She laughed at that. Every good detective she knew trusted their little voice.

They finished off their juice and headed for the door. She didn't notice until they were almost to the front door that there wasn't a kitten in sight. More than likely all curled up together on a bed somewhere.

Chapter Ten

December 4th, 2016
Las Vegas, Nevada

SARGE HELD OPEN the glass front door to the security firm's office for Pickett to go through. There was no name on the door or the front of the building at all. It was just after two in the afternoon and Crowly had agreed to meet them in his office where he could access all the old files.

The weather had become even nicer if that was possible, with bright blue sky and yet no heat, something you didn't often see in Las Vegas. Sarge wished he and Pickett were just out walking instead of working, the day was that nice.

Crowly met them just inside the front door and shook both their hands. There was no receptionist, but a desk for one looked used.

Crowly was a short man, more round than anything, but he dressed in clothes that fit his shape and his sports jacket was tasteful. He looked to be around sixty, maybe slightly older, but Sarge couldn't tell for sure.

Crowly was mostly bald and had piercing dark eyes and a booming voice. There was no doubt to Sarge that if this guy wanted, he could blend in completely with the Las Vegas tourist crowd.

And Sarge also had no doubt that this guy didn't miss many details.

Crowly's office was impressive in its own functional way. He had a massive computer with three screens on his huge wooden desk, a draft board covered with blueprints against one wall, and a large worktable in the middle with six chairs around it. The table was also covered with building blueprints.

A massive area in one corner was filled with tubes of blueprints.

Crowly indicated Sarge and Pickett grab chairs and pull them around behind his desk so they could see his screens. Then Crowly sat in his desk chair and brought up his computer.

"Will tells me you are interested in the security we did for the Landmark after it was shuttered."

"Please," Pickett said. "We're working on the cold case of that girl's body that was found in the building by the furniture inventory crew."

"Yeah," Crowly said, shaking his head. "A hard one to forget and I have no clue how she got in there. That's bothered me for twenty some years now."

Sarge could tell Crowly wasn't lying about that.

"So could you run us through your setup for that building, as much as you remember, and the time frame of your security."

"Don't need to remember it," Crowly said, opening a file on his screen showing a ledger of dates, blueprints of the Landmark property, and other details. "We scanned in all the old jobs before storing everything. Comes in more handy than I imagined it would when I was spending the money to have it done."

"Glad you did," Pickett said.

"We can now certainly pull all the different files of every job together easily," Crowly said. "I have no idea how I did anything without computers now."

Sarge laughed. "We've wondered the same thing at times."

"So here's what we did," Crowly said, expanding the size of the ledger on one screen so they could read it clearly. "We set up the exterior and building cameras and fences as they were working on shuttering the place. We were fully tested and up and running when the last member of the crew boarded up the last door and left."

"Anyone on site or just all recorded monitoring?" Pickett asked.

"Two guards on site at all times," Crowly said, "twenty-four-seven. One stayed with the monitors and another did rounds every hour. Everything recorded and logged in. Considering what I was getting paid to guard that place, I didn't cut corners at all."

Sarge was impressed.

"Anything unusual happen in the first week or so?" Sarge asked.

Crowly brought up another file that was clearly an hourly log of the guards. He quickly scanned through the log entries for the first two weeks, well past the time that Sarge and Pickett knew that Heather Winston had gone missing and the fake Heather came back.

"Nothing," Crowly said. "In fact, in my final notes, except for finding that girl's body in there, nothing at all unusual happened during that entire time. And we guarded that building from the time it was shuttered to the time they blew up the tower for those movie people."

"Who paid for all that?" Pickett asked.

"Bank's insurance company," Crowly said. "Far cheaper for them to pay us for years and cover their asses than to pay out if some kid got in there and got hurt."

Sarge had to agree with that as well.

"Is there any chance you managed to save the security footage from that time?"

Crowly smiled. "You know that was twenty-five years ago."

Sarge knew from the smile that Crowly had them.

"I know," Pickett said, smiling back. "Figured it couldn't hurt to ask."

"Yeah, we got them all," Crowly said. "I had everything digitized."

"I think I could hug you," Pickett said.

"Thanks, but my wife and your boyfriend here might object," Crowly said, winking at Sarge.

Sarge was right. Crowly didn't miss a detail.

"But you can tell Will to send some more work my way at times," Crowly said.

"Be glad to," Pickett said, smiling at Crowly.

Sarge could tell Pickett really liked Crowly. Sarge liked the guy as well.

"So what time period are you looking at? The time before they found the girl?"

"No," Sarge said. "Basically the second week after you started the security. We think she went in there that week."

"Not possible," Crowly said, shaking his head. "But I'll give you the files and the blueprints of our security system and monitors and you can see for yourself."

"And the names and contact information you might have of the guards on during that week as well," Pickett said. "If you wouldn't mind."

Crowly shrugged and in five minutes he handed them two thumb drives with all the videos on it and the guard logs and the names of the guards and the blueprint layouts of the security cameras.

"Get a couple bags of popcorn," Crowly said. "Watching an empty building is some damn boring movie time."

Sarge laughed. "Spent a bunch of my life on stakeouts watching empty buildings. I know the feeling."

"I bet you would," Crowly said. "Anything more, just call me. And if you figure out what happened to that girl, please let me know. I would love to clear that from the old memories."

Sarge didn't blame him at all.

Chapter Eleven

December 4th, 2016
Las Vegas, Nevada

PICKETT CALLED ROBIN and told her how helpful Crowly had been. And what they had from him.

Then she and Sarge stopped at a grocery store on the way back home and got some great steaks and fresh vegetables for dinner. They already had enough popcorn.

They went into Sarge's big computer room and loaded up all the data to his system, checking it for bugs as they went.

Then they spent the next hour in there with the blueprints of the exterior of the building on the screen, studying the entrances, the camera angles, everything.

Crowly and his team had been amazingly effective. They covered every boarded up door or window on one camera or another, and the entire four sides of the fenced-in property was covered as well with cameras.

Pickett was getting a sinking feeling they weren't going to find anything at all, but they needed to look. Somehow, Heather Winston went missing and got into that building during the week they had recorded in front of them.

After an hour, they went back into the kitchen. There were still no kittens in sight, but Pickett had a hunch they would be showing up as soon as she and Sarge started making noise in the kitchen.

Pickett started working on the salad while Sarge got the steaks ready to grill. After the steaks came off he would get them a bottle of wine from his fantastic wine room.

He had just put the steaks on when he said, "Think there might have been another way into that old hotel?"

"From where?" she asked. "Sewers, electrical, something like that?"

"Anything like that," Sarge said, nodding.

Picket had just finished the salad so she grabbed her phone. "I'll get Robin to send us all the construction details of the Landmark. Construction started in 1961, but the place didn't open until July of 1969. Who knows what might have been built during those years."

Robin answered and Pickett quickly explained what they were thinking and what they needed.

"Should all be public records," Robin said. "I'll get it all to you in the next hour or so."

"Thanks," Pickett said. "You might save us endless hours of staring at a video of an empty building."

Robin laughed. "I'll see what I can do for the cause."

As Pickett hung up, Nose came slowly down the stairs, clearly just waking up.

Shortly behind her were two yellow kittens, also half-asleep. Again cute didn't begin to describe those three.

Sarge laughed. "I see the smell of steak finally reached the upstairs area."

"It's reached my stomach as well," Pickett said, taking the salad over to the small dining table between the living room and the kitchen. "The steaks smell wonderful."

The kittens gathered in the kitchen as Sarge put the steaks on two plates and then with cloth napkins and silverware, carried it all to the table as well, making sure he didn't step on a kitten on the way.

"Want me to pick the wine?" Pickett asked.

"Please," Sarge said and he moved back through the herd of cats to get two glasses of water.

Pickett got out a wonderful red pinot and took it back to the kitchen and Sarge opened it as she put two wine glasses on the table.

The three cats just watched the entire process, not really knowing what to make if it.

And when she and Sarge finally sat down at the table, the cats went to the living room and spread out.

Thirty minutes later, she and Sarge had just finished the wonderful steak dinner and Sarge was starting to clear the dishes into the dishwasher when Robin called back, all excited.

"There was a utility tunnel built from a building near the back of the south parking lot," Robin said. "The parking lot and that block building was never fenced off when the hotel was shuttered because no one realized that tunnel was even there, since it didn't appear on any of the final plans in 1969. In the final plans the electrical was brought in from a different side and the water and sewer were hooked into the city in a different direction. The old tunnel was just left and taken off the final construction plans."

"Big enough for someone to walk through?" Pickett asked.

Sarge turned from the sink with that statement, staring at her.

"More than big enough," Robin said. "Originally it ran all electrical, water, and sewage pipes on and off the property, so it had to be large."

"So who would have known it was there?" Pickett asked.

"We find the answer to that question and we might just find our killer," Robin said.

"Thanks," Pickett said and hung up.

"So?" Sarge said.

Pickett just smiled. "What movie would you like to watch tonight?"

"Another way underground into the building, huh?"

Pickett nodded. "Not on the final construction blueprints that Crowly had, so he wouldn't have known to watch it. Built when construction started in 1961 but then not used when the hotel was opened in 1969."

Sarge nodded. "One mystery solved, another one created."

"This case seems to do that, doesn't it?" Pickett said.

She just hoped that at some point the answers would lead to an end and to who killed Heather Winston.

At least in one day they had taken an impossible cold case and opened it back up wide. That was at least a start.

Part Three
YET ANOTHER SURPRISE

Chapter Twelve

December 5th, 2016
Las Vegas, Nevada

SARGE HAD JUST finished showering and dressing and Pickett had made coffee and given the kittens their morning treats when Robin called.

Sarge sipped on his coffee as Pickett put the phone on speaker.

"Morning," Robin said. "Will's friends came through and we got a hit on the fake Heather Winston DNA preliminary findings when we ran them through some data bases this morning."

Sarge was stunned. He hadn't given that much hope at all.

"We found a family match with her mother who was in the local database for a number of theft and assault charges. The fake Heather's real name is Connie Downs," Robin said. "She was a classmate of Heather's in high school. She went missing about the same time as Heather did and there is still a missing person's case open on her."

"How in the world did she pull that off?" Pickett asked.

"She was the same height, same hair color, same eye color," Robin said. "And they looked like sisters in their school pictures. Kind of creepy actually."

"Family differences?" Sarge asked.

"Completely different," Robin said. "Heather was from a stable and fairly happy family. From what we can figure out quickly, Connie came from a poor home and no father, with an abusive alcoholic mother who ended up in jail more often than not."

"Connie wasn't liked at school I'll bet," Pickett said.

"No way of really knowing quickly," Robin said, "but their yearbook had just Connie's photo in the student listings while Heather was all over the yearbook with pictures in clubs and other activities."

Sarge nodded. An unpopular girl taking the place of a popular one. No wonder the parents were figuring out something was wrong fairly quickly, even with the fake Heather in college.

"So we got a classic reason why the switch," Pickett said. "But Connie didn't do this alone and she didn't kill the parents alone. So who knew about the tunnel into the hotel? And why do all this for Connie?"

"I'm betting it wasn't for Connie," Sarge said. "She was just a side benefit. I think someone was going after Heather on this all along. Connie ended up just an easy distraction in case everything fell apart."

"Got a hunch you are right about that," Robin said.

Pickett was also nodding.

"So the way I look at it, we have a mess," Sarge said.

"You think?" Robin asked and they all laughed.

"We have a woman who has been leading a fake life now for twenty-five years," Sarge said. "We don't know who helped her set that up and possibly kill the parents, but we're all fairly certain she couldn't have done it alone or even come up with the idea. And we have no idea who knew about that old utility tunnel into the Landmark."

"My problem," Pickett said, "Is why the Landmark in the first place?"

"Wondering the same thing," Robin said. "Why not just kill Heather instead of locking her in a room where she might have been discovered. And eventually was."

"Told you we have a mess," Sarge said. "Any ideas on what to even do next. We could expose Connie and pressure her to talk."

"We'd need some active detectives involved with that," Pickett said. "Let's give us a few more days to dig up more before we go down that road."

"I agree," Pickett said.

"I do too," Sarge said. He didn't want to turn this mess over to the active detectives just yet. They wouldn't have the time or the energy to push it like they could.

"So Heather must have had a pretty good enemy or two," Pickett said. "I think we go that way, see what we can find without spooking the fake Heather any more than me might have already."

"Agreed," Robin said.

Sarge nodded, but he was still stuck on one aspect that seemed to be making no sense.

"I'm still thinking the Landmark being shuttered had something pretty major to do with this," Sarge said. "Any luck on finding reports about things going on in shuttered hotels?"

"Actually, yes," Robin said. "Twice over the years raids have been done on shuttered hotels."

"Raids?" Pickett asked a half second before Sarge could.

"Why would anyone raid a shuttered hotel?"

"High school and college sex parties," Robin said. "Abandoned and closed-down hotels full of rooms and beds."

"Seriously?" Sarge asked. "I'm trying to wrap my mind around there being enough students in the local universities and high schools who would do that sort of thing."

"The raids didn't find local kids," Robin said. "Or at least not many. Most of the kids arrested for trespassing in those raids were from the LA and central California schools."

Sarge just leaned against the kitchen counter, shaking his head. It made such perfect sense now that he thought about it.

"Free rooms in Las Vegas for the weekend," Pickett said.

"How far apart were these raids?" Sarge asked.

"One in 1993 at a shuttered motel on the old Boulder Highway and another in 2004 in a shuttered Strip hotel," Robin said.

"So this is likely still going on," Pickett said.

Sarge just nodded. He had no doubt at all.

Chapter Thirteen

December 5th, 2016
Las Vegas, Nevada

PICKETT AND SARGE and Robin talked for another half hour about where to go next on this case. They settled on trying to figure out why anyone would want to kill Heather.

Robin said she would dig up some addresses of Heather's closest friends in that first year of college, before she had her switch to fake Heather, and bring the names to breakfast.

When Robin mentioned breakfast, Pickett realized just how hungry she was. Normally they just had their coffee and then headed out immediately for the buffet at the Golden Nugget, but this morning they had talked for a while first.

The kittens were long past their morning laps of the complex and now were all asleep in the sun in the living room. At the moment they were still spread out around the room.

It took her and Sarge only a minute to get their jackets and get headed for breakfast. The morning air was crisp and again the day was going to be clear and sunny.

She loved the walk they made every morning. Not only did it feel like quality time with Sarge, but it felt great to just be able to get out and move around.

"You know," Sarge said as they got to Fremont Street and turned toward the Nugget, "someone local has to be organizing these sex parties and figuring out how to get into each shuttered hotel. And then spreading the word into California. Seems pretty risky and time-consuming."

"That is does," Picket said.

"So why do it?"

"They have to be making money on it in some fashion," Pickett said. To her that was clear.

"Filming it all like we found in the tunnels?" Sarge asked.

"Maybe," Pickett said.

She didn't want to think about what they had found down in the storm tunnels under the city. People coming into town for weddings had been kidnapped and held prisoner and filmed every minute of every day and the films streamed or sold.

It had been a horrific sex operation. It had taken her months to stop having nightmares about what they found down there.

But by finding it, they had rescued hundreds of people.

She glanced over at Sarge as they walked and she could tell he didn't much like the idea either of this being another sex ring.

"Doesn't feel right," she said. And it didn't.

He said nothing.

They were almost at the door to the Nugget when Sarge said simply, "We need to find one happening now, if they are still going on. We need a list of the shuttered hotels and motels and figure out which ones might be used for these parties. And how often they happened."

Pickett nodded, but again that didn't feel right.

"And we should be able to find some older people who participated and wouldn't mind admitting it and telling us about it now."

"Why would that help besides maybe find the person behind it all?" Pickett asked.

"Because if we see the rooms, the setup used now, talk to some who came in for a party, we might be able to figure out why. And what, if anything, they had to do with Heather getting locked in that room."

Pickett shook her head. "I'm guessing the why is because high school kids and young college kids would love the excitement of it all. A forbidden sex party, a dangerous sex party, all in Sin City. I might have gone along on one at that age, to be honest."

She smiled at his shocked face.

Then as he held the door open for her, he laughed. "Honestly, I might have as well. Especially if it had been with you."

"You silver-tongued devil, you," she said.

But she had to admit, as a freshman in college, if college-aged Sarge had invited her to one of these sex parties in an old shuttered hotel, with a chance of getting caught and arrested for trespassing, she would have gone along.

Just for the thrill of it.

And the fun of being with Sarge.

Chapter Fourteen

December 5th, 2016
Las Vegas, Nevada

SARGE HADN'T REALIZED just how hungry he had gotten until the wonderful smells of the buffet hit them going up the escalator. Since it was Pickett's turn to buy, he didn't even bother to take off his jacket before heading to the buffet to get his omelet started.

After they all had food, the three of them talked about the chance the parties were still going on and the reasons they had gone on for so long.

"More than likely just be tradition," Robin said. "College and high schools have a lot of strange traditions. I could see something like this going on every year from most schools. A secret party whispered about all year. Only the popular kids getting the invite and instructions."

Sarge had to agree with that and it made the most sense. But they still needed to find the person feeding all the hotel information to the different schools. And finding safe ways into the shuttered hotels and setting the rules for each hotel.

That kind of information had to come from someone local.

And someone who had access to hotel information in general. That just couldn't be a large list of people who had been around for twenty-five or more years.

Robin said she and Will would see if they could figure out who that person might be while Sarge and Pickett interviewed a few of Heather's old friends from the time before fake Heather.

The first woman they called to talk with after breakfast was Cinda Blessing. Cinda agreed to talk with them over a break, so they met her outside her accounting office at 10:30 in the morning. The day was growing warm enough that they could sit on the concrete steps of the building facing the traffic.

Pickett sat beside her while Sarge stood facing them both a few steps down.

Cinda was a large, round woman who dressed for her size and had an infectious laugh and almost a twinkle in her blue eyes. She clearly enjoyed life. Sarge liked her almost at once.

Robin had showed them Cinda's picture from high school. She had been thin and trim back then.

"Why are you investigating Heather's week-long disappearance after all these years?" Cinda asked.

Sarge smiled at her. "Just trying to tie up a few loose ends and after we do we promise to give you the entire story, if you'll help us now."

Cinda smiled back and said, "Sounds like a deal to me."

"First off," Pickett said, "please don't mention this to Heather if you are still in contact with her."

Cinda looked sad and shook her head. "After that week of her being gone, she was never the same. We haven't spoken in years. But honestly, why don't you just ask her what happened?"

"She can't say what happened," Pickett said, looking sad.

Sarge was impressed at how Pickett sold that with the look.

Cinda nodded and said, "Oh."

"So do you know where she disappeared from, exactly?" Sarge asked.

"No," Cinda said

Sarge could tell she was hedging on that answer, so he decided to give her a little help.

"Was it from one of the sex parties held at the shuttered Landmark?"

Cinda jerked, then smiled. "Yeah, the last time I saw her before she disappeared was that night in the Landmark. That place was creepy, but I have to tell you, Danny and I had some fun that night. I got pregnant that night with our first kid and Danny and I were married three months later. Our kid could never

---

figure out why, at times, Danny and I would just call him The Tenth Floor and then laugh."

Both Sarge and Pickett laughed along with Cinda.

"The poor darling," Cinda said, shaking her head, "to this day he still doesn't know what that is all about."

"You know how often those kinds of parties are thrown?" Sarge asked.

"Only one I ever heard about," Cinda said. "But being married and pregnant, I doubt I would have heard of others."

"Do you know who Heather was with that night?" Pickett asked.

"Not a clue," Cinda said. "Some guy she said was from California, a junior, and handsome and she said she would introduce me. But I never ran into her in the hotel and then I got sort of busy, if you catch my drift."

Cinda laughed again and Sarge had no choice but to join her laugh it was so infectious.

Chapter Fifteen

December 5th, 2016
Las Vegas, Nevada

PICKETT REALLY LIKED Cinda and was enjoying their talk. Finally, Pickett got around to the main question they had been wondering about.

"Did Heather have any enemies that you knew about?"

"Oh, yeah," Cinda said, laughing. "A bunch."

"What did she do to cause that?" Sarge asked while Pickett regrouped from the surprise.

Cinda looked at both Pickett and Sarge, a serious look on her face. "You really don't know, do you? I thought that was the real reason you were here."

"Not a clue," Pickett said. "We really are just investigating the disappearance. Trying to figure out why it happened."

"Anyone close to Heather knew why it happened," Cinda said. "She covered too many bets that lost and got in over her head. Way over, more than likely refused to pay off on a couple of bets, made some pretty powerful people around the university real mad."

"Covered bets?" Sarge asked.

Cinda nodded. "I'm convinced she was taking bets like a bookie on some weird shit. Not the normal sports stuff the casinos all cover in their sports books, but mostly celebrity stuff. Who would be divorced, who was sleeping with whom, range of gross on movies on opening weekends, and so on. Amazing what people will bet on when given the chance. Especially in this town."

Pickett was shocked. She had never heard of anything like this.

Cinda went on. "Heather spent a lot of time out and about in the clubs and hotel bars. She also wrote a nasty celebrity gossip column for a small newspaper that was starting to get major attention."

"Column?" Sarge asked.

Cinda nodded. "Heather dished crap on numbers of bigger name stars that were playing here in the casinos. Her favorite targets though were the lounge bands, the small groups, the lower-level magic and comic acts and the Elvis impersonators. She could be one nasty bitch in print to them. But after she vanished for that week, she stopped doing all that, including writing, and became a nasty bitch in person instead. Her columns kept going for a few months, but then stopped."

Pickett tried to wrap her mind around what she had just heard. Sarge was busy taking notes and shaking his head.

"Let me get this straight," Pickett said, "the week Heather disappeared, she planned to meet some handsome guy from California and also owed a bunch of people money and had a bunch of celebrities and musicians hating her."

"You got it," Cinda said. "And since you didn't know any of that, you wouldn't know that Heather back in those days kept amazingly accurate notes in dark blue journals on everything, including the money and her sources on the gossip. I saw her writing in the damn things all the time. You might ask her what happened to those journals. Last time I saw them they were in her pretend office in a storage unit down off of Sahara."

Pickett knew exactly which storage area she was talking about. The place had been there for thirty years and was looking pretty worn these days.

"So do you know if she wrote those columns under her own name?" Sarge asked.

Cinda laughed. "Heavens no. She wrote all that under the name Darling Black."

And that made Pickett glance at Sarge who was just writing that down. Pickett remembered clearly the name Darling Black and how many threats were sent to the small newspaper against her. Pickett and Robin, in their first year as detectives, had been forced to investigate some of those threats. They had gotten nowhere and then Darling Black stopped writing and it all went away.

Cinda was right. Darling Black had been a real nasty bitch. Stunning that the world didn't know she was nothing more than a college student.

But someone clearly must have known.

Someone angry enough to lock Heather, aka Darling Black, in an abandoned hotel to die.

Part Four
DARLING BLACK

Chapter Sixteen

December 5th, 2016
Las Vegas, Nevada

SARGE AND PICKETT thanked Cinda for all the help, then headed for the car. Once inside, Sarge glanced at Pickett. He had noticed her react to the name Darling Black, so she clearly had a memory of the pen name.

"So what was with the name Darling Black?" he asked.

"As Cinda said, a real nasty bitch," Pickett said. "Let's wait until we are at lunch with Robin and both of us can go over what we had to deal with on that name."

Sarge nodded and glanced at his notebook. "I know the storage facility she mentioned. Think they might still have records from all those years ago?"

"It's not that far," Pickett said, shrugging. "Might as well check since our cast of possible suspects just grew to half the city."

"And don't forget the California date."

Pickett laughed. "Seems we are making progress, but in the wrong direction."

Sarge nodded. "Feels exactly that way."

Ten minutes later Pickett had them parked outside the main building for the S&S Storage and Save. The place was in a desperate need of paint and the wire fence looked like one good wind would knock it down. The garage doors on each unit seemed rusted and that was from what Sarge could see from the parking area.

They headed into the small office to be greeted with a cloud of smoke and a woman behind the desk with a 1960s beehive hairdo and layers of purple makeup. She had to be in her eighties.

She ground out her cigarette in a full plastic ashtray and said, "What can I help you folks with?"

Her voice sounded as you would expect from a person who smoked far too many cigarettes: Low and full of gravel.

Both Sarge and Pickett introduced themselves and showed her their badges.

The woman only nodded and didn't introduce herself.

They had decided on the way over that chances are Heather had rented the unit under her own name, so Sarge said, "We're wondering if you have records that might date back into the early 1990s."

"Got them into the seventies," the woman said. "Don't trust them tax people to not bother me, so I keep it all."

"We're looking into a locker that might have been rented by a Heather Winston in 1990 or before," Pickett said.

"She rented it in December of 1988," the woman said.

"Wow, great memory," Sarge said.

"No memory needed," the woman said. "I see it every month when I do the books. We needed some cash to expand, so we had a special that December for a lifetime rental and she paid the two thousand. Ten people did, but she's the only one still here."

Pickett glanced at Sarge. He couldn't believe what he was hearing.

Pickett recovered faster than Sarge. "Does Heather ever come around much?"

"Nope," the woman said. "I can tell you for a fact that she hasn't been here in years and years. Her lock rusted off about twelve years ago and we opened up her unit. It was still full and since she was paid up, we legally couldn't do anything, so we just closed it back up and put one of our locks on it. No one has ever come asking for the key. Got a hunch she forgot the unit was here."

"Can we get the number of the unit?" Sarge asked. "We'll do some checking and see if we can get that freed up for you."

For the first time the woman almost smiled, which Sarge wasn't sure wouldn't crack her layers of thick makeup. "Appreciate that. Let me know if there is anything I can do."

The woman gave them the number and Picket and Sarge thanked her and headed back for their car.

"We need a search warrant," Pickett said as she closed the door and started up the Jeep.

"But unless we tell someone about the real Heather being dead and the fake Heather," Sarge said, "that is going to be damned hard to get. And I'm honestly not believing we could get this lucky."

"Not so sure it's luck in this case," Pickett said. "If this case holds true, all that stuff in there is going to do is expand our suspect list, not narrow it."

"If the contents are what we suspect it to be," Sarge said.

Everything about this case was just getting stranger and stranger. Why would a nineteen-year-old college girl rent a storage unit for life? What did she plan on keeping in there?

And what Sarge really wanted to know was did this young girl have help with all the betting, the money, the research into all the gossip, and everything. She had also been going to college at the time of her disappearance and her grades were top line.

"I think we need lunch," Sarge said after they had sat there thinking for almost a minute in silence.

Pickett nodded, grabbed her phone, and called Robin.

"You are not going to believe what we have found," Pickett said. "Lunch at the café?"

Pickett nodded, then said, "See you there."

She clicked off her phone and got the Jeep out of the parking lot and into traffic, headed toward the Bellagio.

Sarge just sat thinking, trying to make some sense out of all the details. And not a thing was coming together.

Chapter Seventeen

December 5th, 2016
Las Vegas, Nevada

THE BELLAGIO CAFÉ was one of Pickett's favorite places. It not only had great food and choices, but the seating was comfortable and many of the booths were surrounded by plants, which gave a feeling of privacy to every meal even though they were in the middle of a large casino.

Also, the casino machines and games were far enough away that the noise was muted and talking was comfortable. The café was always their choice to have lunch when they were out along the Strip.

Pickett and Sarge had just gotten seated when Robin arrived, carrying a notebook and a folder.

As they were waiting for the drinks, Pickett and Sarge filled Robin in on the details of the conversation with Cinda.

"Darling Black?" Robin said, shaking her head. "Wow, that's a name out of the past."

Pickett said, "Wait, there's more."

She and Sarge told Robin about the storage place and how Heather's storage unit was still there.

"Oh, shit," Robin said. "How the hell are we going to get into that?"

Pickett felt the same way and Sarge just looked concerned. At this point it looked like they were going to have to turn all this over to an active detective and all three of them knew that the case would just run cold again. Active detectives just were so busy with the stuff happening right now around them, a decades-old possible murder wouldn't get much attention at all.

And Pickett didn't blame them in the slightest. Detectives spent most of their days just trying to prioritize which case needed the most attention the quickest. It was always an impossible task and always too much to do. She didn't miss the stress of that part of the job at all. Not for a second.

"Think maybe we can talk with Andor?" Sarge said. "Get him to talk with the chief, let us get into that unit to see if there really is a case worth an active detective's time."

Pickett looked at Robin, who seemed to be frowning. Pickett knew that meant she had no better idea.

But then Pickett realized they might have another way. "Cavanaugh."

Sarge frowned, but Robin nodded.

"Detective Tony Cavanaugh," Pickett said to Sarge. "An old friend, still active but about to retire. Wants to join the Gang when he does."

"And he owes me and Will a favor," Robin said, smiling. "I'll set up a time to meet him after lunch, see what he can do. Something as simple as a search warrant for a storage unit I think might be possible. Good idea."

"So what's in the folder?" Pickett said.

"Photos of the doorframe in the Landmark," Robin said, pulling out the folder from beside her on the booth and opening it up for Pickett and Sarge to both see.

Robin pointed to an area near the top and bottom of the frame. And the destroyed insides of the lock. "Door was nailed closed after the lock was disabled."

"Murder," Sarge said, nodding.

"Might have only been with the intent to hold her for a few days, but then it turned into Heather dying," Pickett said. "Manslaughter or murder, either way trapping her was intended."

At that moment the waitress came with their drinks and to take their lunch order. Then after she left, Robin and Pickett explained to Sarge why they knew the name Darling Black and how they had been assigned to investigate some threats against her.

"I'll pull up the old file on the stuff we did," Robin said.

"Won't be worth much," Pickett said. "Newspaper stonewalled us and then when the columns stopped the entire thing seemed to just vanish."

Sarge nodded. "So I keep coming back to the place where a young college student couldn't have been a bookie and a rising columnist and a student without help from someone."

"And someone was behind nailing that door closed and then helping the fake Heather take over Heather's life," Pickett said.

"And maybe kill the parents as well," Robin said.

"None of this is still fitting together," Sarge said.

Pickett couldn't agree more. But she had a hunch that whatever was in that storage unit might get them going in the right direction. They were almost at a dead end without it.

If they could just get the search warrant without losing the case. That was one of the really major drawbacks about being in the Cold Case Gang task force. They had no standing to go and get search warrants.

And honestly, so far, in all the cold cases she and Robin had worked, they hadn't needed one.

But this time they did. They simply had no choice.

Chapter Eighteen

December 5th, 2016
Las Vegas, Nevada

SARGE WATCHED AS Pickett was clearly excited to see Cavanaugh again when he met them in the parking lot area of the storage facility at a little after four in the afternoon. His head was bald, his sports coat hung loose on his shoulders, and his face looked thin, maybe a little too thin.

But his broad smile and green eyes made Pickett smile as she gave him a hug. Robin gave him a hug as well and then Pickett introduced him to Sarge.

Cavanaugh's grip was firm and his smile real. "Heard a lot about you over the years," Cavanaugh said. "And I'm really impressed you could convince Pickett here to leave her matron ways in the past."

"I doubt I had anything to do with that," Sarge said, laughing.

"Matron ways?" Pickett asked, pretending to frown at Cavanaugh.

"Yeah, you know, like your virginity," Cavanaugh said, "Hard to get rid of but you never miss it once you do."

Sarge laughed and Robin sounded like she was going to hurt herself she was laughing so hard.

Pickett just laughed and then gave Cavanaugh another hug. "Damn it's wonderful to see you again. When you officially joining the gang?"

"Six months from now," Cavanaugh said. "You want to know how many days and minutes exactly? I cross them off my calendar in my office every day."

Again Sarge just laughed. Cavanaugh seemed like a great guy and clearly Robin and Pickett loved him.

Cavanaugh reached into his breast pocket and pulled out a folded piece of paper. "We have permission to search, photograph, inventory, and even remove some things."

"Wow, what did you give the judge for that?" Robin asked.

"Just mentioned this might get some answers on whatever happened to Darling Black and he gave me the whole nine yards," Cavanaugh said. "I hadn't thought of that name for decades until you told me what you guys were doing."

Sarge just shook his head. Had he been the only person in Las Vegas to not know that name?

Cavanaugh and Robin went into the small office and a few minutes later the woman with the tall, beehive hair came out with them. She had a lit cigarette in her hand and walked all four of them down the worn concrete to a second building and pointed to a unit and handed Cavanaugh the key.

It took only a moment for Cavanaugh to get the lock off, but both he and Sarge had to slowly work the rusted old garage door up.

Sarge and Pickett had brought a couple of LED lanterns in hopes they would get the search warrant and also a number of file storage boxes.

About a foot inside the door was a dusty curtain strung from one side of the ten-foot wide unit to the other.

Sarge had the others stay outside and he carefully pulled the curtain aside, sliding it along the cord holding it up, trying not to stir up any more dust than he had to.

Then he stepped back out into the sunlight to let the dust settle that he had disturbed.

With the light of the day shining in, the unit looked like it might have even more than they had hoped. A wooden desk sat against the right wall with a desk lamp in one corner. Some papers were piled to one side and an old computer filled the middle of the desk with a massive printer on the other side.

Everything had a thick layer of dust on it.

"Wow, that setup cost some money in its day," Cavanaugh said, pointing at the computer and printer.

Sarge had been thinking the same thing. Just the printer alone had to have cost over three grand in 1990 money. No telling how much the computer had cost.

Along the back wall were a row of six four-drawer file cabinets and two lamps on top of the cabinets. Some papers were stacked neatly on top of the cabinets.

In the back left corner was a fairly large combination safe.

"What was she doing in here?" Pickett asked.

"Let me take some pictures before we even look," Robin said.

Sarge watched as Robin made sure she didn't miss an angle on any of the stuff in the room.

"You guys don't mind," Cavanaugh said, "I'm going to leave the deeper exploring in the dust to you. I got another appointment to make before dinner. Send me the pictures and inventory for my official file. And keep me up on what you find, would you. This is all damn weird."

Both Pickett and Robin hugged him and thanked him before Cavanaugh nodded to Sarge and headed back for his car.

"Nice guy," Sarge said.

"One of the best," Robin said. "His wife Steph was a dream as well, but she lost a long fight with cancer a few years back. He's going to make a great addition to the gang. Andor said we were going to have a special welcome night for him when he finally retired officially."

Sarge had a gut sense they were right about Cavanaugh being a good member of the gang. Somehow he had managed to get this search warrant and then felt comfortable leaving it to them.

"So how do we start?" Pickett asked.

"We open every file drawer and I get a picture first," Robin said. "And then every desk drawer and the same thing. Carefully and by the numbers we all used to follow."

"Pain-in-the-ass numbers," Pickett said.

"My suggestion after that," Sarge said, "is we take fingerprints. We need to know exactly, besides the testimony of the landlord, who was in this place."

"How many people were in here," Pickett said, nodding.

They all put on evidence gloves and Sarge was about to open a top drawer on the left near the safe and Pickett was moving to the cabinet on the right when he noticed a small wire leading from the drawer.

"Don't touch anything!" he shouted. "Back out carefully a safe distance."

Pickett and Robin did exactly as he told them to do.

He carefully, without touching anything, traced the wire along the top edge of the cabinet and then down the side to where it disappeared behind the cabinet.

The cabinet was either wired to explode if opened wrong or if opened wrong would set off some sort of alarm somewhere. Either way, he wasn't taking any chances.

He moved along the cabinets slowly, looking at each one. From what he could tell, every file cabinet was wired the same way.

And so was the large desk drawer.

He got down on his knees and visually traced the wire from the desk to a switch hidden on the wall behind the desk.

The wires from the cabinets all seemed to come into that same switch.

And above the switch, secured to the wall, were enough explosives to not only destroy everything in this unit, but the entire row of units.

He could hear his blood pounding in his ears and he didn't want to dare breathe.

Those were old explosives.

And when explosives got old, they often got touchy. It was lucky the thing hadn't gone off when he and Cavanaugh had worked that door open.

Sarge slowly climbed to his feet, not touching anything, being very careful to not lose his balance.

His heart was threatening to pound out of his chest by the time he slowly backed out of the storage unit and turned to join Pickett and Robin who were standing in the middle of the drive looking very worried.

"Everything is wired to explode if opened without deactivating a switch under the desk," he said, indicating that they should all move farther away from the unit. "Enough to level the entire row of units."

"Oh, shit," Pickett said.

"Too damned close," Robin said, shaking her head.

Pickett hugged Sarge as they moved away and he hugged her back.

Robin took a deep breath after they had stood for a moment staring at the open storage unit. "I'll call Cavanaugh, have him get the bomb squad out here and get back here himself since this is his warrant."

"I'll get the lady in the office to shut this place down and open that front gate for trucks," Pickett said.

"I'll stay right here and make sure no one gets near any of this," Sarge said.

As Pickett and Robin moved away, Sarge moved over and leaned against another row of storage units. He just kept staring back into the open mouth of the unit, trying to catch his breath and slow his racing heart.

Over the years he had come close to dying a number of times.

But this one might well have been his closest.

And coming close to dying was not something anyone ever got used to.

Chapter Nineteen

December 5th, 2016
Las Vegas, Nevada

IT TOOK THE bomb squad almost an hour to clear the unit, working carefully to not disturb any evidence at all.

Pickett stood hugging Sarge the entire time. His quick mind and sane thinking had saved all of their lives. He seemed fine on the surface but she had a hunch under the stern shell he was feeling this one.

The sun had set and the night air now had a bite to it. Pickett had gotten their light coats from her car, but if they were out here much longer they were going to need heavier coats.

The bomb squad had set up bright lights filling the entire inside of the storage unit with light. They left the lights up making the entire area feel almost as bright as day.

As the squad pulled away, Cavanaugh turned to the three of them. "That bomb was as dangerous as you thought it was, Sarge. Very unstable. Now I got a hunch the chief will want me to stay and help you guys on this."

"I think we could use the help," Robin said. "Thanks."

Pickett agreed to that completely.

"I got one of Will's people bringing us heavy jackets and some hamburgers and fries," Robin said. "What does everyone want?"

After the four of them decided on dinner and Robin got it on the way, Sarge said, "Okay, where were we?"

"About to die an ugly death," Robin said.

"Yeah," Pickett said, "let's skip that step, shall we?"

"Gladly," Sarge said, smiling at her.

"Can't tell you how happy I am to have missed that step," Cavanaugh said.

"We were about to photograph the interior of the drawers without touching anything, then dust for fingerprints," Robin said.

Cavanaugh nodded. "That sounds like a solid by-the-book plan. But I got the lab guys coming in an hour to do the fingerprinting now."

Pickett nodded.

"Good," Sarge said. "That way we won't miss anything."

So carefully, wearing evidence gloves, all four of them went back into the unit.

Robin took pictures as they carefully opened each drawer. Just the grating sound of the old file drawer opening made her tense. This place had become a frightening place, that was for sure.

Every file was labeled with a number. There seemed to be no order to the numbers which meant to Pickett that there was a master sheet somewhere.

The drawers in the desk had the journals that Cinda had mentioned and one drawer was full of computer storage disks.

"We're going to need to take those to Will," Robin said, "to have his people save what is on them, if possible."

"Assuming those will be evidence," Cavanaugh said, "is Will set up for that sort of thing with the city as far as chain of custody?"

"He is," Robin said. "Licensed computer lab for the department."

"Perfect," Cavanaugh said, nodding.

Pickett let out a sigh of relief when they finished the photos and left the unit again, moving back out into the chilly night air.

Right at that moment the truck from the city forensics lab pulled up and right behind it one of Will's assistants with coats and their dinner.

Cavanaugh got the lab guys going on the storage area while Pickett and Sarge and Robin put on coats. They then decided the best place to eat would be in Pickett's Jeep since it had the most room inside.

Pickett went and pulled the Jeep into the storage area, facing it so they could see the lit area where the tech people were working.

Cavanaugh took the offered coat and then joined them and for the first few minutes they ate their hamburgers and fries in silence with Cavanaugh and Robin in the back seat.

Finally it was Cavanaugh who broke the silence.

"You know, from first glance at how much is in there and how it was protected, we might be sitting on one of the most dangerous caches of information imaginable for a lot of people in this town."

"Dangerous enough to kill Heather Winston over," Robin said.

Pickett just nodded. She glanced over at Sarge. He was eating and seemingly lost in his own thoughts.

"What are you thinking?" Pickett asked him.

He glanced at her and then said, "We need armed guards on this place until we get all that stuff moved into a secure location."

"Think we should call Mike?" Pickett asked. Until Sarge said that, she hadn't given the next step much thought at all.

"I do," Sarge said. "And with all the people in the bomb squad and now the tech people working this, word is going to get out and some people out there are going to know exactly how dangerous this place might be to their lives."

"Mike?" Cavanaugh asked.

"Private and well-trusted security firm," Pickett said as Sarge put aside his half-finished hamburger and took out his phone.

"What about Will's firm?" Cavanaugh asked.

"Mike does a different form of security," Pickett said.

"We'll tell you all about him later," Robin said. "But it was Mike's people who went into the tunnels ahead of us on that massive kidnapping and sex-tape case and cleared out any opposition and helped with the evacuation."

Cavanaugh sort of chuckled. "I had heard rumors that the gang had broken that case and gone in ahead of everyone. But I honestly didn't believe it."

"We hate credit, remember?" Robin said.

"I'm starting to understand that now," he said. "And if something comes of this case I'll get the credit, right? And I'll have to do the days of paperwork as well."

"You got it," Pickett said, turning to smile at Cavanaugh.

"Damn, retirement can't come faster."

"Mike," Sarge said into his phone, "we got an emergency situation that is going to need some firepower to guard."

Pickett listened as Sarge explained the situation of the storage unit, the bomb, that it might have been Darling Black's old office, and the location.

"Thanks, Mike," Sarge said and clicked off his phone.

"He'll have his people in place in one hour and come tell us what he has done."

Pickett nodded and finished off her hamburger. Knowing that they would be guarded by Mike and his people suddenly made her feel much better.

Now they just had to figure out if that old information in that storage unit was worth the problem and the near-death experience.

She had a hunch it was going to be.

Chapter Twenty

December 5th, 2016
Las Vegas, Nevada

THE TECH GUYS were just finishing up when Mike appeared beside the door of the Jeep and all four of them got out. Sarge shook Mike's hand and thanked him for the quick reaction.

Mike wore his normal jeans, T-shirt under a dark jacket, and tonight he had on a black stocking cap.

"Anything to do with Darling Black has to be dangerous," Mike said.

"I'm starting to understand that," Sarge said.

Sarge introduced Mike to Cavanaugh and explained that Cavanaugh was only months away from joining the gang, but for the moment was stuck as the lead detective on this case.

Mike laughed. "Paperwork hell."

"Trying not to think about that," Cavanaugh said, shaking his head.

"Between the bomb squad and the tech folks, this will take me a week to cross the final 't' on this mess."

"Got a hunch we are a ways from the end of this yet," Sarge said, laughing.

Cavanaugh just shook his head like a sad puppy and everyone laughed.

"I have this place surrounded by my team," Mike said. "And two have clear sight on this unit there. I'm going to stick around for the night as well on this one. Where you thinking of moving all that?"

"Not sure yet," Sarge said. "Got any suggestions?"

"I have a secure house on the north side," Mike said. "Make it comfortable to work as well. And we can guard any chain of evidence clearly that way."

Sarge noted that Cavanaugh was nodding.

"We got one issue," Sarge said. "We have a big standing safe in there. We're hoping to find the combo in the desk once we get to looking."

"Can I take a look at it?" Mike asked.

Sarge glanced at Cavanaugh who shrugged.

They all went back over to the unit just as the last tech guy reported to Cavanaugh they were all done and the unit was clear. They would have preliminary results for him by noon tomorrow.

"Wow, that's fast," Pickett said.

"Finding an active bomb on site will tend to speed up things some," Cavanaugh said.

Sarge sure understood that, especially in these modern times.

Mike went in and bent down and looked at the dial on the safe, then without touching anything, looked around the safe and under it, since it was on four metal legs about three inches off the concrete.

"We'll open it before we move it," Mike said. "And pull the contents. The safe itself can be secured nicely in the garage of the house I have."

"You can open that safe without cutting into it?"

"Oh, sure," Mike said. "I can get some equipment from my car and pop it for you in a few minutes."

"Please?" Sarge said, not believing that the safe was going to be that easy.

"Be right back," Mike said, striding off toward the main gate.

"So tell me again who this guy is exactly," Cavanaugh said.

"Where Will's company works out in the open and for big name stars and politicians," Robin said. "Mike and his people work behind the scenes, sometimes just along the line of what is legal and what isn't in some cases. Will calls him at times when he needs help on a case."

Cavanaugh nodded.

"Right now there are four or five ex-special forces people guarding us," Sarge said. "Mike was ex-special forces as well."

"Damned good to know considering what has happened here so far," Cavanaugh said.

"Also Mike is the best computer expert I have ever seen," Robin said.

"That's going some considering Will and his computer force," Cavanaugh said.

Sarge could only agree with that.

They all stood just outside the doorway to the unit until Mike got back. No point at starting on anything until they had the safe cleared.

Mike had a small tool kit. He went right to the safe and tried the handle. It was secure and locked.

He spun the dial three or four times, then took out what looked like a small meter and locked it in place against the metal door just to the right of the dial.

Then slowly he moved the dial until something registered on it.

"Right three to twenty-six," he said.

Sarge pulled out his notebook from his pocket and wrote that down.

Mike turned the dial back to the left slowly until something registered again on the dial that Sarge couldn't see.

"Left two to twenty-one."

Mike then turned the dial back to the right again very slowly.

When he stopped he said, "Right one to ten."

Then he eased the dial back to the left until it stopped.

"Back to zero," he said.

He took the device off the side of the safe, then pushed the handle down and pulled the door open.

"Holy shit," Cavanaugh said.

Sarge could only agree. Inside the safe were stacks and stacks of bundles of hundreds of dollars.

They all stepped back and just stared at the vast amount of money in the safe. Sarge just couldn't believe how much there was.

"I'll get some folks out here to take custody of that paperwork nightmare," Cavanaugh said, pulling out his phone and stepping away. "That's going to take real protection to move that amount of money."

"How much do you think is there?" Pickett asked.

Sarge had seen this kind of money a number of times in the past. Once he had helped guard the final cash prize at Binions for the World Series of Poker. That had been two million and it wasn't even close to the amount in that safe.

"Fifteen million," Sarge said. "More than likely more. Each of those bundles is ten thousand."

"So how did a college girl end up with that kind of money in a safe?" Robin asked.

"I think a better question is who was her partner or partners," Pickett said, "and how did they lose track of that kind of money?"

"And what are they going to do when they discover their money has been found?" Sarge said.

"I'm going to get a few more men out here," Mike said, pulling out his phone. "At least until this can be taken by armored car to a secure impound center."

"Thanks, Mike," Sarge said.

"Don't thank me. That money in there is like bait in front of a pack of rats and I don't want my men outgunned."

Sarge didn't like the sound of that at all.

Chapter Twenty-One

December 5th, 2016
Las Vegas, Nevada

PICKETT DIDN'T MUCH like the safe standing open and millions in cash just sitting there. In fact there was nothing about this case she was liking at this moment, from almost being killed by a bomb to not knowing what was in those files.

But she was very glad Sarge had thought of calling in Mike and his people.

Cavanaugh turned back to them after a moment. "Going to take about an hour for a security detail and armored car to get here, and then it will take them about thirty minutes to count and secure that money."

"Afraid we don't have that kind of time," Mike said, coming back to join them. "We have company. Who told you about this place?"

"An old friend of Heather's named Cinda," Pickett said.

"Well, someone knew fairly quickly and right now four armed intruders are working their way this way from three sides. Another is waiting in a van a block down the road from here."

Pickett couldn't believe what she was hearing. Cinda couldn't have been involved in all this. Did that woman play them to find the storage unit and get it open? Was that even possible?

"I'll call for backup," Cavanaugh said, reaching for his phone.

"No need," Mike said. "That will be too late and might get someone hurt. My men will handle it, but I need you four to act naturally and just walk as a group back over to the Jeep. Stay on the side of the Jeep closest to the building and just talk so a spotter for them won't realize they have been made. Keep your guns in their holsters, but be ready to cover. I'm going to bring in the person in their van."

Mike then turned and without another word headed off like he was going back to his car.

"You trusting him on this?" Cavanaugh asked as the four of them turned and walked slowly back toward Pickett's Jeep.

"Completely," Robin said. "Mike's in charge at the moment, we do what he says. That's why we hired him to protect us."

"His people are that good," Pickett said, touching Cavanaugh on the arm to reassure him.

The four of them reached the Jeep and stood facing each other so each of them could see in any open direction. Pickett still felt out in the open, but this was better than standing in front of all those lights in the open storage unit.

"Not hearing anything," Cavanaugh said.

"You won't," Pickett said.

"Mike's men won't fire a shot," Sarge said. "They will just wrap up the attackers for us."

"Deliver them with bows on," Robin said.

Pickett looked along the row of storage units and into the distance. A dark building sort of loomed in the distance, only basic lights were on. It was clearly not occupied.

"Sarge, you know what that building is in the distance there?"

"New apartment construction," Sarge said.

"Let's move around behind the Jeep," Pickett said. "That's close enough for a sniper."

"Have I said how much fun it is to work with you three," Cavanaugh said as they all slowly worked around to the back of the Jeep, putting the car between them and that distant dark building.

"Just a normal day for the Cold Poker Gang," Robin said.

Pickett laughed.

"Trust me," Sarge said, "This is far, far from normal."

"And here I thought all you guys did was play poker," Cavanaugh said.

"Well, we do that too," Robin said.

In the other direction Pickett could see lights from a McDonalds and passing cars.

Now they were covered on three sides at least.

They stood, not knowing what to say for another minute. As far as Pickett was concerned, that was the longest minute she had experienced in a very long time.

Finally Mike came around the corner pushing a resisting and very angry Cinda Blessing ahead of him. That meant all the men were also under wraps.

Pickett just stared at her as Sarge said simply, "I'll be go to hell."

As Cinda got close, she could see the open safe and the massive amount of money.

"That bitch," Cinda said, almost spitting out the words.

More Cold Poker Gang Now Available
from all your favorite booksellers
in trade paper and electronic editions.

"Talking about Heather I assume," Pickett said as Cavanaugh took Cinda from Mike with a nod.

"I'll get her people in," Mike said, moving away and leaving Cinda with them.

"You knew this place was trapped, didn't you?" Sarge asked.

"Of course I did," Cinda said, glaring at Sarge, any sign of the happy accountant long gone.

"And that the money was in the safe," Pickett said.

At that moment there was a sickening thud followed a moment later by the sound of a gunshot echoing over the city.

A hole appeared in Cinda's chest and she slumped to the ground out of Cavanaugh's hand.

"Mike! Sniper!" Sarge yelled as loud as he could as he grabbed Pickett and yanked her into the open storage unit.

"Building to the west!" Pickett shouted.

The shot had come from the dark building she had been worried about a few minutes earlier.

Robin grabbed the shocked Cavanaugh and got him safely into the small place as well, leaving the body of Cinda in the open. She was clearly dead. She had gone down face first and there was a massive hole in the back of her chest where the bullet had come out.

Another shot rang out, but this time it sounded different. Pickett just hoped that hadn't been targeting one of Mike's men, or Mike himself.

"All clear!" The sound of Mike's voice echoed over the complex.

"Get an ambulance on the way," Sarge said, moving quickly back to Cinda's body.

Cavanaugh had his phone out. "Shots fired. One down."

At that moment Mike and another man with a rifle came around the corner.

Mike took one look at Cinda's body on the ground and just swore.

"One of my men is staying with the body of the man who fired this shot," Mike said. "This is Craig, the guy who took him out."

Craig handed Mike his rifle.

Robin turned and started quickly talking with Will on the phone telling him what happened and that Mike was going to need some help with clearing one of his men.

Pickett just stood there above the dead body of Cinda Blessing, wondering who she really had been, and how she fit into all this.

And why she had been worth killing.

Part Five
UNSCRAMBLING THE MESS

Chapter Twenty-Two

December 6th, 2016
Las Vegas, Nevada

SARGE COULDN'T BELIEVE how tired he was by the time he and Pickett got back to the complex at three in the morning. The entire evening and night had turned into a disaster.

Everyone involved had given statements; the money had been moved to safety; the unit locked up and guarded until its contents could be cleared to a safe house as well tomorrow.

The police took everyone's story and arrested the four men that Mike's people had captured. They were not talking.

The body of the sniper and his gun in the apartment construction had been recovered and Mike's man who had shot the sniper was questioned and his rifle taken, but he had been released. It was a clear case of self-defense. No one was doubting that at all. There was no telling how many others that sniper might have killed.

Will had two of the top lawyers in town with Mike and his people and they all walked after giving statements.

Cavanaugh was clearly shaken by the entire thing, but was clearly directing traffic through the entire mess, not letting anyone get off course or question Mike's actions in any way.

Sarge had been impressed with that.

Sarge went into the kitchen and got out a bowl of cut-up melon and put down some toast, then poured them both a small glass of orange juice. They needed a little something to eat before going to bed. They hadn't eaten since the hamburgers earlier.

Pickett had gone over to her old place to use the bathroom and just as the toast popped up she came back, dressed in a bathrobe and in her slippers.

To Sarge she looked wonderful, even as tired as she was.

She came into the kitchen and just hugged him, finally letting him go after she kissed him.

"That could have gone better tonight," he said as he turned to put some butter on their toast.

"It could have ended up so much worse," Pickett said.

Sarge laughed. "Yeah, between the bomb and the sniper, I guess it could have."

She took the knife from his hands, kissed him, and then said, "I'll finish getting this ready. You go change clothes and wash up."

She pushed him toward their bedroom and he did as she suggested, coming back five minutes later after getting out of the clothes stained with Cinda's blood and splashing water on his face.

He'd had some rough nights as a cop over the years, but this one ranked right up near the top of that list.

Pickett was sitting at the counter munching on the toast. She looked a little like she was in shock and Sarge had no doubt that he was as well.

He moved to stand across the counter from Picket. As he did, he realized that only Nose had appeared in the kitchen, looking tired and clearly wondering what was happening.

They ate in silence until Pickett finally said, "What the hell is going on? Heather was only in college and whatever is in those files is twenty-five years old at least."

"Nothing is connecting," Sarge said, nodding. "No idea why Cinda would send us to that storage unit except to have us open it so she could get to the money."

"But if she knew about the money, did she know about the fake Heather and the real Heather's death?"

Sarge shrugged. "I'm betting she might have had a hand in putting Heather in that room."

"Too bad she's dead," Pickett said.

"Maybe not," Sarge said. "She might do more talking dead than alive. And it clearly wasn't one of her people who killed her. So we have an even bigger player in this game at the moment."

Pickett nodded and they sat there in silence and ate.

"Can we go take a shower together," Pickett asked, "then crawl into bed together and just hold each other?"

Sarge looked at the woman he had come to love more than anything and said simply, "I would really like that."

He came around the counter, took her by the hand, and led her toward the bedroom, leaving the dishes on the counter, the lights on, and a very confused kitten in the kitchen.

Chapter Twenty-Three

December 6th, 2016
Las Vegas, Nevada

THEY WERE BOTH up at about their normal time. Pickett felt exhausted, both emotionally and mentally.

The kittens were already done with their racing around and were camped out in the living room, solidly in their bath and nap part of their routines.

She had the coffee made and was sipping on a cup when Sarge joined her.

"Well that was a night to remember," he said, kissing her good morning and taking the coffee she offered.

"That's an understatement," she said. "But a bunch of it I wish I could forget."

"No argument there," Sarge said.

"So how about we call Robin to see how that side of things is going, then head for breakfast with our notebooks to see if we can make some sort of sense out of all this."

"A perfect plan," she said.

She got her phone and called Robin, putting it on speaker.

"Thought you two would be sleeping later," Robin said as she answered.

"The power of a schedule," Pickett said.

"Well, this morning we made a little progress," Robin said. "Mike and his crew and Cavanaugh and a half-dozen uniformed officers got the files and desk and everything out of the storage unit and moved to Mike's safe house. Mike has the place secure and guarded."

"Are we going to be able to go through the papers?" Sarge asked a fraction of a second before Pickett was about to ask the same question.

"The three of us and Cavanaugh are the only ones with permission from the chief to go through it," Robin said. "The chief has been right on top of all this since early."

"Wow," Pickett said. "Great to hear."

"The chief moved Cavanaugh off his other cases until this is put to bed," Robin said, "so he's joining the gang a little early in spirit. And the chief assigned him help on the paperwork which has Cavanaugh smiling."

"What about Mike's guy?" Robin asked.

"District attorney is calling it an open and shut case of self-defense and isn't going to bother to do anything. In fact the DA thanked the guy for saving lives and stopping what might have been a larger disaster."

Pickett just smiled at that. Mike had been doing them a favor coming in so fast and she hated that he and his people had been exposed like that. But who knows how that would have turned out without Mike there last night. Pickett didn't want to even think about that.

"Any identification on any of the crew or the sniper?" Sarge asked.

"Cinda's men were all hired thugs," Robin said. "All had records. Cinda had been a suspect in a number of illegal gambling and robbery operations over the years, but had never been arrested for anything. What was amazing is that they had a tap on her phone for one of the investigations and they heard her hire the thugs and tell them she had a dirty job for them to do, but it would be worth millions of they pulled it off."

"Wow," Pickett said, suddenly feeling a lot better. "That's going to help put her crew away for some time."

"Death in the commission of a felony will make it certain they are all going away for a very long time. And two of them are talking like kids on candy, so we're closing a bunch of cases this morning."

Pickett just laughed and smiled at Sarge, who was also smiling and shaking his head.

"The sniper?" Pickett asked.

"A ghost so far," Robin said. "No I.D. on him. Will has his prints and both his people and the city are doing searches. The guy's DNA will be processed by this evening by Will's people and we should have that into the search system as well."

"To make that shot from that distance," Sarge said, "he had to be trained somewhere."

"Mike thinks the guy had to be ex-military," Robin said, "which is why we think either the prints or the DNA will

bring up an answer. Who he was working for is another question completely."

"Got a hunch some of that information will be in the old files in the safe house," Pickett said.

"Betting the same thing," Robin said.

"You coming to breakfast?" Sarge asked.

"Had that two hours ago," Robin said. "But I'll bring us all lunch later on at the safe house."

She then gave them the address and hung up.

"Well, the morning is going better than I feared," Sarge said, finishing his coffee and turning to get his coat.

"A lot better," Pickett said.

Thankfully. Finally something was going right.

Chapter Twenty-Four

December 6th, 2016
Las Vegas, Nevada

SARGE HAD JUST finished his ham and cheese omelet when Pickett pulled out her notebook and said, "I want to start this from the beginning."

"Make sense of what seems crazy?" Sarge asked, laughing.

"With luck," Pickett said.

He could tell she was feeling better after a couple cups of coffee and breakfast and he most definitely was.

He took out his flip notebook and pen and said, "Fire away."

"We have a young college girl by the name of Heather Winston who died locked in a room in August of 1990," Pickett said. "Best guess at cause of death is heat."

"Check," Sarge said. "And we figured out how she and whoever locked her in there got into the shuttered hotel."

"We know a week later Connie Downs returned," Robin said, "claiming to be Heather and has lived as Heather for twenty-five years now."

"Check again," Sarge said. "We do not know why or if she or someone else killed Heather's parents when they started to get suspicious. Or if that was an accident."

"From there we have almost no information that is not tainted completely," Robin said. "We think there might have been a party there the night Heather disappeared, but we have nothing but the dead Cinda's word for that, who more than likely was lying to us."

Sarge nodded to that. Pickett was right, they needed to toss out completely every lead that Cinda had told them, including the idea that Heather had been Darling Black, the bookie and columnist.

"We do know, for a fact, that there was an office in a well-protected storage unit with millions in a safe and a lot of files," Pickett said.

"And we know that someone rented the storage unit in Heather's name," Sarge said, "about a year before she vanished. It might have been Heather, it might have been someone else."

"We should know that when DNA and fingerprints come back from the storage unit," Pickett said.

Sarge nodded and wrote that down in his notebook as a reminder to check later in the day if Robin didn't bring that information to lunch later.

"We also know that Cinda wanted what was in the storage unit enough to let us go in and open it and take that risk and then attack police with a gang of thugs."

Sarge nodded. "And we know that someone else wanted to stop her enough to kill her."

Pickett stared at her notes. "Let me see if I can express what is not making sense to me at all."

"Fire away," Sarge said.

"I do not believe that Heather Winston had the ability to run a major gambling operation, do a major column, and build bombs to protect her stuff all while going to college and getting perfect grades without help. In fact, I'm betting she was only a front, if even that, for an operation run by someone called Darling Black."

"I agree with that," Sarge said. He was bothered by exactly the same thing. It wasn't that Heather might not have been a capable person, but over the decades he had learned to trust his instincts and everything they had learned for sure pointed to a far more experienced person than Heather.

"We do not know Cinda's part in any of this," Pickett said, "including if she had a hand in killing Heather, which I have a hunch she did."

"Agreed," Sarge said. "Do we know anything about her husband?"

"Nothing," Pickett said.

Sarge wrote that in his notebook as a reminder to find out information about Cinda' husband, if she had one.

"So somewhere out there, clearly still living to this day as evidenced by the sniper," Pickett said, "are the person or people responsible for the bomb, Heather's death, and who know how much more."

Sarge nodded.

"Did I hit the high points?" Pickett asked, looking up from her notebook and smiling.

"You did," Sarge said. "And I wouldn't have the foggiest idea where to start with all this."

"The files," Pickett said. "We start there and we might at least figure out what this is all about."

"I sure hope so," Sarge said, "but first I'm going for some bread pudding."

"A serving for me as well, please," Pickett said. "I'll call Robin and tell her we are heading to the safe house in thirty minutes, see if Cavanaugh is there to meet us."

"Sounds perfect," Sarge said.

And then, not surprisingly after a couple near death experiences yesterday, the bread pudding tasted even better this morning.

Chapter Twenty-Five

December 6th, 2016
Las Vegas, Nevada

PICKETT AND SARGE were met outside the front door of the safe house by Mike. The house was in a new subdivision looking down over the valley and the city beyond. To Pickett it looked like it would be fairly easy to defend.

"Thank you for everything, Mike," Sarge said.

"Yes, thank you," Pickett said.

Mike shrugged. "It's what I do and I'm really honored that Will and his people came to help so much last night at the station and that the chief of police was clearing the path as well. The gang sure holds some sway in this city."

"I think the chief understands completely what you and your team did down in those tunnels a few months back," Pickett said. "He's not one to forget that you more than likely saved some cops'

lives, and more than likely did it again last night."

"Well," Mike said, nodding. "It was nice and allows me and my men to keep doing our jobs."

"Which I plan to pay you handsomely for," Sarge said.

Mike laughed. "Oh, you'll get my bill when this is done."

"So where did all the files end up and any surprises in the moving?" Pickett asked.

"No surprises," Mike said. "All the file cabinets are set up like they were in the unit against one wall near the dining room and the desk is just off the dining room in a small nook. The safe is in the garage and empty. Turned out there was sixteen-point-five million in the safe, all bills older than twenty-five years, so more than likely it had just sat there all that time."

"Another question we missed this morning," Sarge said, taking out his notebook. "Where did the money come from?"

Pickett nodded to that. With luck, they would find the answer to that in those files in there.

"Anyone else here?" Sarge asked.

"Cavanaugh said he was going to take a nap and would be back after lunch," Mike said.

"Robin is bringing lunch about then," Pickett said. "Want me to bring something for you and your men?"

"Thanks," Mike said. "We're fine. Have fun in all that paperwork."

With that he turned and headed up the sidewalk.

Sarge led the way into the modern home. It was nicely furnished with brown cloth and oak furniture. It had light walls decorated in some sort of Native American style art and dark hardwood floors.

Light poured in from all the open windows and the ceilings were high in the living room and dining room area. Very nice and modern. Pickett could see a large kitchen to one side and to the back.

The old file cabinets looked completely out of place next to a massive oak table in the dining room.

"At least we're going to have room to spread out and look at stuff," Sarge said.

Pickett and Sarge both took off their jackets and left them over the back of a chair near the front door, then they both went to the file cabinets.

Sarge walked right up to the first one and pulled open the top drawer.

Then he shook his head and let out a breath. "Somehow still afraid it was going to explode."

"I was thinking the same thing," Pickett said.

Pickett moved up beside him and studied the numbering on the files. None of it seemed to be in any kind of order, almost random numbers, but Pickett had a hunch that was far from the case.

"We're going to need to find the key to the organization for all of these files, or at least work it out somehow," Sarge said.

He opened the first file and they both looked at the contents. Pickett was surprised. The folder held an accounting ledger, detailed handwritten notes, what looked to be contracts, and a couple bills of sale that seemed to have been notarized.

Sarge closed that file and picked another about three-quarters of the way back into the drawer. Same thing exactly. Accounting ledger, notes, contracts, and bills of sale for something.

Pickett wasn't sure what she was expecting, but it sure wasn't anything like that.

There were different names on the bills of sale, different names on the contracts, and different names on the accounting ledger. Only the odd number on the file seemed to hold any meaning as to why these files were in the same folder.

"We got to find the master list for these numbers if there is one," Pickett said, turning to go look in the big desk tucked in an alcove off to one side of the dining area.

She opened the big drawer with the ledgers and took out the top one.

Inside it looked more like a diary instead of a ledger. It was going to take them some time to read them all.

So she and Sarge moved them from the desk to the big oak dining table, making sure to keep them in the same order they were stacked in the drawer.

There was nothing else in that drawer.

They went through the other desk drawers, carefully putting the contents in places on the table.

No sign of any kind of numbering system at all.

Pickett glanced back at the files. "That numbering system had to be easy to remember, yet hide the true nature of the files from anyone who got in."

Sarge nodded. "But with something like that, even when young, I would have been deathly afraid of forgetting the system."

"So there has to be something to tell us what the numbers mean," Pickett said.

They went back to the desk and completely pulled out each drawer, making sure there was nothing taped to the bottom of the drawer or that the drawer had a false bottom in it.

Nothing.

Sarge picked up the wooden chair that had been in front of the desk in the storage unit and made sure nothing was taped under the seat. Then he tested the wood in the legs to make sure nothing was hollow there. Solid.

Then Sarge got down on his back and using his phone as a flashlight, slid in under the desk, looking for anything there.

"Nothing," he said as Pickett helped him back to his feet.

She was disappointed that the solution hadn't come easy. Nothing about this case seemed to be coming easy or straightforward.

Pickett turned with Sarge to look at the piles of stuff on the table and the file cabinets that were all full.

Pickett knew the organizing system had to be detailed out in all that stuff somewhere.

But where? At that moment it seemed like they were looking for a needle in a very large haystack.

And there was no doubt in Pickett's mind they were going to need help.

Chapter Twenty-Six

December 6th, 2016
Las Vegas, Nevada

SARGE FELT DISAPPOINT-MENT that they hadn't found the key to the strange file numbering system in the desk. It had to be somewhere, but the question was where.

He and Pickett went over and each picked up a journal. The journals looked like they had come out of a stationery store, with green cloth cardboard covers.

At the top of the inside cover the person writing in the journal had put a number and it was circled. And the pages were all numbered.

Sarge sort of leafed through the book, not really reading, but noticing that some entries were only one page and other entries went on for a while. And the dates seemed to jump all over the place.

Suddenly it dawned on him what he was seeing.

He was holding journal number two and an entry about a purchase of a car started on page forty-seven.

"What journal number do you have?" he asked Pickett.

"This has a five inside the front cover.

"Go to a page where an entry starts," Sarge said.

She flipped quickly a ways into the journal and stopped.

"Page thirty-two," she said.

Sarge stood and moved over to the first file cabinet and opened the top drawer. The hanging files seemed to be numbered randomly in two, three, or four digit numbers.

"Still missing something," Sarge said. He went back over and picked up the journal numbered with a one and looked at the first entry. It was dated September, 1989. Just under a year from the time Heather was locked in that room. She would have been just starting her first year in college.

He went back over to the first file cabinet and Pickett stood and followed him. He opened the top drawer and looked at the first file.

921.

"Got it," he said. "The ledgers are the key. He pulled out the file labeled 921 and motioned that Picket should join him back at the table.

"9th month, page two, first journal," Sarge said.

He opened the file, then opened the journal. The entry in the journal matched the names in the paperwork in the file.

Pickett kissed him on the cheek. "Damn, what's it like to be so smart."

"Not smart," Sarge said, "just lucky. Especially finding you."

She kissed him again and laughed. "That was pretty lame, but I loved it."

"Good," he said, smiling at her. "Got lucky again."

She laughed and they set about testing his labeling theory. It seemed that the person who had done the journal always went through the entire cycle of nineteen journals with an entry before starting over.

So the second file was the day after the first file, but the journal entry was in the second journal, second page. And so on until the 20th entry was the second entry in the first journal.

They tested that with about a dozen files and the system held.

So Sarge wanted to see now what the last entry said, the last file said, right before she went to that hotel. Assuming, of course, that it really was Heather Winston who had done the journals.

It took them a moment to find, but the last dated entry was not in August when Heather was locked in that hotel room, but on December 20th of the same year.

The entry gave the date and then simply said, "New car smell turning rancid. Took twenty-five of the forty-one. Shutting down for now."

Either Heather hadn't been locked in that hotel in August when she vanished and was replaced by Connie, but instead went into the shuttered hotel after December twentieth, or these journals had been done by someone else.

All Sarge could do was stare at the entry and wonder exactly what it meant. Like everything in this case, nothing was making sense.

Chapter Twenty-Seven

December 6th, 2016
Las Vegas, Nevada

PICKETT COULDN'T BELIEVE that last entry and when it was done. Something was very off here, of that there was no doubt.

"We need to start over and check everything," Pickett said after a moment of silence while they both thought about what that last entry could mean.

"I agree," Sarge said. "Everything. Every detail, right from the first missing person's report on down."

"So we start where we should have started," Pickett said, "right now before we go into these files. Who was the detective on the missing person's case for Heather Winston and why didn't it get closed?"

"And who was the detective on the Connie Downs missing person case," Sarge said. "And the detective on the mummified body in the hotel. Let's find that out and go talk with them."

Pickett nodded. "Not sure why we missed that step on these cases."

"We don't miss any step now," Sarge said.

Pickett felt right about that. They had built all of this on misinformation and bad data. That just made her angry at herself.

They now needed to correct some of the bad information and get on a track to solving all this. And maybe then they could dig into those files.

Sarge picked up the phone and called Andor who could get to all the original files at headquarters quickly. Sarge put the phone on speaker.

Andor answered without a hello. Instead he said, "You guys had some fun last night I hear."

"Just testing out the possible new recruit," Sarge said. "Cavanaugh did fine. A little training and he might be able to keep up with us."

Both Andor and Pickett laughed.

"Just glad you guys are all right," Andor said.

"Thanks, we are too," Sarge said. "But this case has gotten so twisted, we figured we would get back to the beginning on this. Could you get us the names of the different detectives who handled the Heather Winston disappearance in August of 1990, the Connie Downs disappearance in August of 1990, and the discovery of the body in the Landmark in the spring of 1991."

"I was headed down to headquarters in thirty minutes," Andor said. "I'll look it up first and call you back."

"Also check if you wouldn't mind," Pickett said, "how they got the DNA from the mummified body and also what they did with the body and the personal stuff. And also why they even bothered getting DNA at that point in time."

"No problem," Andor said. "Watch your backs on this one."

"Mike and his team already are," Sarge said.

"Good," Andor said.

Then he clicked off.

At that moment Robin came in carrying three bags of wonderfully smelling hamburgers and fries. Pickett realized she was hungry.

"Making progress?"

"Actually yes," Sarge said.

Robin quickly put the food in the kitchen and came back out.

Sarge explained to Robin what they had discovered about the numbering system.

"Wow, simple but effective," Robin said. "Especially if those journals and most of the stuff in those files had been blown up. The remaining stuff would be useless without the entire picture."

"Exactly," Sarge said.

"So you got any news?" Pickett asked. "And if so, can you tell us about it over lunch. My stomach just decided to start rumbling."

"I got news and I got lunch," Robin said.

The kitchen in the modern house was just off the dining area and it had a large table looking out over a garden. Picket said she didn't feel comfortable at the moment just sitting in the window like that, so they moved to the counter and sat on the stools there.

"So what's the news?" Pickett asked after they each got started eating the fantastic burgers and fries. If Cavanaugh didn't hurry up, one of them might eat his as well.

"Got back all the preliminary results on the fingerprints and DNA in the storage unit," Robin said. "It all belongs to Heather Winston."

Pickett just stopped eating and stared at Sarge, who had a burger halfway to his mouth, frozen in front of him.

"So who was the body in the Landmark?" he asked after a moment.

Robin looked at him, then at Pickett.

"I'll get the final file," Pickett said. She retrieved the file that was dated in December and let Robin read it.

Robin looked at her, stunned.

"We have a mummified body that couldn't get fingerprints," Sarge said, "and somehow, for some reason, someone took DNA from the mummified body in 1991. And kept that on file."

"And that body would have needed hot summer months to mummify like that," Pickett said.

"We are missing something major here," Robin said.

Pickett could only nod to that and go back to eating.

And what she really wanted to know was who exactly was this Heather Winston?

And where was she still living? Because Pickett now had no doubt that body in that hotel was not Heather Winston.

Chapter Twenty-Eight

December 6th, 2016
Las Vegas, Nevada

SARGE JUST SAT eating his burger, trying to let the details of what they knew settle into his mind. He could feel that part of the solution was right in front of him, but he couldn't spot it.

"So what we think happened," Robin said, pushing the remains of her hamburger and fries away, "is that Heather Wilson killed someone in that hotel room, planted her own DNA somehow, and then replaced herself at home with another girl."

"No way could she do it alone," Pickett said.

Suddenly Sarge realized where they had been making their mistake. They had never checked Heather Wilson's real birth certificate.

Suddenly all the pieces clicked into place. If his hunch was right, that is.

"Robin," Sarge said, "I need you to get some information as quickly as you can."

Robin shrugged and pulled out her notebook.

"Any background information, including birth certificates and so on of all four of the Winston family, including the brother. Including where they got their money and so on."

She wrote that down.

"You got an idea?" Pickett asked, smiling at him.

"If I'm right," Sarge said, "all four of the Winston family are part of all this."

"So why would anyone kill the parents?" Robin asked.

"I'm betting they didn't die," Sarge said. "Either look-alikes in the car or faked deaths covered up by enough money."

Pickett sat back, looking stunned at what he was saying. "The brother looked much older than his age, didn't he?"

Sarge nodded.

"So who planted the fake DNA on the body?" Robin asked.

"We have Andor checking on the detectives on all three cases," Sarge said. "When we get the names you might want to run some financials on the detectives from the time period if you can."

Robin nodded and picked up her phone. A moment later she was talking with Will and telling him what they needed and how fast they needed it. And to try to trace the deaths of the parents and if any bodies or another couple went missing about the same time.

At that moment Sarge's phone rang. It was Andor.

"A detective by the name of Saul Sawyer was on the body and responsible for pulling the DNA," Andor said. "He was shot and killed a year later. They never found the shooter."

Sarge felt his stomach twist into a knot.

Sarge quickly told Andor what they were thinking and told him to cover his tracks carefully.

"Had a hunch after last night that would be the case," Andor said. "I want in and got the information without alerting anyone or even triggering any warnings. One of Doc's computer people helped me make sure."

Sarge let out the breath he was holding. "Great thinking. We'll be back with you as soon as we figure out what all these files are about."

"Just be damn careful," Andor said and hung up.

Sarge relayed what he had found out from Andor and Robin immediately called Will back to tell him to cover their tracks even more and look into Detective Saul Sawyer's financials.

"So you are thinking the entire Winston family thing was a cover?" Pickett asked.

"Sure starting to feel that way," Sarge said. "With only her fingerprints in that unit, that last entry, all that money, and three suspicious deaths, one that we know was covered, it sure feels that way."

"And if you are right," Robin said, "there is a chance that all four of the Winstons are still alive and out there."

"We need to get some eyes on the brother," Sarge said.

Robin nodded. "Will's people can do that. I want to keep Mike focusing on keeping this place safe for the moment."

"I agree," Pickett said.

Sarge completely agreed.

Robin was about to call Will when he called her.

She listened for a moment, shaking her head.

Sarge just watched, more worried about news than he could remember being before.

Finally Robin told Will about getting some eyes on the brother and then nodded.

Then she hung up.

"Will already has a team watching the brother," Robin said. "He hasn't surfaced yet today."

Sarge nodded. He had been afraid of that. This entire group or pretend family might now be so far underground as to be impossible to find.

"The family itself didn't exist before Heather went to her senior year of high school," Pickett said. "Their records show them moving into town, but that was the moment all the records started. Will thinks they are all fake."

"So they came into town, set up whatever was going on in those file cabinets, made a ton of money fairly quickly, and then faked their deaths over the next two years."

"The brother didn't," Pickett said. "Why not?"

Sarge knew the answer to that. "They actually didn't leave, that's why."

Pickett nodded. "I was thinking the same thing."

"But I bet not one of us thought to get a picture of Bob Steven's wife, did we?" Sarge asked, smiling.

Both Pickett and Robin just stared at him, then Robin said, "Shit." And grabbed her phone.

As Sarge smiled, Robin told Will to pull up a picture of the brother's wife and do facial recognition with Heather Winston.

She held.

Sarge smiled at Pickett.

Less than thirty seconds later Robin said, "Well, guess we better put even more people looking for them."

She nodded, then said, "Thanks."

"We found Heather Winston," Robin said. "Married to her pretend brother under the name Judy Winston. They were married four months after she disappeared and was replaced and during the same time frame as her last entry in the journal."

"And I bet their first child came along a few months later, right?" Sarge said.

"Nailed it in one," Robin said.

Chapter Twenty-Nine

December 6th, 2016
Las Vegas, Nevada

PICKETT SAT BACK on the barstool and tried to make sense of all of this. Heather Winston, her parents, more than likely fake, and her fake brother who became her husband, all arrived in town at the same time. They set her up in high school and the brother in college.

But why and what were they doing and where did all the money come from?

And more importantly, why did they leave all that money in that safe with a bomb? When they were quitting, why not just take it all?

What was their scam and why shut things down? Who were they afraid of?

"We need to figure out what they were doing," Pickett said.

Sarge and Robin both nodded and all three of them stood and headed into the dining room with all the files.

The file cabinets looked so out of place in the modern dining room and had a faint smell of mold as well.

They all started from the beginning of the files, making notes, going over each entry. They took each file out, each looked at it and they didn't move on to the next file until they agreed to what it was, how much money was involved, and any other detail that was in the file but that they didn't yet understand.

It became clear fairly quickly that no matter what the object in the ledger might be, the entire thing was about cars, which actually surprised Pickett at first, but the deeper into the files, the more amazed she became that such an operation could exist.

They quickly figured out what each initial stood for on the bills of sale. A Cadillac Eldorado was just CE.

There were thirty different companies and hundreds of fake names selling the cars and seemingly they sold to every dealer in town. Records of fake bank accounts being opened and then closed a few months later were throughout the records.

By the time Cavanaugh got there an hour after they had started, Pickett was convinced she knew where all the money came from. It was from selling cars.

A lot of cars.

They spent fifteen minutes getting Cavanaugh up to speed and how they were now looking for the brother and his wife and kids.

"Might also want to get a search going for the parents," Cavanaugh said.

"If your hunch was right, they are still alive somewhere."

Robin nodded to that and stepped off to one side to call Will.

Then they told him about the cars.

"All that money," Cavanaugh said, looking confused, "and all this and the bomb and the sniper and everything is about cars?"

"Seems that way," Pickett said.

Sarge nodded, then said, "That's what all this paperwork is about anyway."

"That makes no damn sense," Cavanaugh said, shaking his head.

Pickett agreed with that.

Sarge looked at all the files. "We know only Heather Winston did all these books and handled all that money. But to move that many cars, legally or illegally, there had to be a lot of people involved."

Suddenly Pickett understood what they had missed.

"We only have money coming into these ledgers," Pickett said. "Nothing going out that we have come across yet."

Sarge looked at her, clearly surprised.

"I heard that and you are right," Robin said, stepping back closer to the table, her phone back in her pocket.

"So how many cars are we talking about?" Cavanaugh asked.

"From my best guess," Sarge said, "and considering we are only a quarter of the way through so far, I'm guessing around eight thousand cars."

Pickett nodded. "The sale prices seem to be ranging in the four to six thousand dollar range. So that math works to get to forty million in the safe as the last entry noted."

"That means they were selling from ten to twenty cars a day for the entire time they were in operation," Cavanaugh said, looking stunned and staring at the files. "How was that possible?"

"And who did the selling?" Robin asked.

"And where did all the cars come from?" Pickett asked.

That question bothered her more than any of the other hundred questions she had.

Chapter Thirty

December 6th, 2016
Las Vegas, Nevada

SARGE AND PICKETT and Robin and Cavanaugh worked together to finish going through all the files. It took them three hours and they came up with a total of eight thousand and fifty cars sold, or at least recorded by Heather Winston in those records.

Cavanaugh had gotten permission for two of Will's people to come in here and spend the night digitizing every piece of paper and every page of every journal. Sarge was going to feel safer about all of this when that was done and all this information stored off-site.

So when they finished, Robin headed home to help Will while Sarge and Pickett also headed home. Mike's men shadowed all three of them and Mike said he would have men stationed around Sarge and Pickett's place all night.

Sarge had to admit he felt better having backup. No telling exactly how deep and how powerful a cesspool they had uncovered here.

Sarge and Pickett agreed to meet Cavanaugh and Robin the next morning for breakfast at the Golden Nugget and plan what to do next.

After the heavy breakfast and then the hamburgers for lunch, neither he nor

Pickett was that hungry, but they both agreed they needed to eat.

So when they got back to the complex Pickett worked to make them a light salad with some ham and cheese while Sarge sat on the floor in the living room and watched three kittens chase after a string he had tied on a stick.

They seldom caught the string, but they were sure cute chasing it.

"You ever feel like that we're the kittens in this case?" Robin asked after laughing at a pileup of orange fur.

"How's that," Sarge asked, keeping the string just out of reach of the three kittens.

"We're chasing this thing and just not catching it," Robin said, putting two bowls of salad on the table, then going back for glasses of water and silverware.

Sarge could only agree to that.

Sarge dropped the stick and the string in the middle of the floor and stood. Instantly all three kittens seemed disappointed and didn't care anymore about the string. It wasn't trying to escape, so no point in even touching it. But all three kept an eye on the string while pretending not to.

Sarge and Pickett talked for a time about the case, but both of them were so tired, nothing seemed to make sense.

They finally decided to just table the discussion until breakfast and picked a romantic comedy to watch.

Sarge was pleased that Pickett nodded off to sleep before he did. When he was young, he might have thought of carrying her into bed, but as it was he just shut off the movie, woke her just enough to get her to walk toward their bedroom, and then turned off the lights.

The three kittens were nowhere to be seen.

But the next morning the kittens were back in their normal routine and he felt a thousand times better. Pickett had made the coffee for him and as they stood drinking in the kitchen Pickett asked, "Should we walk over today?"

"Drive," Sarge said. "No point in making it any harder on Mike's men than we already are."

Sarge didn't like the idea that their normal routine was disrupted, but he had a hunch it wouldn't be for long. This entire case was unraveling quickly.

The kittens were settled in the living room as he and Pickett headed out the front door. Everything felt normal until Pickett asked a simple question just as he pulled the door closed.

"Whatever happened to Darling Black?"

And instantly this case felt even farther from being solved.

And Sarge hated that.

Chapter Thirty-One

December 7th, 2016
Las Vegas, Nevada

PICKETT WATCHED FOR any sign of Mike's men as they went to her car in the parking garage and then pulled out to drive the short distance to the Golden Nugget parking garage.

She didn't see a sign of any of the security, but she knew they were there and watching. And that told her just how good they really were.

The normal wonderful smells of waffles and bacon hit her as they went up the long escalator to the second floor. The place didn't look too busy, with almost everyone seated against the big windows overlooking the pool.

Robin was already sitting at the table with a number of notebooks beside her just about as far as they could get from those windows. She waved them over before Robin could pay.

"Already paid for all four of us this morning," Robin said.

Pickett could see in Robin's eyes that there was news. Good or bad, Pickett couldn't tell.

At that moment Detective Cavanaugh came up the escalator and Sarge went to get him into the restaurant and to their table. Two minutes later all of them were getting their breakfasts and four cups of coffee were on the big table.

Sarge had also asked the hostess to not seat anyone close to them this morning so Pickett felt that they had some privacy.

After they had all eaten for a moment and Robin had gotten her daily update on the three kittens, Pickett turned to Cavanaugh, who was looking tired, but not as tired as yesterday.

"Get everything photographed and saved?"

"All done," Cavanaugh said, nodding as he worked on a large slice of ham. "And this place is better than I remember it for breakfast."

Sarge nodded. "And they change the selections regularly."

Cavanaugh just shook his head and kept eating.

"So what's the news?" Pickett asked Robin.

"Bob Steven and his wife, formally his sister, have vanished completely," Robin said. "However their two kids are still in college and acting as if nothing has changed. We have people on them."

"They might not know anything?" Pickett said.

"I'm betting on that," Cavanaugh said, nodding. "But that said, what do we know?"

Pickett and Robin both took out their notebooks at the same time. Sarge was only a second or so behind. Cavanaugh just watched and laughed.

131

"From the beginning," Robin said, "We know that a young girl that looked similar to Heather Winston died in the old Landmark Hotel after it was closed up."

"A week later a fake Heather Winston took her place in the family," Pickett said. "We have no idea why."

"We know that about four months after the fake Heather Winston was trapped in that hotel room," Robin said, "the real Heather Winston, or whatever her real name might be, walked away from about fifteen million in a storage unit while setting explosives to blow up everything. It is pretty certain she never returned to the storage unit even though she lived here in town all those years, married to her pretend brother. She raised two kids like a normal parent."

Pickett found that just amazing.

"The files in that storage unit show pretty clearly that they were selling cars to build up the cash in that safe," Sarge said.

Pickett nodded to all of that.

"We also know," Sarge said, "that Cinda Blessing knew about the money and the danger of the storage unit and tried to take it, but was killed by someone else who knew about the storage unit and what it contained."

"Or wanted to stop her," Pickett said.

"That's pretty much it," Robin said.

"So we know things," Pickett said. "But we have no answers to the many, many questions of how and why."

Robin, Sarge, and Cavanaugh all nodded.

"So why not try to start from the real beginning of all this, at least the one we know," Pickett said.

Again all three nodded.

"We know that two couples, an older couple and a younger couple, arrived in Las Vegas and set up fake identities as a family and somehow started selling cars."

"For cash," Sarge said.

"And no idea where they got the cars they sold or how they paid for them."

"If they paid for them," Pickett said. "Any kind of transportation or theft ring would have to be vast to get that many cars in that short of time."

"Let alone sell them," Sarge said.

"We did some preliminary traces last night on some of the cars listed," Cavanaugh said. "All were bought and sold aboveboard, many by reputable dealers. The paper trail is clean on all of them."

Silence around the table.

The sounds of the tourists talking and laughing from the other side of the restaurant mixed with the faint sounds coming from dishes being bussed and kitchen work behind the buffet.

Pickett could feel the frustration of this case starting to close in around her. She needed to clear her mind.

"Bread pudding break," she said, sliding her chair back and standing.

Sarge came with her and Robin and Cavanaugh both passed on the offer to bring them one.

As they walked back to the table, Sarge said, "We need to tie up some connections, first."

"Like what?" Pickett asked as she set her dish of bread pudding in front of her chair and sat down.

"How did that DNA get planted on that body and why did it lead us to the brother?" Sarge asked.

"You think she married her real brother?" Pickett asked.

"In most cases DNA evidence is pretty solid stuff," Sarge said. "But in this case I don't trust it as far as I could throw the sample."

"But it just might give us some more answers," Robin said, grabbing her phone.

Pickett worked at the wonderfully sweet bread pudding while Robin asked Will to do a very deep background search on Heather's DNA. Where did it come from, relatives that might be in the system, and so on.

"Only going to take Will's people a minute to run the program," Robin said. "Didn't think to do it before now."

Pickett watched as after a moment Will started talking. Robin just nodded slowly, writing some notes in her notebook, which Pickett knew meant the news wasn't good.

"Thanks," Robin said after a moment and clicked off her phone.

She looked at Pickett, then said simply, "We got a distant relative connection to a family in Washington state by the name of Winston. They were killed in a house fire. The entire family perished. Two parents, a college aged son and a senior in high school daughter."

"When?" Sarge asked.

"Two weeks before the family appeared here in Las Vegas," Robin said.

"Bodies confirmed in the fire?" Cavanaugh said.

"Confirmed and identified by family," Robin said. "Somehow these imposters must have taken some DNA from the family and made sure the DNA was in the system as them here."

"Brother got his DNA in by filing it," Cavanaugh said. "Two months after they got here. That's how he got his into the system. He purposely put his DNA in as part of a pilot program back then for a university study."

"So we really have no idea who this family is or where they came from?" Pickett asked. "Right?"

All three nodded.

Robin glanced at Cavanaugh. "Sorry to say but the lead detective on the dead girl's case in the Landmark inherited just over two hundred thousand the same week as she was found."

"More than likely got him killed," Cavanaugh said, shaking his head.

Again silence around the table.

"Will says they are looking for a possible family or two couples," Robin said, "that vanished at the same time back then, but he thinks it is unlikely they will find anything."

"Not sure how much it would help us anyway," Pickett said. All she wanted to know was what happened here in Vegas and who was that dead girl in the Landmark?

Chapter Thirty-Two

December 7th, 2016
Las Vegas, Nevada

"MAYBE IF WE just created a list of questions about all this," Sarge said, "and then put them in an order of importance, we might be able to start carving at this mess."

He really, really needed some organization at this point in time. So much information they had thought they knew and then didn't, he wasn't keeping some of it straight.

"Sounds like a good idea," Pickett said. "I'll start. Who was Darling Black and what did he or she have to do with any of this?"

All four of them wrote that down. Robin added, "Why did she stop at the same approximate time as Heather pretended to vanish for a week."

"She didn't," Pickett said. "That information came from Carla. Actually her columns went to December."

Sarge nodded and wrote that down.

"What was being sold to make that kind of money?" Cavanaugh asked. "The records from the files want us to believe it was cars, but I sure can't imagine how that could have been done without a huge organization."

"Agreed," Sarge said. "I'm betting it was some sort of information. We need to see if we can break that deeper code on those records."

Robin nodded. "I'll get some computer people on it right after breakfast, now that we have all the records digitized."

"Who was the girl in the Landmark?" Pickett asked.

Sarge wrote that down and put a star beside it in his notebook. The most important question as far as he was concerned.

"Who killed Cinda Blessing and how much did she really know?" Robin asked.

Sarge wrote both of those questions down separately.

"Why if the parents and brother, or husband, of Heather were involved, did only Heather go to the storage unit?" Sarge asked. That question had bothered him since they got the information back from the lab techs.

"Maybe," Cavanaugh said, "she was the only one involved."

Robin nodded. "There are a number of reasons why two couples might vanish and assume new identities."

Sarge nodded to that. Two couples in trouble, wanting to get away, taking advantage of a tragedy of a family to do it.

"Warrants?" Pickett said. "Robin, when you get a chance have Will search for outstanding old warrants for a father-and-son combination. Bail skipped around that time."

Sarge again just nodded. A long shot, but might give them an idea of what this group was good at.

He wrote down the question in his notebook, "Heather alone?"

Cavanaugh's comment about maybe it was only Heather stuck with Sarge. He put a star beside that question as well.

"Maybe," Pickett said, "there were some gems of truth in what Cinda told us about Heather."

Sarge quickly flipped back through his notebook to his notes when they talked with her.

Pickett was doing the same. Picket said, "Cinda said Heather had made a lot of people angry by not covering losing bets on celebrity stuff."

"Could that have been accurate?" Sarge asked.

"And it was Cinda who told us that Heather was Darling Black," Pickett said.

"We need to pull up all of Darling Black's columns," Robin said, scribbling in her notebook.

"The woman, if her notebooks and files are any indication, was a master of codes," Cavanaugh said. "Maybe she was using those Darling Black columns as a form of communication for some reason."

"At this point," Sarge said, writing that down in his notebook, "Anything is possible."

"So how would we even find out if Darling Black was Heather?" Pickett asked.

Robin looked up and smiled. "How about we ask her to come talk with us?"

Sarge stared at the grin on Robin's face.

Cavanaugh looked stunned.

Pickett just sort of laughed and said, "I know that look and it can't be good."

"How about we get a reporter for the *Las Vegas Sun* to write an article about Darling Black," Robin said, "and how the police are looking to talk with her about a cold case. Just get some information because they feel she might be able to help solve the old murder. Promise to keep her identity secret."

"Get the word out on the streets," Cavanaugh said. "I can do that through the station as well."

"If Heather was Darling Black," Pickett said, "she's not coming out."

"But if Darling Black was someone else," Sarge said, "he or she might appear after all these years. And might just have a detail we are missing."

"Worth the shot," Robin said. "And I got a friend at the *Sun* who could do it."

Sarge nodded. An extreme long shot, just as finding the original names of these people was a long shot. But at this point, they didn't have much more than that.

Part Six
COLD, THEN HOT

Chapter Thirty-Three

December 10th, 2016
Las Vegas, Nevada

PICKETT WAS SLOWLY getting frustrated at the complete lack of progress. For three days now nothing at all had changed, no matter how many questions they asked or what they did.

She and Sarge had settled into a routine again. Mike had his people still on guard and close at all times. Pickett didn't want to know what that was costing Sarge, but he told her he would tell her later, that right now safety was far more important than money.

Robin and her computer people had figured out that the cars mentioned on the

records were actually all cars sold, and the money in the storage unit had nothing to do with the sales of the cars. The real money from the sales went through normal channels both with the dealer purchasing the cars and the banks financing the cars for the end buyers.

But Heather had used those car sales, that she somehow had gotten information about, as a way of tracking some other money flowing into the storage unit.

But not a clue as to where the money was coming from.

For three days an interstate search had been in full swing for Bob Steven Winston and his wife, otherwise known as Heather. But it was as if they had simply just vanished off the face of the planet.

Their two adult kids were both worried to death about their parents and seemed to have no idea what had happened.

Both adult children had offered their DNA and a family history had appeared. Bob Steven and Heather had not been related, but were actually married in Illinois the year before they moved to Las Vegas.

They had been reported missing in Illinois three months after the wedding and no sign of them had ever surfaced until now. Their adult children suddenly found out they had real family in the Midwest. Pickett could only imagine how that was making them feel.

There was no clue as to the real identity of the fake parents, but no one was taking any bets that they had actually died in that car wreck.

Now Pickett and Robin and Sarge were again meeting for breakfast to try to come up with anything they could dig at for the day. Pickett didn't feel good about their chances.

They had all gone through the buffet for the first time and were eating when a middle-aged woman with a wide smile and a tourist look about her walked over to their table. The woman had short brown and gray hair and wore no makeup. She had on a multi-colored blouse, a suit-like pink jacket over the shirt, and dark slacks. She had a dark tone to her smooth skin that gave her a look of ageless beauty.

Pickett saw her coming first and cleared her throat, a signal she and Robin had used as a "heads-up" signal for decades.

Robin glanced up, saw the woman and even though she didn't seem to tense, Pickett saw her gun hand move down to her lap.

Pickett was ready to go for her gun as well if the woman tried anything.

Sarge just kept eating, since the woman had walked up to their table from behind him.

The woman just smiled and said, "I understand you detectives are looking for me."

Sarge jerked and glanced around.

"Depends on who you are," Pickett said.

As Pickett got over her surprise, she realized the woman looked vaguely familiar.

"One of my pen names when I was younger, now back a ways I must admit, was Darling Black," the woman said. "Always loved that name."

Pickett just sort of nodded and indicated the woman take the empty chair at the four-chair table.

"We are looking to talk with you," Robin said. "Thanks for stopping by."

"You had breakfast yet?" Sarge asked as the woman sat down as if what was happening happened every day. Pickett just shook her head. The man was unflappable.

"Actually," the woman said, "already eaten. Sitting over there with my husband and son and his wife. My real name is Melita Henson. That's my husband Al and my son Ben and his wife Toni."

"Great to finally meet you," Sarge said, smiling.

"We really appreciate the new remodeling you are funding," Melita said.

"Least I can do," Sarge said, shrugging, "to keep our building up."

Sarge then introduced Pickett and Robin with their full detective names, then said simply, "Melita and her husband have a condo in the Ogden."

"Yup, we come down from Portland for the late fall through early spring," Melita said.

Pickett just shook her head. Darling Black lived in the same building as they did.

Robin just laughed.

"So how did you hear we were looking to talk with the Darling Black part of you?" Sarge asked.

"I write novels under a number of pen names," Melita said, "and the reporter who did the story in the *Sun* is a friend of mine. I called her when I read the article and she told me who you three were. I was going to call you later today when I saw you here."

Again Pickett just shook her head.

"So what exactly can I do to help in some murder case?" Melita asked. "Can't imagine what Darling Black might know. I was pretty young back then."

Pickett glanced at Robin who just shrugged.

"Do you remember," Pickett said, "back after you stopped using that pen name that a body was found in the Landmark Hotel?"

Melita shook her head. "Afraid I don't."

Pickett could tell she wasn't lying or hiding anything.

"Can you tell us why you stopped your column so abruptly?" Robin asked.

"Enrolled in the University of Washington English program to get an MFA in creative writing. Got a full ride, actually. Got kind of too busy that fall to keep doing that silly column."

"When was this exactly?" Pickett asked.

"I went to Seattle in late August of 1990," Melita said.

Pickett nodded. The same point the woman supposedly was locked in that room to die.

"Did you ever know a Heather Winston?" Sarge asked.

"Name sounds familiar," Melita said, nodding. "I think she was a year ahead of me in school. Blonde popular type."

Pickett nodded. "That describes her."

"So what exactly does any of this have to do with my Darling Black columns?" Melita asked. "They were mean and sort of stupid, but not much else. But they did cause a stir, which for a high-school girl was fun and exciting."

"We had a very unreliable source that said Heather Winston was Darling Black," Sarge said.

Melita laughed and shook her head. "Not unless Heather Winston was my 'Deep Throat' source. I wrote all those columns."

"Source?" Pickett asked.

"Sure," Melita said. "I was a high school girl buried in getting the best grades I could for that scholarship. I couldn't have gotten into some of those clubs if I had wanted, so I had a source for what I wrote."

"Ever meet this source?" Sarge asked.

"Nope," Melita said, smiling. "But it was great cloak-and-dagger fun. Twice a week I got an envelope without a return address on it, mailed from the University Station post office. It had pictures, dates, and names. The only deal I had with the unknown person was that I would use all the information they sent in my column and not change a thing. I couldn't have done that column without all that information. But some weeks it was difficult to fit it all in."

Pickett couldn't believe it. Could Heather have been sending some sort of signals for something through Melita's column? What might that have been?

"I know this is going some," Robin asked Melita, "but any chance you might have saved all those envelopes and letters?"

"My husband hates it," Melita said, smiling, "but I save everything. It's all in storage here along with my parents' stuff in my old family home. My nephew and his wife live there while going to college, but I doubt they would mind a visit."

"Please," Sarge said.

Pickett and Robin both nodded.

"Glad to help if I can," Melita said. "As long as you promise me the full story when you are done. What little bit I have gathered sounds like it would be great material for my Stripe mystery novels."

Now it was Pickett's turn to be shocked again.

"You write the Randy Stripe novels?" Pickett asked. "I love those books."

Melita just nodded thanks.

"Deal," Sarge said. "The full story once we figure it all out."

"Deal," Melita said, standing. She handed Sarge a card. "After you are done with breakfast and back at the Ogden, call me."

"About an hour," Sarge said.

"It will be fun digging out those old files," Melita said.

She headed back toward her family as Pickett just sort of stared at Sarge and Robin.

"We either caught a break," Robin said. "Or this is just going to confuse us even more."

"I wouldn't bet against the confusion," Sarge said.

Pickett laughed. Sadly, neither would she.

With that Robin grabbed her phone to have Will and his people do a quick check on Melita.

With this case, no one could be trusted.

Chapter Thirty-Four

December 10th, 2016
Las Vegas, Nevada

SARGE WAS GLAD that Melita's history and family all checked out. He and Pickett enjoyed the walk after breakfast back to the Ogden, purposely not talking about the case. Robin had decided to go back to her office to be there if they needed to check on something quickly.

Just an hour after the conversation in the restaurant, Sarge and Pickett met Melita in the lobby of the Ogden and used Pickett's car to get out to the Spring Valley area.

The home had clearly been built as a nice, modern home in the eighties. It was still well-kept with what looked like a new coat of off-green paint and the trees were large and offered shade.

Melita let them in, saying that her cousin and his wife were both at work but had said it was fine for her and two detectives to go to the basement.

The basement was filled with a family room that not only had some kids' toys, but a large-screen television filling one wall.

Melita unlocked a door to one side of the family room and pushed it open, clicking on the light.

"Since all of this is my stuff," she said, "My husband and I are the only ones with keys."

Sarge was impressed that the back room of the basement was bright, with tile floors and all four walls covered in shelves. Some boxes sat up on wood pallets off the floor and boxes filled every shelf, all clearly labeled.

An empty wooden table filled the center of the room, clearly used for sorting onto the shelves.

"Wow, organized," Pickett said.

"My husband calls it obsessive." Melita said, laughing. "But it comes in handy. I print out and bring a copy of every one of my books here, along with an electronic backup copy."

Melita went right to an old file box with the label DB on the side and pulled it down from the shelf, turning and placing it on a table.

"Haven't opened this since I put it back here and headed to college."

"Wow," Pickett said. "We're honored you are letting us look at it now."

Melita laughed. "Nothing to be honored about. Just old paperwork that should have been tossed decades ago."

"Glad you didn't," Sarge said.

Melita opened the box and inside Sarge could see very organized envelopes. Each one had been sealed and then ripped open.

"Chance of DNA?" Pickett asked, pointing to a ripped envelope.

"A real good chance," Sarge said, smiling.

Sarge quickly put on some evidence gloves and opened one envelope. It had two pages of a typed letter in it with no signature. A list of details about some local bands and a stage act.

"My columns are in the folders against the back," Melita said.

The letter in Sarge's hand was carefully worded and exact. Sarge had no doubt it was a code of some sort. But it was going to take a computer expert to crack it.

Melita shook her head. "Wow, looking back at this, I was sure stupid to use this information without ever checking any of it."

"High school," Pickett said.

"Being young doesn't excuse everything," Melita said.

"Oh, it does when you get to be Pickett and my ages," Sarge said.

"I think you might call it envy," Pickett said, laughing.

Melita laughed as well.

"Would you mind if we take these with us and have everything scanned and analyzed?" Sarge asked. "I promise we'll return it all to you as is."

At that moment Sarge's phone buzzed and he glanced down to see Mike's number.

Sarge answered it.

"Board yourself in the house where you are, keep the door locked," Mike said. "My man on you has five armed intruders working toward the house you are in. I'll be there with reinforcements in ten minutes."

"Melita's family," Sarge said.

"Already protected and under guard." Mike clicked off.

Sarge stuffed the phone back into his pocket. "We have company."

"How the hell did they know what we are doing?" Pickett asked.

"That is a question for later," Sarge said. He moved quickly over and closed the basement door and locked the handle. He didn't much like the idea of being trapped in a basement room, but at this point this was their best bet of survival.

Then he came back across the room and had Pickett help him tip the heavy wooden table over on its side facing the door. It looked to be solid oak and would give them some cover. Especially if the attackers started firing through the walls.

He put the box with the Darling Black files behind the table as well.

"What's happening?" Melita said. "What about my family?"

"It seems we have led some really bad people right to you," Sarge said. "We have special forces protecting your family and backup coming here in ten minutes."

"All for those stupid columns?" Melita asked as Pickett pulled her down onto the floor behind the heavy wooden table.

Sarge moved over and stood behind the door, his gun drawn. A brick fireplace wall there would protect him from shots coming through the door or sheetrock walls. But even so he would crouch when he heard someone coming, make himself a smaller target.

"No," Pickett whispered to Melita, just barely loud enough for Sarge to hear as well. "Not just the columns. For millions of dollars and numbers of deaths. We think those letters sent to you were a code and there are some very angry people who don't want some secrets in that code revealed, even after all these years."

"Oh, shit," Melita whispered.

"That pretty much describes how we feel," Pickett whispered.

The sounds of steps on the staircase coming down from upstairs cut through the silence.

Mike said ten minutes.

Only three had passed.

This was not looking good.

Not looking good at all.

Chapter Thirty-Five

December 10th, 2016
Las Vegas, Nevada

PICKETT CROUCHED BESIDE Melita.

How the hell had it come to this? What did those men coming in actually know? And how had they been following them with Mike's men watching things.

Or had they actually been following Melita?

Either way they were in a very bad spot, trapped in a basement room, and unless they could hold on until Mike and his men got here, this would turn very ugly very quickly.

The invader's footsteps on the stairs were clear and not really trying to be silent.

Then from almost directly above the storage room there was a loud thud.

Pickett had a hunch that was a body hitting the floor. She just hoped it wasn't Mike's man.

"Find out what that was," a man's voice said from outside the storage room.

Pickett couldn't believe what she had just heard. That was Bob Steven Winston's voice.

She glanced up over the table and Sarge just nodded from where he was crouched behind the door against a brick fireplace. He clearly had recognized the voice as well.

The doorknob rattled as someone tried it.

"Stay silent and low to the ground no matter what happens," Pickett whispered to Melita.

She nodded and curled down into a ball on the tile floor.

"Darling Black," Bob Steven said, "if you and those two detectives are in there, your only chance of living is to open this door."

Silence.

"Break it down," Bob Steven's voice said from the other side of the door. "I'm getting tired of all this screwing around."

Pickett rose up and saw that Sarge had moved slightly away from the brick wall to get an angle on the door.

She had her gun trained on the door as well.

He glanced at her and then nodded. He put three fingers in the air, then two, then one.

Pickett and Sarge both opened fire at the door and the wall on both sides of the door.

The intense sound of the gunfire was like a hammer smashing into them in the small file room. She had fired her gun a number of times in closed spaces and it was always a shock at how loud it was.

They both quickly fired six times, spacing their shots at waist high and along the wall and door.

Then Sarge ducked back to the brick and Pickett back behind the wooden table.

"Son of a bitch!" Bob Steven said. "Light the place up."

At that moment the firing started and the files above the table were shaking as shots plowed into them.

Bullets hit the table with loud thuds, but the table held.

Dust and splinters were flying everywhere.

Pickett used her body to cover Melita's.

Then, suddenly the gunfire ended as three quick pops stopped it cold.

Pickett figured help had arrived.

But neither she nor Sarge or Melita moved. Pickett wasn't sure she even wanted to take a deep breath.

Then Mike's voice said, "Clear. You all right in there?"

"I am," Sarge said, moving over through the swirling dust to help Pickett up.

"I am," Pickett said.

Then both she and Sarge helped Melita up.

She seemed fine and uninjured. Just completely in shock. Pickett didn't blame her in the slightest. That wasn't something Pickett had ever wanted to live through.

"I bet that's not the kind of research for one of your mystery novels you were ever hoping to get," Sarge said to the shaking and wide-eyed writer.

"No," Melita managed to say, shaking her head as Pickett held her up and Sarge went to unlock the door. "Not in my worst nightmares."

"Oh, trust me," Pickett said. "What you are about to see on the other side of that door will be the real nightmare."

And she was right. Five men's bodies were sprawled in pools of blood in the once-nice family room. One of Mike's men stood on the stairs with his gun slung over his shoulder.

Mike stood among the bodies, close to the door.

Sarge shook Mike's hand and said simply, "Thank you."

Pickett and Melita moved toward the door. Pickett wasn't sure if Melita's legs would hold her, but then Mike stepped forward and put his arm under Melita's.

"Thanks, Mike," Melita said. "Seems I owe you once again."

Pickett glanced at the white, dust-covered face of Melita, then at Mike, who just smiled.

Clearly Mike had done her a favor at some point in the past. It was going to be interesting to see what that was.

"Always my pleasure," Mike said, taking Melita from Pickett and helping her through the bodies and to the stairs.

Outside the sirens were getting closer.

Pickett moved over to Sarge and just hugged him.

Damn he felt wonderful.

And it felt even better that he hugged her back.

Then together, they both stepped over the very dead body of Bob Steven Winston and headed up the stairs.

About halfway up Sarge said, "Cavanaugh is going to love the paperwork on this one."

All Pickett could do was laugh.

Part Seven
FOLLOW THE MONEY

Chapter Thirty-Six

December 14th, 2016
Las Vegas, Nevada

SARGE WAS HAPPY that after four days since the shootings, things had finally calmed down enough to be able to walk to breakfast again.

And both he and Pickett had helped each other through the nightmares of reliving that fight in that closed room.

It had taken them all the rest of the day and all the next day being interviewed to finally be done with the major investigation part of the fight. Of course, the department had their guns for the investigation, but they both had other guns, so neither of them had worried about that.

And since they were retired and it had clearly been a case of self-defense, the chief hadn't even asked them to sit

aside. Part of that had to do with them not officially being on the force as well. Insurance wasn't an issue it seemed.

Poor Cavanaugh had found himself in a paperwork nightmare, as Sarge had known he would be. He had three assistants on it and it was still burying the poor guy.

Will and Robin's people had once again swooped in to help Mike and his people, but they didn't really need it. The house had secret security cameras and pretty much everything had been recorded, including the fight in the basement. That had helped a great deal.

It was two days ago that Robin had gotten permission to get the box of Darling Black letters. She had spent the last two days having them digitized and then running all sorts of comparisons with the columns, the letters, and the paperwork from the storage unit.

Melita and her husband had gone back to Portland and Mike was pretty convinced the men had been after the letters, not her. Neither Mike nor Melita would tell them how they knew each other. And after asking once, Sarge didn't press. So much about what Mike did was behind the scenes. Better to not know.

At breakfast today Robin was going to tell them what she had found in the study of the letters, if anything.

But there were still so many questions. Where was Heather Winston? Who was the dead girl in the hotel room? And what was so important in that storage unit and those files that so far eight people had died, not counting the girl in the room and maybe the parents. Two at the storage unit, six in the house.

For Sarge, they still had a long way to go to get this case solved.

The December day was cold, but not biting. He liked the walk to the Nugget breakfast more in the winter than in the summer. The air had a cleaner smell to it, fresher.

He and Pickett had just turned onto Fremont Street when something occurred to him.

"Cabin in Big Bear," he said.

Pickett glanced up at him, a puzzled look on her face.

"We need to check to see if the cabin at Big Bear that the parents had been at when they supposedly died was still in the family. Or maybe under another name."

He had a hunch that if it was, they would find Heather there.

Pickett nodded. "That just might be possible."

Before they even had a chance to sit down, Sarge told Robin his idea and she got on the phone to Will and his people.

Sarge and Pickett turned to get breakfast since the smell of ham and waffles this morning seemed even more wonderful than normal.

Pickett and Sarge were waiting for their omelets in the buffet area when Robin came over to them. "Cabin changed

names three times over the years, but always from one corporation to another, owned by the same name. D. Black."

"Not the Melita Darling Black?" Pickett asked, clearly as shocked at Sarge felt at the very idea.

"Nope," Robin said.

"Thank heavens," Sarge said.

"Checked that completely and it has nothing to do with Melita or any of her family. Got a hunch it is Heather, but all sales were done with cash, so nothing but the tax records are traceable."

"She's there," Sarge said, nodding. "It would make sense."

"But is she still alive?" Pickett asked.

Sarge had no idea the answer to that question, because it was clear that Bob Steven Winston had some pretty powerful backers. And since he failed, more than likely his wife, who had clearly been behind a lot of this, had failed as well.

Sarge heard himself think that, then realized how Bob Steven Winston and his men had gotten on Melita's track. Heather had known who she was all along and where she had lived.

"I'm betting," Sarge said, "that Heather is there and still calling the shots."

"Mike?" Pickett asked.

"Mike and Cavanaugh," Robin said. "Cavanaugh and a couple of men need to go with Mike to check that out. We don't want Mike's men out on a limb without official backup again in this case."

Sarge agreed. "I'll call Cavanaugh."

"I'll call Mike," Robin said.

"And we're not going?" Pickett asked.

Sarge laughed. "One gunfight for two retired cops is enough for one week, don't you think?"

Pickett smiled. "I am in total agreement."

Sarge laughed at the complete relief showing on Pickett's face.

Twenty minutes later the three of them were eating breakfast while Mike and his men and Cavanaugh and two other detectives were headed to the cabin at Big Bear. Mike said their hope was to take her alive.

Sarge normally wanted to be on the front line, but after the fight four days ago, he just wanted her arrested if she was there.

And besides, they still didn't know why all this was happening. And who that poor girl who got baked to death in that room was.

They had other work to do.

Chapter Thirty-Seven

December 14th, 2016
Las Vegas, Nevada

PICKETT WAS VERY relieved that Sarge didn't think they needed to be there to arrest Heather Winston, if she was at the cabin. Pickett didn't think they needed to do it either, but if he had wanted to go, she would have been at his side.

So now they had to sit and wait. And try to figure out the rest of this mess.

After all three of them had mostly finished their first round of breakfast and were sipping their coffees, Pickett turned to Robin. "What did the computers dig up?"

"We know the car buying cover was nothing more than that," Robin said. "A cover."

Pickett and Sarge both nodded.

"We also know that Heather was the one who licked those envelopes. Except for Melita's prints, the only other ones were Heather's, the same as the ones in

the storage unit. In fact, the envelopes and printer match envelopes and the printer from the storage unit."

"So Heather was Darling Black's source," Pickett said, nodding. She had figured as much, but good to have evidence now prove it.

"Any idea why?" Sarge asked.

"The information in the Darling Black columns came directly from the letters," Robin said, "with very little changes at all. Melita didn't change much, not even the writing, especially toward the end as she clearly got more interested in getting ready for college. And the columns after Melita left for college were written completely by Heather."

"So in a way Heather really was Darling Black, filtered once," Sarge said. "Cinda was right about that."

Robin nodded, then went on. "Best the computers can figure when putting the information from the files with the letters is that the code indicates a time and a fairly exact place."

"For what reason?" Pickett asked.

"That is the big question," Robin said. "We ran all the times and places against all known crimes or other events. Nothing."

Sarge just shook his head, clearly discouraged.

Pickett felt the same way.

"Let me see if I can get this straight," Pickett said, doing her best to grasp all the real information they had so far. "Heather gives a young columnist information to feed into her column."

"Yes," Robin said simply.

"The column must have been used to publicly pinpoint something at a time and place," Pickett said.

Robin nodded.

"Heather got paid large sums of money for the information she was putting through the column," Pickett said. "So we are missing the front of this puzzle and the back of this puzzle."

"How's that?" Sarge asked.

"We don't know where or how Heather got whatever information she was passing on," Pickett said. "And we don't know what was done with the information on the other side to make it worth so much money and so many lives twenty-five years later."

Sarge and Robin both nodded.

"We have the center, you are right," Robin said.

"So what kind of places were pin-pointed by the articles?" Sarge asked.

"Addresses that were vacant lots at the time, parking garages, a few old casino parking lots, and so on," Robin said. "The times were from the middle of the morning to late evening."

Suddenly Pickett had an idea. This was all about money, but far larger sums of money than the forty million that had been in that safe at one point.

Pickett looked at Sarge and smiled, then at Robin. "This all started fairly quickly after she and her fake family moved to town. Right?"

Robin and Sarge both nodded.

"So we didn't ask a few questions we needed to know," Pickett said. "First off, did anyone else from Heather's former town move here ahead of Heather's fake family?"

"Tough to find, but possible," Robin said. "What are you thinking?"

"Drops," Pickett said. "This town constantly has vast sums of money in transit. And without some of the modern technology we have now, back in 1990 it was much harder to track all that money."

Sarge nodded. "Had my share of armored car robberies back when I was starting off. Someone almost always ended up dead."

Robin and Pickett both nodded.

"If an exact location is known through a code in the paper to both an inside person and a pickup person, a drop from a money car would have a lot less likelihood of being tracked."

Sarge suddenly sat back in his chair. "If Heather's notes were right and she had over forty million in that safe when she pulled the plug, how much money are we talking about overall?"

"More than I want to think about," Pickett said. She turned to Robin. "Any total of how many dates and places there were in those notes?"

"Over the length of the column there were over a thousand," Robin said.

"Heather had the fake cars she was selling making her from three grand to six grand," Pickett said.

"That's forty million easy," Sarge said. "Just for Heather's cut, which more than likely was small."

"Wow," Pickett said as Robin picked up her phone.

Chapter Thirty-Eight

December 14th, 2016
Las Vegas, Nevada

SARGE LET HIS coffee soothe him as he and Pickett waited for Robin and her computer people to dig out even more information.

And wait for word from Mike and Cavanaugh. They wouldn't arrive up there for another forty minutes. Sarge might have to have a couple of pieces of the wonderful bread pudding by then.

And maybe some bacon and a waffle first.

He had a hunch Pickett was right, that the times and places were drops, more than likely of bags of money from casinos.

And if that was the case, this was a skim operation of large proportions, more than likely connected to a larger skim operation. Otherwise, even back in 1990 it would have been caught easily.

So for this to work, this had a lot of inside help and some powerful people involved. No wonder people were dying now. Chances were some of those powerful people were still around.

Robin was about to hang up, but Sarge had an idea and stopped her.

"Hold on," Robin said to someone on the phone.

"Possible to run all those dates and locations and see which major casinos were close to them?"

Robin nodded and then said into the phone, "Thanks, call me at once when you have something."

Then she clicked off her phone and turned to Sarge and Pickett. "Already did that. I noticed earlier that the locations were all close to the various Hughes Casinos, including the Landmark when it was still in operation."

"Oh, no," Pickett said, sitting back.

Sarge knew exactly what she was thinking. For the longest time it was rumored that Hughes skimmed vast sums of money from his casinos and took it with him when he left Las Vegas. It had only been rumors and some people thought that Hughes had nothing to do with it if it had happened. But it was one of those rumors that never seemed to die.

And Hughes left and started selling off his casino properties right about the time all this was happening.

"We might as well be chasing Bigfoot," Pickett said.

Sarge laughed. "We'd have better luck with Bigfoot."

"So you thinking this might have been a skim of a skim?" Robin asked Pickett.

"Only way money wouldn't be missed or traced back then," Pickett said, nodding.

Sarge agreed. By the Hughes era, the mob had been mostly chased out of town and the vast skim of money the mob had sent east was staying in town, for the most part, as large corporations started to move in and buy and build casinos. But those skim operations could have still been working easily for a few years, especially from the Hughes properties.

"The date that Heather shut down," Sarge said, sitting forward. "Does that correspond at all with any major casino sting operation?"

Robin grabbed her phone again.

"That would explain why she left money in the vault and rigged everything to blow," Pickett said, nodding. "If the entire operation was getting shut down, if they traced it to the storage unit, they needed to find money and everything destroyed."

Sarge knew that Pickett was right. Finally an explanation for that setup in the storage unit.

"Articles headed to your phones," Robin said and hung up her phone.

Sarge got the article a moment later and started reading at the same time Pickett and Robin did. A huge sting operation had been started in the summer of 1990 because of an informant, but the raid didn't happen until December, at the exact same time as Heather shut down.

And two days before the last Darling Black column was published.

But it was the next to the last line of a third article that mentioned that the case had been delayed when the informant vanished suddenly in August.

He read that line aloud.

Robin and Pickett both nodded.

"Looks like we have found who was in that room," Sarge said.

At that moment Sarge's phone clicked.

Sarge put the phone to his ear.

"We're here and it looks like the cabin is occupied," Mike said. "Cavanaugh has the warrant and we're going in."

"Good luck," Sarge said and hung up.

"Mike?" Pickett asked.

Sarge nodded. "They are going in."

Chapter Thirty-Nine

December 14th, 2016
Las Vegas, Nevada

PICKETT FORCED HERSELF to go back to the buffet to get all three of them a helping of bread pudding. She was so nervous, she wasn't hungry, but Robin was on the phone with Will and his people and Sarge was on the phone with Andor at the police headquarters, trying to have someone dig into the file and pull out the informant's name who vanished.

So bread pudding seemed to be a task she could handle for them at the moment.

She was convinced they had figured out the entire scheme.

It was logical that Bob Steven would try to defend their names and the money they had gotten. So more than likely he had hired the sniper who killed Cinda at the storage unit.

And since he died in the battle in Melita's basement, he was clearly in charge there.

So now, to really finish this off, they needed to capture Heather alive. Pickett was convinced that wasn't going to happen. But Mike and his men, with the detectives were sure going to try to make it happen.

And if they did get Heather alive, this could finally be done.

Pickett carefully fixed up three dishes of bread pudding, putting just the right amount of rum sauce over each one, then carried them back to the table.

She wasn't sure she could eat any of hers, but waiting was easier with a fork in her hand.

Sarge smiled and thanked her. "Andor is digging. Said it shouldn't take too long."

At that moment Robin hung up. "Three of the major players in the scam of the Hughes properties died in the raid. Two unnamed others considered major players were never found and the money was never found."

Pickett nodded and started into her bread pudding, letting the sweet and familiar taste calm her some.

Both Sarge and Robin did the same.

"Anyone have any idea how much was skimmed?" Sarge asked between bites.

Robin shook her head. "Guesses run from three hundred million into the billions, but all that is Bigfoot country. No one really knows for sure. All anyone knows is that a skim operation was taking place and they shut it down."

Pickett laughed. "Heather's storage unit sure confirms a lot about the fact that the skim happened."

"It does at that," Robin said.

At that moment Sarge's phone rang. He glanced at it and nodded, then clicked it on and said, "Hi, Mike."

Pickett and Robin watched as Sarge nodded, then said, "Great news. Keep her protected."

Sarge hung up. "They captured Heather alive."

Pickett said, "Yes!"

"Fantastic!" Robin said, laughing.

"If they can get her back here and under protective custody," Sarge said, "we might just get a few more answers on this."

Pickett frowned at Sarge. "You still think there are more people than Bob Steven and his men trying to shut this down?"

"I do," Sarge said, nodding. "With billions on the line and reputations to protect, if any of the major players are still alive, they are going to make sure Heather never says a word."

Pickett pushed her unfinished bread pudding away.

What next? She wasn't sure she wanted to know, actually.

Chapter Forty

December 19th, 2016
Las Vegas, Nevada

SARGE WAS STUNNED when he heard that Heather lasted exactly four days in custody.

She was being transferred for a court hearing with six cops around her and in full body armor when a sniper put a bullet through her head.

No sign of the sniper was found, so a totally professional hit. Someone had been worried about being brought out into the open after all the years and didn't want that to happen.

That would have been the end to that if not for the fact that Heather had been giving extensive testimony, on advice of her lawyer, in hopes of getting witness protection.

All carefully recorded. But sadly, from what Cavanaugh told them a few days later, she didn't know names.

She didn't know about the girl being killed in the Landmark, and she had no idea what had happened to the girl who wrote the Darling Black columns for her until she surfaced.

What he and Pickett and Robin had worked had been the system Heather used. She explained it all in detail.

Cavanaugh did learn that her fake brother and future husband, Bob Steven, had known about the scam from the summer and had been so worried about her that he had helped her fake her own disappearance and put in the fake Heather in her place.

Their kids knew nothing about anything. The newspapers and the police made that clear almost from moment one.

The original parents had been fake, just cover for them. Heather and Bob Steven were paying them. The two had actually died, for real, in the auto accident by Big Bear.

After Heather was killed, Mike and Sarge figured that Sarge and Pickett and Robin were clear. The case was over as far as they were concerned. Sarge ended up paying Mike far less than what Sarge thought it was worth, but Mike would have none of taking more money.

"Those are my rates," Mike had said. "Trust me, you didn't get a deal."

So now, just six days before Christmas, Sarge and Pickett were headed toward breakfast actually talking about what they were going to do for the holiday.

Details such as where to put up a tree, that sort of thing. And if they wanted to do a Christmas Day party or not.

Sarge did, Pickett wasn't so sure yet.

They had just reached the main door to the Golden Nugget on Fremont Street when Sarge's phone rang.

It was Andor.

"Finally dug out the informant's real name and description," Andor said. "I sent it to Robin and she should have it for you when you get to breakfast. Her name was Dawn Gilbert. Twenty-five, unmarried, worked in the cage at one of the Hughes properties."

"Thanks," Sarge said. "Anything we should know?"

"Parents still alive," Andor said. "They never knew what happened to their daughter. You going to want to tell them? They live here."

"Yes," Sarge said. "We'll do it."

"Thought you would," Andor said. "Great job. See you at the game after Christmas."

With that Sarge put the phone back in his pocket and on the escalator up to the buffet he told Pickett what Andor had said.

Pickett just sighed. "Finally they will get closure."

Sarge could only nod to that. Too bad they would never know who locked her in that room.

Or would they?

He quickly dialed Andor back and asked him for the testimony about Dawn's case and her friends and who she had implicated.

Then, after they all got settled and they had all looked over Dawn's information and when exactly she vanished, Sarge said simply, "Let's delay telling her parents for a day to find her killer."

"And how would we do that?" Pickett asked.

"We cross-reference," Sarge said. "Andor is sending her testimony and we figure out which person on there knew about the old tunnel at the Landmark. And who had the most to lose. And who was closest to her who might be able to lure her there."

Chapter Forty-One

December 19th, 2016
Las Vegas, Nevada

THEY HAD ALL studied Dawn's file and then had finished breakfast when the file from Andor came to Robin through Will.

Pickett had a hunch she knew who had killed Dawn, but she wanted to wait for the testimony.

That made it clear. Dawn had a boyfriend who had worked in the back counting room at the Landmark and then been transferred to another Hughes property when the Landmark shut down. She said in her testimony that she had asked him a couple of times about strange bags of money in the cage.

Pickett was convinced those questions had gotten her killed.

His name was Jarman Jones, divorced and a few years older than Dawn.

All three of them agreed it was most likely him. And he had the knowledge of the Landmark tunnel after it was closed up.

Robin got Will on researching Jarman Jones carefully, including his finances back at the time of the scam. Then the three of them went back for seconds.

Twenty minutes later Will got back to Robin.

Pickett sat intently listening for any hint as Robin nodded and wrote as fast as she could in her notebook. Then she said, "Thanks."

"He's alive," Robin said, "rich from that period of time, a claimed large inheritance, and works casino security with his own private firm."

"He had a lot to lose, didn't he?" Sarge asked. "If Heather lived?"

Robin nodded.

"Damn it all to hell," Pickett said. "Did Will figure out how much money the guy inherited back then?"

"Five hundred million," Robin said.

"He's our main guy," Sarge said, grabbing his phone. "I got Mike."

"I'll call Cavanaugh," Robin said.

Pickett just sat and shook her head.

Thirty minutes later they were headed in Robin's car for a meeting near Jarman Jones Security main building. Jarman had an office there and Robin had one of Mike's people call to make an appointment in one hour to make sure he was actually in the building.

Cavanaugh had gotten a warrant and in fifteen minutes Mike had his people stationed around the building and out of sight.

Mike had told Sarge that Jarman employed ex-military and that Jarman himself was a highly trained sniper who practiced daily at a number of private ranges. So there was a good chance Jarman was good for Dawn's murder, but maybe Heather's murder as well.

The guy was dangerous and would be trapped.

The headquarters was a flat two-story office building with a wide parking lot and about thirty cars.

The plan was that Sarge and Pickett would go in under the guise of needing home security for their new home. They would be stationed where they could see the stairs up to Jarman's office when Cavanaugh and the police arrived.

Their main job was to get innocents who happened to be in the lobby to cover if fighting broke out.

Mike and two of his men were covering the two back exits until the police could move around into position.

Everyone was convinced that Jarman would see the police coming and try to make a break for it. In which direction and how was the key?

"You ready?" Sarge asked Pickett as they headed, arm-in-arm toward the front three steps and the glass doors of Jarman Jones Security.

"Rather be putting up a tree," Pickett said. "But since we are here, let's get this bastard."

"Oh, I like the sounds of that," Sarge said, smiling at her.

They went in and gave their names to the receptionist, then moved over to one side.

The lobby wasn't that big and was full of some large indoor plants. Only one other couple was in the room and they were sitting reading magazines like they were in a doctor's office.

The front windows were clean and clear and the parking lot was obvious beyond the windows.

Sarge and Pickett both stood and watched as five police cars came rushing in and stopped along the front of the building.

Then Cavanaugh, moving fast for an old guy, bounded up the stairs along with three uniforms and two other detectives, bursting into the main foyer.

"Looking for Jarman Jones," Cavanaugh said, showing the warrant with one hand.

Pickett and Sarge moved over in front of the couple who were now standing, looking shocked.

"You need to get out of here now," Pickett said, showing the couple her badge.

She took the woman's arm and Sarge took the man's arm, but then something to Sarge didn't seem right. The guy was carrying a gun.

This guy looked like Jarman Jones with a wig on.

More than likely the guy had decided to investigate new clients by listening to them talk in the waiting room.

Sarge went to take the man by the arm as if helping him, then slammed Jarman hard into the wall and shoved him down over the couch, holding him in a way that Jarman couldn't get to his gun.

Pickett instantly seemed to understand what had happened and snapped the woman's arm up behind her back and shoved her face-first into another wall.

"Cavanaugh," Sarge said, "I would like to introduce you to Jarman Jones."

Sarge used the barrel of his gun to brush off the wig from Jarman's head.

Two detectives converged on Jarman and two cops on the woman and just like that it was over.

"Jarman Jones," Cavanaugh said, starting to read him his rights, "you are

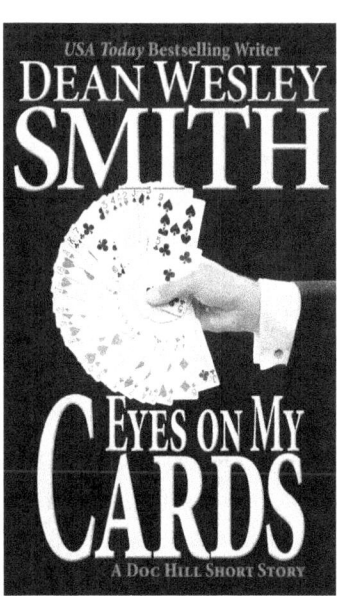

under arrest for the murder of at least Dawn Gilbert. Got a hunch we'll add a few more on that list shortly."

Sarge laughed as Cavanaugh finished reading him his rights and took the guy out into the cool afternoon air.

For the first time since they got this case, a sense of relief washed over Sarge. They were almost finished.

Almost.

Only one more thing to wrap up.

Epilogue

December 20th, 2016
Las Vegas, Nevada

PICKETT WATCHED AS Sarge knocked on the well-kept suburban home's front door just to the south of the Spring Valley area of Las Vegas. Mr. and Mrs. Harold Gilbert had lived here for over forty years. They clearly kept their home up and loved it. It had a new roof and a fresh coat of tan paint. Even the windows were clean which was almost impossible to do in the winter in this area.

The day had turned cold, with steel-gray skies, but not cold enough for Pickett to need to wear a heavier jacket. She hoped to make it through the entire winter without a heavy jacket.

A young woman answered the door, clearly about college aged. She had a bright smile and long blonde hair. More than likely she resembled what Dawn had looked like when she died.

"Looking for Mr. and Mrs. Gilbert," Sarge said, opening his badge and showing it to the young woman.

Then Sarge introduced them both as the young girl's eyes got round.

"My name is Connie. My grandparents are in the back sunroom. Is everything all right?"

Pickett assured her that nothing was wrong, they just had news.

"Oh, about my aunt Dawn I bet," Connie said, nodding.

Pickett said nothing to the young girl. No need to, she understood.

Connie led them through the well-furnished and comfortable home to the back, where what looked to have been an outdoor porch area had been glassed in. It was comfortably warm and had a view of a valley and the mountains in the distance.

In the summer it would have to be air-conditioned to stay useful, but Pickett had no doubt it was.

"Grandma, grandpa," Connie said, "the police are here to see you."

Connie moved over and stood against the wall, watching and waiting.

Pickett introduced her and Sarge as both of the Gilberts stood and shook their hands. The Gilberts looked to be in their late seventies and both seemed to be in good health. Pickett hoped that in another fifteen years she could be in as good of shape.

"It's about Dawn, isn't it?" Mr. Gilbert said.

Sarge and Pickett both nodded.

Pickett went on to tell them about how her daughter had been trying to do the right thing, but was trapped in a room at the closed Landmark and not found until the following spring.

Both of the Gilberts just nodded, but Pickett could tell they were both sad and relieved.

Pickett then went on to tell them they had arrested her killer yesterday.

Both the Gilberts looked relieved at that.

After all the questions they had were answered, the Gilberts walked Pickett and Sarge to the front door and thanked them for finally allowing them to know what happened.

"Sorry to have to do this at the holidays," Sarge said.

Mr. Gilbert just shook his head and brushed that aside. "Actually, after all these years, knowing is a great gift."

"Very much so," Mrs. Gilbert said. "Thank you."

Pickett and Sarge rode in silence back toward their complex. Pickett couldn't imagine what that couple had gone through, losing a daughter and not knowing what happened, yet still raising three other children.

Impossible to imagine.

It was as Pickett pulled into the parking garage and parked that Sarge said, "We need to talk about what we are going to do for the holiday?"

"A tree would be nice," Pickett said, smiling at the man sitting beside her.

"We have kittens," Sarge said, smiling back.

"So we anchor it solidly," Pickett said. "Let them play and be kittens."

"I was hoping you would say that," he said, "because I have a fifteen foot tree being delivered at four this afternoon."

"And if I hadn't wanted a tree?" Pickett asked, laughing.

"I would have had to head the guy off at the pass," Sarge said. "But I left the choice of decorations on the tree up to you."

"How about up to us," Pickett said.

"We better get something before he gets here," Sarge said, "because I'm not climbing a ladder to decorate the top of a tall tree."

She started the car back up. "Well then, let's get going. We've got a lot of decoration shopping to do if we're going to get ready for a Christmas party."

"Christmas party?" Sarge asked, staring at her as she backed out of her spot and headed for the entrance to the garage.

"We live in one of the largest condos ever created in this town," Pickett said. "If we can't throw a party, not sure who can."

Sarge just laughed. "Sounds like fun to me. But you know, we would be starting a tradition."

"After these last few weeks," Pickett said, "some fun and tradition is what the doctor ordered for us and all of our friends."

"Especially on our first Christmas together," Sarge said.

Pickett glanced over at the man she loved more than anything. He was smiling.

And she was as well.

It was going to be a great Christmas, she had no doubt about that at all.

Coming Next Issue in *Smith's Monthly*

#7...April 2014

#8...May 2014

#9...June 2014

#10...July 2014

#11...August 2014

#12...September 2014

#13...October 2014

#14...November 2014

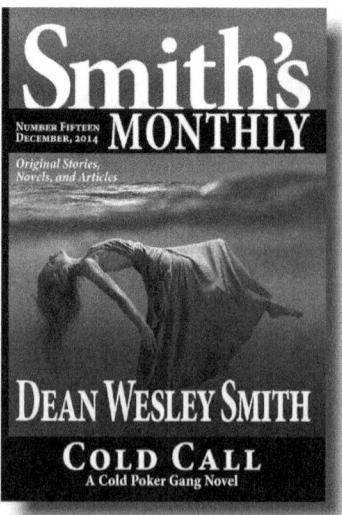

#15...December 2014

#16...January 2015

#17...February 2015

#18...March 2015

#19...April 2015

#20...May 2015

#21....June 2015

#22...July 2015

#23...August 2015

#24...September 2015

#25...October 2015   *#26...November 2015*   *#27...December 2015*

#28...January 2016   *#29...February 2016*   *#30...March 2016*

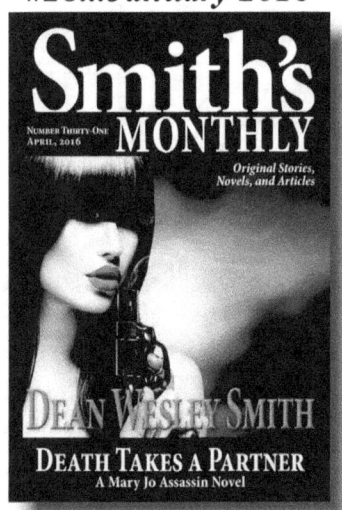

#31...April 2016   *#32...May 2016*   *#33....June 2016*

#34...July 2016

#35...August 2016

#36...September 2016

#37...October 2016

#38...November 2016

#39...December 2016

Thank You!!

I would like to thank the following wonderful people who support my blog and my work through Patreon. Your support is very important to me. Thanks!

Irette Y Patterson
Kathryn Rooney
Erick Lindman
Christopher Ridge
Raphael Husbands
James Gotaas
milady133
Danica Oakley
Kenny Norris
Kate MacLeod
Leah Cutter
Leigh Anderson
Robert J. McCarter
Jennette Heikes
Jamie Curierre
Albert Lemke
Marsha Kessler
Diane Darcy
Robin Brande
James Husum
Terry Mixon
Shantnu Tiwari
Chong Go
Maria Grace
Gnondpom
David Hendrickson
Fen

Sherman Cox
Miguel Angel Alonso Pulido
Marian Goldeen
Michelle Tatam
J.R. Murdock
Gunnar Gunderson
Jesse P Thurston
coraa
Martin Barkawitz
David Beers
Leslie Claire Walker
Nancy Hendrickson
F.I. Goldhaber
Michael J Lawrence
Barbara G. Tarn
Anthony St. Clair
Ann Tucker
Karl Gallagher
T. Thorn Coyle
Cristof Jones Harrison
Tasha Turner Lennhoff
Brenda Smith
Kari Wolfe
Mary Jo Rabe

And a very special thank you to
Betsey Wilcox.